CRUSHER

CRUSHER

Blaine C. Readler

CRUSHER

Visit us at: http://www.readler.com

E-mail: blaine@readler.com

ISBN: 978-0-9834973-9-4

Printed in the United States of America

To Chris and Dan, for understanding that life is essentially silly—that the trick to true happiness is relaxing enough to appreciate the joy ride, while paying sufficient attention to keep the car on the road.

ACKNOWLEDGEMENTS

A humble thanks to my first and forever editor, for cleaning up the text, and keeping me alive these last twenty-eight years.

A grateful nod to Michael Ilacqua for the cover design:
http://cyber-theorist.com

Check out his new book:
http://thephantomparadigm.com

Your assumptions are your windows on the world. Scrub them off every once in a while, or the light won't come in.

—Isaac Asimov

Chapter 1

Darren blinked. Sharon had warned him a week ago. She was on to him, and if she caught him with that floozy one more time, the engagement was off. "After I *warned* you!" she screamed. Darren held the phone away. Even from a tiny speaker the size of a dime, her furious voice could hurt his ear.

"I didn't *do* anything!" he said into the phone, then moved it a foot from his ear.

"Tanya saw you with her. Don't lie!"

He clutched the phone with both hands and yelled into it. "We work together! How can I *not* be seen with her?"

"Tanya saw you kissing her, you slimy toad!"

He stared at the screen. How do you answer a bare lie? "That's a lie!"

People say that so often as yet another lie. It wasn't fair. They ruin the declaration.

"Why would Tanya lie about something like that?" Sharon cried. "It's off, toad. I don't want to see you ever again."

"Why would she lie? She hates me, that's why. She never liked me—" The phone beeped. "Sharon? You there? Sharon?"

He snorted and slammed it down on the table, then picked it up and made sure he hadn't broken it. The floozy was a woman he'd dated in college years before. They'd been in the accounting program together, and the fact that he'd gotten her a job at the firm only meant that they shared the same education and careers. To Sharon, instigated by Tanya, no doubt, it was much more meaningful.

Darren slumped into his comfy chair and flicked on the TV. After a few minutes, he turned it off. He was tired. Not end-of-the-day pleasantly exhausted tired, but grainy not-enough-sleep tired. He kept hearing sounds at night. Scuttling sounds, like mice. No, bigger. Like rats. He would get up and check it out, but never find anything. Then he'd lie awake until he heard it again. Once he knew it was there, it was impossible to go back to sleep.

The tinkle of his phone launched him from the chair. Expecting it to be Sharon, maybe with an apology, he didn't even look at the screen, and he was irritated that it was his aunt Melba. Not that he didn't want to talk to her. Okay, he didn't want to talk to her. She was bossy. She didn't actually boss you around, it was more like she knew the right way to do everything, and she wouldn't drop a subject until you had stumbled onto it.

And she was a hippie.

"Darren, hello dear. You are indeed an angel," she said.

"Huh?"

Unless you represented the establishment—anybody she didn't like—you were honey, pussycat (reserved mostly for women), sweetie, or angel. This was different. "Angel" wasn't a nickname here, it was a noun.

"Oh, don't be humble," she said. "You are truly a sweetie."

Another noun. "Uh, I don't understand. What did I do?"

"What did you do? Why, just help me finally get centered. I was getting so close to finding my prime chakra when the hospital called. They might as well have thrown a grenade at it—the chakra, that is. Not that I condone references to war. Let's consider that grenade a metaphor. Come to think of it, you can't actually throw a grenade at a chakra, so of course it would have to be a metaphor, now wouldn't it—?"

"Aunt Melba."

"Yes, sweetie?"

"I don't know what you're talking about. Was the hospital calling about Crusher?"

Crusher was his cousin who'd managed to sustain massive brain injuries when he tried to fake an accidental fall from a high-dive board for the funny home videos TV show. He hadn't spoken an intelligible word in over two months. The doctors had recently been referring to his condition as a persistent vegetative state. As a kid, Darren had spent a couple of weeks with his cousin each summer, and he suspected that the doctors would have concluded the same diagnosis before the accident. He had once watched Crusher crack open a walnut with his teeth, and bite his tongue so hard it bled.

"Honey, if you wanted to surprise me," Melba said, "you shouldn't have copied me on your email."

"What email? Aunt Melba, I really don't know—"

"Darren, sweetie, we'll have to postpone this little cat and mouse game. My masseuse is here. We're going to find that chakra if it kills us. Not that I condone references to violence. Anyway, thanks so much again, you arch-of-angels."

Arch-of-angels. Oh boy. She normally reserved that for the far-left Democratic candidate. She seemed awfully cheerful for having effectively lost a son just months before. On the other hand, it wasn't Darren's basement that the dope had been living in the last ten years. He might be cheery too if he were standing in her all-hemp-no-trace-of-dead-animal sandals.

He went to his computer. "What the hell?" he squawked. There it was in his sent box. An email to the hospital administration office, offering to take Crusher off their hands. There was even an e-form with permissions all filled out and attached.

He shook his head in a vain attempt to wipe away the grainy thinking. As he watched, a message came in. The hospital had arranged to have an ambulance drop off Crusher later that day—no extra charge. Crusher had been on disability ever since he'd skewered his hand with a nail gun, and the hospital would be only too happy to extricate a Medicaid patient from an expensive bed.

Who the hell had done this, fabricate his request *and* approval? Aunt Melba? She was a whacko, but lying was against her religion, whatever that was this week. No, she obviously wasn't aware of the fraud—

Something else was happening on the computer monitor. He gasped and sat back. Words had appeared across the screen. Astoundingly, they spanned the entire width, on top of multiple windows. He'd never seen that before. The message read:

Hello, Darren. I have invited myself into your life. You will be surprised when you find out who I am. I know that you are sitting now. You should stay that way for awhile.

"What—the—hell?" Darren muttered.

The words disappeared, and new ones formed.

I know that this is probably shocking. You will adjust.

Darren's brow furrowed. "Who are you? *Where* are you?"

I am nearby. As to who, that is the current topic.

He glanced around, but the room was empty. "How many fingers?" he asked, holding them up.

You're testing me?

"Yeah. How many fingers?"

Lift them higher.

He raised them a few inches, still glancing around.

A little higher.

He held them up, checking the line of sight through the window.

Three. Now four. Now just one. I believe that is a rude gesture.

"Damn it!" Darren cried, pushing his chair back. "Where the hell are you?"

Not quite yet. You're still adjusting.

Darren's arms tingled with goosebumps. This was too freaky. Well, there was one way to take care of it. He reached over and shut down the computer. After a few seconds the monitor went dark, and he sighed with relief.

But then, with horrible impossibility, white words re-reappeared on the black screen.

We really have to get through this initial adjustment, Darren. I need your help.

With a little yelp, he switched off the monitor, and the white words disappeared.

Darren sat, frozen in disbelief. But he had seen it. There was no getting around it. The computer was definitely off. How could this person continue to output on his monitor?

He heard it. The rustling. The same furtive scrabbling he'd pondered as he lay awake in the dark.

He had a hunch. He stood up and leaned forward to look behind the monitor. What he saw was incomprehensible at first. It seemed that someone had dropped globs of molten silver into a pile on the table. The computer cable had been pulled out of the monitor, and strands of bare silver arched up out of the globbed mass and into the monitor connector.

"Good God!" he muttered, and a tendril of silver lifted and … waved at him.

Darren jumped back with a gasp. He tried to imagine what it could be—maybe a silver-painted octopus. But octopuses have suckers and two distinct eyes. He'd seen black, shiny ovals, but if they were eyes, their lids were shut. And there had been at least half a dozen. Maybe more like a huge, misshapen silver spider. Or a disembodied hand, a silver hand.

Again the rustling. The monitor shook a little, and a tendril the size of his little finger curled over the top. Two more tendrils followed, and together they lifted an indistinct mass of silver onto the monitor top. Several of the black ovals moved around to face him, sliding along like leaves blown across the surface of a pond. These were clearly eyes, or what served as eyes. The shape of the beast—or whatever it was—morphed, changing dimensions a little, apparently to better balance on top of the narrow perch. Darren expected it to talk, or bark, or whistle, but it sat watching him through an array of small black ovals.

"What—what *are* you?" Darren finally asked hoarsely.

A nub appeared next to the eyes, and reached outward, like a snail extending its eye tentacle. It stretched, and then thickened, until it formed what was evidently meant to resemble a finger. The fake appendage crooked, and wiggled up and down. Darren was mesmerized by the fantastic sight and didn't notice at first that another identical finger had extruded on the opposite side. They were both wagging up and down with growing urgency. It dawned on him that they were gesturing downward.

"Oh! You want me to turn the monitor back on?"

The beast paused, and then eased itself back and disappeared behind the monitor.

"I'll take that as a yes," Darren said, and reached to push the monitor button. He stepped back, keeping his distance.

Some rustling, and then words appeared.

Okay. You jumped the gun, but now we're past that phase. Ahead of schedule, and that's good.

"What phase?" Darren asked.

I told you. Your adjustment. Now we need to talk about the next phase.

"Hold on. My adjustment?"

You're still here.

"Right."

Your cousin will be arriving soon. I arranged that. He is integral to the next phase.

"Whoa! Hold on. Who—*what* the hell *are* you?"

A full response is not possible using English, or any other Earth language. Let's just say that I'm an alien.

"That much is pretty obvious."

I believe the proper term is "space alien."

Darren sighed, and pulled the chair back to sit down. He was still keeping his distance. "I've taken enough recreational drugs to recognize a hallucination. You are real, or I've gone insane."

I can't gauge your sanity. In any case, I am real. You need to prepare a bed for your cousin.

"Not so fast. I'm still on phase one. Where did you come from? Another star? Outside the solar system?"

Another star would, by definition, be outside the solar system, but yes. I was part of a survey crew. Against my better judgment, my colleagues decided— immediately upon arrival—to investigate what they took to be Earth's most advanced form of transport, to measure your level of technical progress. Unfortunately, that happened to be a jetliner.

"Why was that unfortunate?"

They didn't understand the primitive degree. They assumed that the heat shooting out the back of the engines was just due to an inefficient power source.

"So?"

So, in their haste, they failed to comprehend that the engine's motive force was due to inertial reaction.

"Still don't get it."

The inertial reaction of great volumes of air, air that is sucked in from the front.

Darren finally got it. "Oh, my God! The airliner that made an emergency landing a week ago—one of the engines blew up! That was *you?*"

Not me personally. I managed to bail out at the last second.

"But … but, your ship must have been really small."

It's relative. You're just big.

Darren sat back. This couldn't really be happening. He wasn't ready to accept that he was nuts, though. "How did you learn English?"

We arrived nearly a week ago.

"But, how did you—where did you—"

Using your own name as a WiFi password is not very secure. Your neighbor has figured it out, by the way.

"Wait a minute. You learned English off the internet?"

There's plenty of online children's books, and news stories come with pictures and video.

"But, in a *week*?"

Has your species developed interstellar travel?

"I see your point. But, why didn't you seek help from, like, the authorities?"

You are joking?

Darren didn't want to be from a species that couldn't figure out interstellar travel. "Uh, joking. Of course. But, why me?"

I already told you that. Because of your cousin. But first, I need to be charged.

"Charged?"

Well, fed.

"What do you eat?"

Energy.

"I see. I'm not sure I have any left in the cupboard."

Again, a joke?

"Yes, a joke." Darren made a mental note to use the joke ploy any time he stumbled. "How do we charge you?"

Your microwave oven would be the easiest.

"Now, *you're* joking?"

No. Microwave radiant energy is easily absorbed.

"As evidenced by exploding eggs."

What's your point?

"Um, when we were kids, we were told never, ever put pets in the microwave."

I see. The egg absorbs the energy as heat. I will be storing the energy.

"Fine. It's your yolk. Um, do you want me to show you where the oven is?"

I know where it is. It would be easiest if you carried me there.

Darren stared at the screen. He wanted to ask if it was joking, but he knew it wasn't. "I might hurt you."

You can't possibly.

"You might hurt me."

That is possible, but I won't.

"And I should … you know, believe you?"

We don't lie.

"How do I know that's not a lie?"

Good point. If I wanted to hurt you, I already could have.

"How do I know *that's* not a lie?"

Do you know how to travel between stars?

"Okay, okay. Maybe we can compromise."

Darren rooted around in the kitchen and came back with a pot, which he lay next to the monitor. Rustling was followed by three black ovals peering around the edge, and then more rustling, and words appeared on the screen.

Are you serious?

"What's wrong? It's plenty big enough."

I've traveled hundreds of light years to get here, and you're going to carry me in a cooking pot?

"I don't have to carry you at all. I could just call the police," Darren said.

I wouldn't be here when they arrived. Then you'd be in trouble.

"What happens when you run out of charge?"

Something banged from behind the monitor, and Darren wondered if space aliens could get angry. Seconds later, silver appendages curled over the edge of the pot and pulled the beast inside. Watching it move, he now thought it looked more like a squid, one that could look in all directions at once. He put the lid on, but it didn't go all the way down. A pencil-thin rod was holding it up an inch. Darren pushed harder, but the lid didn't budge. He leaned with all his weight, and he saw the lid denting around the beast's protesting obstruction.

Darren let it go and walked to the microwave, holding the pot out in front of him. He didn't doubt that the beast was telling the truth about being able to hurt him.

After crawling inside the microwave chamber, his guest held up one appendage, which then separated into five little ones in front of

Darren's eyes. "Are you waving goodbye, or what?" Darren said.

The pantomimed hand wagged back and forth.

"You are trying to tell me something, though?"

The faux fingers bent forward and back up, clearly an affirmative. They curled together into what might be a fist, and then sprang back open.

"Five minutes? You want me to run the oven for five minutes?"

The fingers melted back, and the beast spread all the appendages wide, ready to absorb "food."

"I'll take that as a yes," Darren said, and closed the door. He dialed in five minutes, and hesitated. This ran against everything he'd learned. You don't put something live in a microwave. He jabbed the ON button. He wasn't even sure this thing was alive.

The microwave was still running when the ambulance arrived with Crusher. Darren told the orderlies to lay him on the small bed in the spare bedroom. His cousin wouldn't care how big his bed was, since he wasn't aware of anything. Darren had visited him once in the hospital. He'd gotten the willies then, just as he did now. There had never been a full deck behind the handsome face or those dazzling blue eyes, but now there was clearly nothing. The eyelids blinked, the mouth twitched now and then, and sometimes the head would turn as though following you, but Darren didn't need the doctor to tell him this was all reflex—there was about as much behind the movements as a clam closing when touched.

The microwave dinged its completion as the orderly was reciting verbal instructions about the care. Afraid that the space beast would try to get out, Darren yelled, "Hold on! I'll be right there!"

The orderly stopped, surprised. The apartment was small enough to see that there was nobody else. "It's, um, habit," Darren said. "Sort of a ritual when I'm making a meal."

The orderly looked from Crusher to Darren, probably wondering which one he should be giving the instructions to.

After the orderlies left, glancing skeptically one last time over their shoulders at him, Darren hurried back to the microwave, where he found the beast still sprawled on the glass platter, as though relaxed under the warming rays of the sun. The dark ovals looked like sunglasses. Completely motionless, the creature actually looked dead. Darren was wondering if he should have perhaps heeded his caution, when the tip of one of the appendages lifted and gave him a little wave.

The space alien crawled back into the pot without protest, and Darren returned the gesture by leaving the dented lid behind. Back at the monitor, it wrote:

Your cousin has arrived?

"Mind, body, and soul—minus the mind and soul."

I am relieved. We can proceed with phase two.

Relief was an emotion. Wasn't it? A little more insight into the creature's makeup? "What is phase two? I can't see Crusher providing a lot of insight."

Phase two is acquiring rhodium. My stock was lost in the accident.

"I see. What happens if you don't get it?"

I will expire.

"Oops."

But first, I will lose rational functioning.

"You'll go crazy?"

In a sense. My actions will become unpredictable.

Darren remembered the dented lid. "No sense procrastinating. What do I do?"

Simply take me to Crusher.

"That's it? Phase two is going to Crusher?"

That's the first step. Your part. Beyond that, you will do what you would have done anyway—keep him alive.

"I don't get it. There's got to be more to it. The rhodium's not going to find its way to Crusher on its own."

Of course. I will work with Crusher to acquire it.

"With Crusher? There's not much to work with."

There are facilities that can be useful.

"How will you use them? He has no video input connector, you know."

A joke, I presume. Animals use electrical impulses in the operation of their nervous system. Electrical signal control is one of my specialties.

Darren shrugged. "It's your funeral."

Yet another joke?

"In a way, yeah."

A berserk space alien that ate microwaves for sustenance was the joke. Darren told himself this. Then shuddered.

He carried the alien to Crusher, and the beast waited in the pot while Darren placed the folded towel under Crusher's head as instructed. He wanted to ask what that was for, but he sensed that his multi-eyed guest was getting impatient. Another emotion, perhaps?

From the pot, the alien pointed to Darren's pocket. He took out his phone and saw that there was a text waiting: *Remember, keep Crusher alive.*

That was odd, as though a parting message.

He looked down, but the beast had already crawled out of the pot and positioned itself next to Crusher. Darren had seen the beast morph its appendages, and wasn't surprised when half of them stretched one way towards Crusher's feet, and the other half towards his head. Darren's eyes widened in astonishment, however, when the alien's main body began to stretch as well. Like clay rolled between your palms, the alien continued elongating, coiling near Crusher's feet. The black ovals stretched as well, forming candy cane stripes along the extruding rod. It grew thinner and thinner, until Darren thought it might disappear altogether. When it was finally as thin as a toothpick, it stopped. The tip next to Crusher's head wiggled a little, as though checking itself out, and then dove underneath his cousin's neck. Darren stared, wondering what it was doing. It dawned on him that the coils near Crusher's feet were contracting, getting smaller. He leaned over to look on the other side of Crusher, but there was nothing there. Where was the space alien going?

And then Darren saw it. A spot of red had formed in the towel where Crusher's head met his neck. He squatted down for a better look, and gasped and fell back when he saw the long silvery thread coursing up into the base of Crusher's skull.

"Shit!" Darren shouted. "Holy hell!"

He panicked, caught in indecision about what to do. Should he grab the silver thread and pull it back out? He knew how strong the beast could be. If it resisted, Darren might only succeed in mincing what remained of his cousin's brain. In the end, all he could do was watch in horror as the last of the alien intruder disappeared inside, like a strand of slurped up spaghetti.

Darren squatted next to his vegetative cousin, panting, his heart racing. His head spun with colliding thoughts. He tried not to imagine what the alien thread was doing inside, but failed. The horrendous images got the best of him, and he suddenly shivered and crab-walked away from the small bed, crashing into a cardboard box. *What have I done?* he thought. His cousin had been a retard, but his cousin nonetheless.

Darren closed his eyes. *Had been* he told himself. Past tense. The dolt cousin who'd touched his tongue with the jumper cables just to see what would happen had already left this Earth before the alien wiggled inside. Aunt Melba had talked to the doctor about pulling the plug, but there was no plug to pull. All they could do was stop feeding him, and she had considered that—was still considering it.

He closed his eyes and took deep breaths, practicing the calming yoga exercises Aunt Melba had taught him long ago. Thrashing sounds pulled him back. Crusher was jerking around on the bed, his arms and legs twitching randomly, his head turning one way, and then twisting the other. The eyes, though, remained as unseeing as always.

Darren couldn't take it anymore, and left the room. He paced the small apartment, trying to ignore the sounds coming from the other room. After twenty minutes, the noise stopped. He peeked inside and found his cousin lying quietly. Darren would have guessed he was sleeping, except that his eyes were open, staring off into infinity.

A walk around the block settled Darren a little. He'd intended to walk farther, but he worried about leaving his invaded cousin alone, and hurried back. He couldn't bear to be near him, but felt guilty when he left. This was hell.

His anxiety peaked a couple of hours later when Darren could no longer ignore his duty to feed his ward. He cooked up cream-of-wheat with a dissolved vitamin pill, and took the bowl to the spare bedroom. He'd watched the aid at the hospital feed Crusher, and it had looked easy then. A few little pokes with the spoon around his mouth, and his cousin would open and swallow on reflex. Now, however, if Darren didn't see the man's chest slowly rise and fall, he would have thought he'd died. Try as he might, no pokes or prods would open that stubborn mouth.

"Fine," Darren said. "It looks like my problem's going to solve itself sooner than later."

With that, the sightless eyes swiveled towards him. And focused.

Darren nearly jumped away. His skin crawled at the sight of that look. It was *seeing* him. They then swiveled back to gaze at nothing, but the mouth twitched once, twice, and then flopped open.

Darren stared at the dark cavern, carpeted by a wet, red tongue. He half expected a shiny alien head to spring out. The tongue wiggled a little instead. Darren took the cue and lay a spoonful of cream-of-wheat on it. Nothing. He moved the spoon back and forth on the rough, wet surface, and the mouth sprang shut and swallowed. Darren held the handle of the spoon, but the rest was trapped inside. He gave it a tug, then pulled it slowly out through resisting lips.

This was going to take patience.

Spoonful after spoonful found its way down the gullet, each a bit easier than the previous. The mouth seemed to be learning the routine.

Darren knew damn well what was doing the learning, but he didn't want to think about that.

He was washing up when his phone tinkled. It was Aunt Melba. "Hello, sweetie," she said. "Has he arrived?"

His panic flooded back for a second before he reminded himself that she'd wanted to pull the plug anyway. "Yeah, as much as he can arrive."

"I understand, honey. I've asked my Path Shaman to log you in as a Class Two Angel. I'd have asked for a Class One, but that requires meta-powers proof."

Darren had no idea what she was talking about, and he didn't ask. Recognition was confirmation, no matter how bozokian, and that made him feel guilty.

"Is he comfortable?" she asked. "No, that's a stupid question—like asking what deodorant my blouse prefers."

Darren noted for future reference that his aunt did indeed wear deodorant.

She sighed. "I guess it's meaningless to ask anything about him, other than whether he's still breathing. I tell you what, if my Loud

Yoga doesn't knock me out tomorrow, I'll stop by. I'll bring some chia-seed pudding. I know that's your favorite."

"Loud Yoga?" he said after she'd disconnected. He reminded himself that he'd have to stop pretending that he liked her organic, non-GMO, low-carbon-footprint concoctions.

Maybe he could feed it to Crusher. That might teach the alien to explain atrocities before acting.

The alien's abduction of Crusher's voluntary nervous system proceeded quickly as the afternoon wore on into evening. Actually, it wasn't as much abduction as picking up the abandoned reins. Darren imagined thousands of microscopic silver strands testing millions of neurons in turn, mapping their responses.

On the other hand, the beast might simply be devouring the dope's brain from the inside out. If so, the consumption was coincidentally causing fingers and toes, eyelids and lips, arms and legs to animate in an ever-more coordinated fashion. By the time Darren checked in one last time, his cousin—or, rather, the alien—was sitting upright, staring at his open palm.

"Good night, you trouble-making son-of-a-bitch," he said.

Crusher's head lifted, swung towards, him, overshot, eased back, and the blue eyes seemed to finally find him. Darren lifted his middle finger, and walked away to bed.

Ж Ж Ж

Darren slept deeply, luxuriously, for the first time in a week. No need to wonder what was causing the rustling. The wonderful respite lasted only a few hours, though. He sat up, wide-eyed at the sound of banshees. He didn't really know what a banshee was, but if there had been one in the apartment, it would have sounded liked this.

As quickly as it came, the scream fell away to silence.

Darren took a deep breath, letting his heart ease back to a mere gallop, and then crawled out of bed. He knew where to find the banshee. Crusher was sitting on the bed, staring at the far wall. "What the hell was that?" Darren asked.

Crusher's head turned and his eyes found Darren with no trouble. Crusher blinked. His mouth opened, and then closed. He blinked. His mouth opened, and a protracted monotone issued forth, like when the doctors tells you, "Say ah." After few seconds, the mouth closed.

"A ways to go yet with the talking, I see."

Crusher blinked.

"I'm hoping the scream was some kind of breakthrough you only have to do once. If not, maybe you could practice putting the pillow over your face.

He blinked.

"Good night," Darren said and walked away. Another "ahh" followed him down the hall.

Ж Ж Ж

Darren woke late the next morning. He felt groggy, but replenished. He shuffled down the hall, and stopped short at the spare bedroom. He didn't remember closing the door. From inside came mutterings. He put his ear close. It sounded like a grown man imitating baby talk—a consonant repeated over and over, followed by a different one, and then a vowel—on and on. He opened the door and found Crusher still sitting on the bed. The abducted head turned to look at him. The motion was the same calculated stiffness as before. The alien was letting head movements go for the time being to work on the much more difficult act of talking.

Crusher blinked twice, and then a flurry of them. It looked like he had something in his eye, or was maybe holding back tears. "You trying to tell me something?" Darren asked.

Two blinks.

"What?"

Darren held up his hand to stop the flood of random gibberish. "That's not going to work. Hmm, maybe you're hungry?"

Two determined blinks.

"Okay. That's easy enough. I hope you liked the cream-of-wheat."

That was followed by a burst of quick blinks. Crusher's head turned slowly one way, and then the other.

"Too bad. I'm afraid it's cream-of-wheat for the time being."

Darren tried to ignore the flurry of panicked blinks as he walked away.

He returned ten minutes later, but no matter how he poked and prodded the spoon around Crusher's mouth, the lips refused to open. "You really hate cream-of-wheat, eh?" Darren asked, but the blue eyes just stared at him.

Darren sat back. "Well, what the hell do you want, then?"

Crusher lifted his hands slowly, palms out, and pushed against Darren. "Fine!" Darren yelled, backing away, "No porridge for you!"

His alien-piloted cousin started to stand up, but fell back. He tried again, and this time managed to stay on his feet. His head turned to look at Darren, and he held out his elbow.

"You want me to walk you somewhere?" Darren asked.

Crusher blinked twice.

"Oh! I understand. The bathroom. Thanks for, uh, waiting."

Crusher's walk was unsteady, and Darren had to work to keep him upright. He stopped when they came to the bathroom, but his ward refused to go in. Instead, Crusher staggered on, and Darren ran to catch up before he fell headlong. Crusher led them to the kitchen, and stopped in front of the microwave oven.

"You want something besides cream-of-wheat? Maybe some tater-tots?"

Crusher ignored him, and used one hand to lean against the counter while he opened drawers with the other.

"Maybe that's where you keep food in your tiny space ships, but not here on Earth. Look, why don't you just pantomime what you want to eat—"

Crusher had pulled out a screwdriver, and was holding it out unsteadily, his hand swaying back and forth like he might be trying to gauge were to poke Darren in the stomach.

"I don't get it. What's that for?"

Crusher's hand swung to the side, and the screwdriver hovered in front of the microwave.

"What? You want to cook it? You're going to ruin Crusher's teeth—"

Crusher dropped the tool, and poked clumsily at the oven's control panel with his thumb until the door popped open. He then leaned unsteadily forward, and made as though to stick his head inside.

"My God!" Darren said. "You want a recharge? Inside Crusher's *head*?"

He turned his head and blinked twice.

"You'll *kill* him!"

The alien twisted Crusher's head back and forth in disagreement.

Darren took a deep breath. "It would hardly matter, I guess. There isn't really any 'Crusher' anymore." He helped the alien zombie stand upright. "I have some bad news, though. The microwave doesn't work with the door open."

The zombie's hand pointed at the screwdriver lying on the floor.

"Ah! I understand. You want me to—what?—disable the door safety switch?"

A hand swung up to execute an unsteady salute.

ж ж ж

It took nearly an hour to render the microwave head-capable. The manufacturer had a litigation-vested interest in not making the job easy. Crusher—the space alien—knew what to do, and it was on Darren to do it. Progress proceeded as arduous communication barriers were overcome via pantomime and hit-or-miss suggestions. "This screw? No? This one? Is the next step even a screw at all? Oh, yeah? Well, screw you!" Sheet metal covers and bolts covered the entire counter when Darren was finally done. "Ready to bake your head?" Darren asked.

The alien had Darren punch in a twenty percent cycle—effectively defrost. The creature pantomimed that he—the silver alien—would be absorbing most of the energy anyway. Shaking his head at the ridiculous situation, Darren helped him insert his head, and then he hit the GO button.

The oven hummed and vibrated a little, changing pitch every ten seconds as the twenty-percent cycle kicked in. Darren half expected sparks to fly, or Crusher's hair to burst into flames, but the recharge proceeded without incident.

Almost.

About halfway through, Darren thought he heard a bell, but assumed it had come from the oven. And so, he was standing, arms crossed, watching Crusher's head get baked, when a scream caused him to jump and spin around.

Aunt Melba stood there, staring wide-eyed. A jar of chia-seed pudding slipped from her fingers and exploded onto the kitchen floor.

"I can explain," Darren said.

Chapter 2

"See, Aunt Melba?" Darren said. "Crusher is fine."

He had helped the space alien, disguised as his cousin, to the living room, and they were all sitting looking at each other. That is, Darren and his aunt were looking at each other—Crusher mostly stared at the floor.

"But, why did you have his head in the microwave?"

She didn't seem angry, just enormously perplexed.

"I didn't put him in there—he wanted to! I was just helping him."

"Darren, honey, he can't 'want' anything. He's a vegetable, remember?"

"No! He's, well, not. Crusher!" he said, addressing his zombie guest. "Raise your right hand."

The blue eyes slowly turned to Darren, and then he slowly raised his left hand.

"Oh, geez," Darren said. "Is that our right hand?"

Crusher slowly turned to look at his raised hand, then lowered it, and raised the other.

Aunt Melba looked surprised, but then skeptical. "That's not exactly an IQ test."

"Okay," Darren said. "Let's see ..." Inside Crusher's head was an alien who understood interstellar travel. "What's two plus two?"

Crusher stared at him a moment, opened his mouth and uttered two seconds of unintelligible gibberish, then blinked.

"My God!" Aunt Melba exclaimed. "He's ... trying to talk!"

"He's learning. He can't seem to get that part working. Talking seems, um, *alien* to him."

Crusher's right hand was still raised, and he slowly lifted his middle finger.

"Hey!" Darren called. "None of that!"

Aunt Melba's eyes had grown wide with wonder, though. "My Lord! It's a miracle!"

Her world was filled with miracles, mystical powers that would lift her from the mundane work-a-day life, if only she could tap them. "Maybe his chakras have kicked in," Darren said.

He was kidding, and he regretted making jokes about her beliefs. It was such an easy target.

She was nodding, though, with raised eyebrows. "I think you're right, sweetie. Poor Crusher just needed some help finding his way back."

"From … ?"

She looked at him, puzzled. "Dreamtime, of course."

"He was just dreaming?"

"No, no. The Australian Aborigines understand the truth, that we're surrounded by another dimension out of time."

Darren had read about their creation story. He didn't think she had that quite right, and in any case, she was mixing metaphysical metaphors, since chakras—whatever they were—belonged to Hindu traditions.

He wasn't about to debate, however. If she was handing him an out, he was going to run with it. "Could be," he said. "Chakras are … you know, cool."

She had leaned over and taken Crusher's hand. "You were probably coming back from a very cold place. But the microwave oven is not the way to warm up, understand, son? Those microwaves are toxic. They'll ruin your DNA."

Darren didn't know much physics, but he knew this wasn't true. If she was letting squid-head take the heat, though, so be it.

The doorbell rang, and he went to answer it. He opened the door to find a young woman, about his own age. She wore blue jeans and a subdued, loose cotton top. Her brown shoulder-length hair was also loose, and could have used some brushing. Any makeup she might have applied was far too subtle to detect. She smiled. "You must be Darren?"

She had an accent. Darren guessed Dutch, but that was mostly because he worked with a Dutch man who was equally relaxed about his appearance. Her eyes were the color of cinnamon, and Daren decided that eye makeup would have done an injustice. "Yes," he said. "What can I do for you?"

She held out her hand. "Adelaide. It's nice to meet you. My mother asked me to meet her here."

"I'm sorry. You must have the wrong address."

And he was sorry about that. Something about her was appealing. Maybe the way the corner of her mouth turned up in a hint of a smile after each sentence, as though she was encouraging you to join her in the intimacy of the subject.

Her smile broadened. "If so, then you must also be at the wrong address."

He shook his head. He didn't understand.

"Melba told me about you—you *are* Darren, correct?"

He stared at her, and shook his head again. "I, uh, I'm confused. I didn't know Aunt Melba had a daughter."

In fact it was impossible. Aunts can't hide something like this, not when Adelaide was essentially his own age.

"Oh, I'm not really her daughter. My father was her husband."

"Ah. From Uncle John's first marriage—you're German!"

That conspiratorial smile again. "You make it sound like an accusation."

"No! Of course not!"

It was, though. Born of habit. Darren's grandfather had nearly died as a POW under the Nazis during WWII, and then on top of that, Uncle John's first wife—apparently Adelaide's mother—had fought for, and won, child support. Neither reflected on Germany or Germans, but within the extended family, the word had taken on a nefarious suggestion by association.

"Adelaide!" Aunt Melba called from within. "Is that you?"

"It is!" she called back, then looked expectantly at Darren.

"Oh! Come in," he said. "She's in the living room."

Darren led the way, and his aunt stood and gave Adelaide a big hug. "We're going to have so much fun!" Melba said.

She started to introduce Adelaide. "We, uh, met," Darren said, then to her step-daughter, "Welcome to America. When did you arrive?"

"A month ago." That *smile*. "I'm not a tourist, you know. I am a US citizen."

"Really?" Darren said, sounding far more surprised than he intended.

"Really," she confirmed. "By birth."

"You were born in America?"

"I was born to an Ameri-*can*."

"Yeah. Of course." He felt like an idiot.

"We're taking an apartment together," Melba explained. "Here, in this complex."

"Oh, yeah? Well, that's quite a coincidence."

His aunt gave him a you-know-better look. "There are no coincidences. I've decided to live close by so that I can help you take care of Crusher."

Help me? Darren thought. *He's your son.* On the other hand, he did have to keep them from getting too chummy. He shuddered to think about her discovering the truth—that what she thought was her son was really just a convenient shell for a space alien.

"And, this must be Crusher," Adelaide said, kneeling before him and taking his hand. Crusher's head turned slowly until he was looking at her. She looked up at Melba, surprised. "That seemed like a conscious reaction."

"Oh, it's conscious, alright. He's coming back."

"I thought the physical damage to his cerebral hemispheres was irreversible—"

"Oh, that's all nonsense. Doctors think that physical structure is everything. They don't understand that it just provides support for the aural soul. Crusher took refuge in dreamtime, but it's time to come back. Isn't it, dear?" she asked him.

His head started to slowly turn in her direction, but then stopped halfway, as though deciding it wasn't worth the effort.

Melba was peering at her son, and Adelaide took the opportunity to throw Darren a little knowing glance. Her eyebrow said it all. Like him, she saw no use in trying to introduce Melba to the hard knocks of reality.

"He's improved since coming from the hospital?" Adelaide asked him.

Darren shrugged. "Maybe a little."

Now he wished the alien would make Crusher look more like the vegetable he was.

"Perhaps we should take him to see a doctor," Adelaide said.

"No!" Melba exclaimed. "No doctors. He lay in that hospital bed for a whole month while the 'doctors' poked and prodded him. He waited until he was free from their 'science' to come back. No, no doctors."

Adelaide capitulated and gave a little shrug.

Melba's phone sang a little song, and she pulled it from her purse. "Oh! It's my aroma therapist. I have to take this," she said and hurried out.

Adelaide grinned. "She's a sweet person. In German we might say *Suesse*. A little off kilter, but in a *Suesse* way. When she found I was coming to America, she insisted I stay with her."

"You know, she was all for the alimony from the beginning. 'Kids aren't accidents of nature,' she used to tell your father."

Adelaide laughed. "When I was young, my mother would tell me that I was an accident waiting to happen. That didn't prevent her from taking the money, however," she said, and then excused herself to use the bathroom.

Aunt Melba hardly knew her a month ago—there was no blood connection, after all—and here she was taking her in like a long-lost daughter. And yet, Melba could seem so cavalier towards her own son. Despite her infatuation with all things mystical, Melba had a logical core. The truth was that Crusher had departed when he'd faked that fall from the diving board. Fawning over the body left behind was pure sentimentality.

Until, that is, a space alien fooled her into thinking Crusher was coming back.

Said space alien was now clumsily jabbing his finger at his open mouth. "Not until they go!" Darren whispered. "Normal humans don't stick their heads in microwaves."

Just then Adelaide returned while Crusher's finger was still jabbing. "He's hungry," she said.

"I think it's just reflex," Darren said. Crusher's finger had paused mid-air, and slowly fell.

"When was the last time he ate?"

"Just last night."

"How much?"

Darren could have lied. "A small bowl of cream-of-wheat."

No, he couldn't. Not to those cinnamon eyes.

She knelt in front of Crusher and took his hand. "Can he walk?" she asked.

"Sort of a Frankenstein waddle," Darren said.

She glanced back at him. "He can probably hear you."

"Okay. Like a two-year-old, then."

She gave him a disapproving look, which made him wince. "Crusher would agree," he said in defense. *If he were actually there*, he thought.

Adelaide helped him up, and led him in a waddle to the kitchen, where she sat him at the small table. "Let's find something he won't choke on …" she said, opening the refrigerator. She looked at Darren. "Do you actually live here?"

"Sorry, today's the day I normally do my food shopping," he said. What he didn't add was that this typically consisted of loading up with more frozen entrees.

"One dessert yogurt, and … well, at least you have milk," she said, looking far into the back. "I guess it's cream-of-wheat again." She opened the milk, sniffed, and recoiled. She looked at Darren aghast. "This has practically turned into cheese. You didn't use this last night, did you?"

"What? No! Heck, no!"

Apparently he could lie to those cinnamon eyes. He doubted that the alien had bothered to tap into Crusher's sense of taste, though. He could claim extenuating circumstances.

She sighed. "Well, Crusher, I hope you like strawberry yogurt." She looked at the date and sighed again. "It's only a week past the sell-by date."

Darren watched as she opened the container and carefully placed a spoonful into his mouth. Then, like a mechanical automaton, the lower jaw snapped up, the throat swallowed, and the jaw dropped open again. The whole time, he kept his eyes glued on Darren, who saw that the automaton's finger lying in his lap was pointed at the disassembled microwave.

After three spoonfuls, the sound of the front door opening was followed by Melba's voice. "Adelaide, dear! You ready to look at the apartment?"

Upon hearing this, Crusher's hand swung up and knocked the approaching spoon from Adelaide's hand, sending a splatter of yogurt to join the scattered globs of chia-seed pudding already decorating the floor.

"Oh!" Adelaide exclaimed. "We've made a mess … and it's on top of an existing mess." She looked at Darren.

"Don't look at me. Aunt Melba threw it on the floor."

Darren waited until the two women left, then held his hand out towards the microwave. "Okay, let's cook up a space alien."

ж ж ж

Darren shook his head as he scanned down the online price sheet. "Are you sure you need a whole ounce?" he called to Crusher, who was in the bedroom watching TV. A three-syllable response came back that sounded like someone talking with a novocaine-numbed mouth. Darren took it to be a "Yes." He leaned back in the chair and put his hands in his pockets. "It costs a thousand dollars an ounce! I haven't got that kind of money!"

He had that kind of money in a retirement account, but there was a penalty for early withdrawal, and, besides, Crusher wasn't capable of signing an IOU on behalf of the alien.

Darren paged down to the shipping details. Ha! He needn't feel guilty about being a Scrooge. "They require three weeks to ship the stuff. Can you wait that long?"

The response sounded like the same three syllables, but an octave higher. "I'll take that as a 'No.'"

The front door opened, followed by Melba's "Yoo-hoo! We're back!"

Adelaide came into the living room and leaned over to look at the laptop screen. "It's not really the best time to invest in rare metals."

"Oh yeah?" Darren said. "Why?"

"Prices have peaked. The latest squabbles in the South China Sea have caused panic. Precious metals are one of the most volatile investments available."

Darren looked at her. Floppy clothes and unkempt hair could hide worldly sophistication. "Really? Are you, like, an economist?"

She laughed. "I'm a graphics designer who lost money investing in gold."

"A graphics designer? Now there's a portable profession. You could work anywhere."

"Actually, I'm a graphics designer when talking to potential clients, and a graphics artist when talking to myself. You're looking to buy rhodium?"

"Uh, yeah."

She didn't say anything. She had just explained why this would be dumb.

"It's for one of my, uh, clients."

"You have clients?"

"I'm an accountant—a CPA."

"Clients ask accountants to make investments for them?"

"No. Not usually. This client is, um, special."

"Special," she said.

"Special" indicates something interesting, but you can't know what. "It's not as an investment. It's a, uh, science project."

She nodded. "Secret stuff."

"Yeah. You know … secret. He needs it right away. He's sort of desperate. And I want to help him. It's important but, um—"

"Secret," she said. She peered at the screen again. "Rhodium. Don't they use that in catalytic converters?"

"I remember seeing that."

She rubbed her chin. "How much are you looking for?"

"Apparently about an ounce."

She nodded thoughtfully. "I might be able to help you. I have a friend who works at a catalytic converter factory."

"He could … steal some?"

"Oh, no! He's the plant manager. Maybe he could resell it to you."

"That would be great. He's, uh, your boyfriend?"

Why did he ask that? It was like he had his own space alien pulling strings inside his head. He wasn't even available. Sharon wasn't serious about breaking the engagement. Was she?

Adelaide grinned playfully. "If you mean, are we dating? No."

Darren felt his cheeks burning. "Great! I mean, about the rhodium."

"Of course," she said with mock seriousness. "The rhodium."

From the bedroom came the sounds of babbling nonsense, like someone pretending to have a conversation with the television. "He's practicing," Darren explained.

ж ж ж

"Here's the pole with the bird's nest," Darren said, parking the car next to it. "Man, that must be a big bird," he added, peering up at it through the windshield. "Maybe I'll just park a couple of spaces over."

Adelaide sat next to him, with Crusher in back, staring at his knees. Melba had left for an acupuncture session, and Darren didn't trust leaving the space alien alone. Adelaide's "friend" Tony had told her to meet him here.

"Why all the way in the back?" Darren asked. "There was plenty of parking near the lobby. And then all the way in the back of the *back* parking lot, besides."

"I don't know," she replied with furrowed brow. "It is strange."

"This must be him," Darren said, nodding at a BMW coming towards them.

Adelaide gave the driver a wave as he parked and got out. Tony was tall and handsome, probably once the star high school football player. Darren disliked him immediately, and wondered why. Maybe it was the smile that was more smirk than smile. Maybe the way he winked at Adelaide. In any case, he looked like someone of authority.

Darren and Adelaide got out, leaving Crusher to stare at his feet, and Adelaide gave Tony a quick hug, adroitly evading the kiss he tried to plant. Darren shook Tony's hand, and judging by the powerful grip, was ready for Tony to try to wrestle him to the pavement.

"You must be the guy looking for rhode," Tony said.

Darren guessed that was the street name, like "meth" for methamphetamine. "Uh, yeah. I need about an ounce."

Tony eyed him. "You know the value of that amount?"

Darren sighed. "A thousand dollars."

Tony nodded. "About right."

"I, um, I could pay you something for it—"

Tony held up his hand. "No way. That would be unethical." He glanced at Adelaide, as if to prepare her. "I could steal some for you, though."

"You would … steal it?" Darren said. He wasn't sure he'd heard him correctly.

"Sure," Tony said, glancing again at Adelaide to make sure she was listening. "They can afford it. Believe me."

Pretty frivolous for the plant manager.

"I can't get you a whole ounce all at once," Tony went on. "They'd notice that. We'll get the rest after the next shipment."

"Oh, man," Darren said, glancing around, afraid somebody might be listening. "I don't want to get you in trouble."

"Nah. I do it all the time." He gestured at the BMW. "How do you think I bought that? Hell, I can get a hundred dollars just for the powder the line workers wash off their hands."

"Powder?" Darren said.

Tony snorted. "Sure. You think we buy rhode in bullion bars?"

"I hadn't thought about it."

Tony snorted again at his ignorance. "The trick is avoiding getting greedy. That's how you get caught—taking too much at one time."

Crusher had gotten out of the car, and now waddled Frankenstein-style towards them.

"Who the hell's that?" Tony asked.

"My cousin," Darren replied. "He took a twenty-foot dive aimed at five minutes of television fame, and found mashed potatoes for brains instead."

Crusher's head slowly turned to look at Tony.

"What's he, a tardo? He gives me the creeps."

"He's aspiring to attain 'tardo' status. So … what do we do next?"

"We wait until Joanie gets off shift. She's the line supervisor. I give her a cut. She has access to the rhode safe."

"You don't?" Adelaide asked.

Tony hesitated a split second before answering. "Yeah. Of course. There's a surveillance camera, though. Pulling rhode is part of Joanie's job."

Adelaide glanced at Darren. She was apparently finding the situation strange as well. "You're the plant *manager*," she said.

"Sure, but, you know, I can't just do whatever I want—look, the tardo's really freaking me, staring like that."

"Crusher!" Darren barked. "Back to the car. Now!"

"He's not a dog," Adelaide chided. She took Crusher's hand and guided him to the car.

"So," Tony said quietly, "like, what's up with you and Adelaide?"

Darren considered telling him that they'd just come from a pay-by-the-hour motel. And Crusher had watched. "She's my half-sister," he said.

He thought about that. A half-sister meant that they shared a parent. He wasn't anything to her, other than hopefully attractive. Or at least not unappealing.

"I see," Tony said. "Cool."

"Yeah," Darren said. "Cool."

He really didn't like Tony.

Tony glanced off, and then back at Darren. "Wait in the car with Adelaide," he said, and walked off towards a guard who'd appeared at the edge of the parking lot.

Adelaide sat in the back seat, holding Crusher's hand. "I apologize," she said when Darren climbed into the driver's seat. "This isn't what I was expecting at all."

"I figured. It's like the Mafia has decided that catalytic converters are the newest hot illicit ticket."

"Certainly not what you'd expect from a plant manager," she said, her brow seemingly permanently furrowed. "I feel guilty."

"You didn't know. You wouldn't have brought us if you thought—"

"No. I mean, I feel guilty about that as well, but he thinks he's going to bed with me again."

"Again?" Darren said.

Her furrowed brow turned puzzled at his critical tone. "Yes," she said. "I hate leading him on."

They watched Tony talking to the guard a hundred feet away. "We'll be receiving stolen goods," Darren said.

"It is a crime," Adelaide agreed.

"Maybe we should call the whole thing off."

Darren hadn't gotten the last word out of his mouth when

Crusher wailed like he'd been stuck with a spike. Adelaide sat back, alarmed. Tony glanced over.

"Okay!" Darren yelled. "We'll do it! Now put a cork in it!"

Crusher immediately fell back to his natural catatonic state.

"What in heaven's name happened?" Adelaide asked.

Darren took a deep breath, buying time to think. "Crusher was—is—friends with this special client. He, uh, knows how important the rhodium is."

He looked at her sideways. Was she buying it?

"Crusher is friends with one of *your* clients?" she said.

"Yeah. In fact, well, it's like this. They were sort of drinking buddies."

That sounded safe enough.

"Crusher was drinking buddies with a scientist? From what Melba told me, I would have expected him to be part of an ATV club—you know, where they ride around the woods scaring animals."

"I guess there was more to him than we thought."

She patted Crusher's hand. "Sometimes the bright qualities aren't obvious."

And sometimes the brightest quality was the ability to suck milk through a straw into one nostril, and have it pour out the other, thanks to a hunting accident that damaged his nasal cavities. He was shooting arrows straight up to see how high they'd go, and he watched as one returned to sender. She never knew the real Crusher.

Tony came back and leaned into the open driver's window. "Carl's cool. I gave him five bucks to get lost. The shift is almost over. Joanie will be coming out any minute."

"You paid the guard to go away?" Darren asked.

"Yeah. Don't worry about it. That one's on me." He glanced around, seeming nervous.

"Something wrong?" Darren asked.

"Huh? Nah. Carl said there's a new guard starting today. No problem."

To Darren, "no problem" usually meant *There is a problem, but I'm going to ignore it.*

People began streaming out a door, spreading out to cars

parked closer to the building. Tony waved and called, "Hey Joanie! Over here!"

A thick-set woman dressed in tight black stretch-pants and a colorful flower-patterned blouse hurried towards them, and Darren stepped out to greet her. Adelaide got out as well. Darren leaned back inside the window. "Crusher! Stay!"

"He's not a *dog*!" Adelaide hissed.

Joanie shook his hand as she looked them up and down, considering.

"You know them?" she asked Tony. She could have been a precinct desk sergeant.

"Sure," he replied. "No problem."

There it was again.

"I don't know," Joanie said, glancing around, just as Tony had done a minute ago. "There's a new guard today. Word is that he's been planted by management."

"But Tony," Adelaide said, "you *are* the management."

Joanie snorted. "Yeah, well so am I, but that doesn't mean a rat's ass on the floor."

Tony was blushing, holding up his hand as though to interject.

"No," Adelaide said, "I mean, as plant manager, surely you would have known if—"

"What are talking about?" Joanie barked, desk sergeant mode.

Adelaide glanced from her to Tony, speechless.

Joanie laughed, a loud cackle. "Tony told you he was the plant *manager*? Ha! And you *believed* him? Ha!"

Tony was blushing hard now, and his eyes widened as he looked past Darren. Another guard had come out of the door, and stood watching them.

Something bumped Darren's elbow. "Crusher! I told you to stay in the car!"

The alien zombie stood staring straight at Joanie. "Who the hell is this creep?" she asked, dividing her glances between him and the new guard. "Look," she said, "I don't trust the new guard. I'm outa here."

Crusher opened his mouth, and out came a deep honk, like a fog horn.

"What the hell!" Joanie cried. "Somebody tell this freak to shut up—"

Crusher grabbed her hand, and she froze, staring at his forehead.

A red dot had appeared—a bindi (if he were a Hindu woman) the sixth chakra, according to Aunt Melba, the third eye. The bindi sagged and stretched downward. It was blood, noticed also by the rest, judging from the collective gasp. The blood trickled down across the bridge of Crusher's nose, and then descended his left cheek and across the corner of his mouth. The collective gasp became a groan as the tip of a little blood-covered worm poked through the hole.

"Crusher!" Darren yelled. "Go back!"

All eyes stared, hypnotized, by the little worm, oblivious to Darren's outburst. Crusher lifted Joanie's hand, and planted her palm squarely across his face. She didn't resist, seeming dazed, paralyzed.

What the hell was the alien thinking?

And then he saw that Joanie's hand was dirty, covered with soot, or perhaps a powder of some sort.

A powder.

"Crusher!" Darren exclaimed. "Are you crazy? How much do you think you'll get?"

Joanie's trance broke, and she yelled, trying to pull her hand away, but Crusher held fast. "It's, it's—" she cried, "it's *licking* me!" The weirdness finally got to her and she screamed, thrashing, struggling to get away against Crusher's determined strength.

Darren tried to help her, but Crusher used his other hand to ward him off.

"What's going on here?" demanded the new guard, suddenly next to them.

It was the voice of authority—true authority, not the tentative, untested lightweight authority of a normal hired guard.

"Officer," Darren said, for this was clearly what he was, an undercover cop, "my friend here is—"

The cop ignored him, grabbing Joanie's wrist instead and yanking it away from Crusher's face. The tip of the alien's tentacle was gone, retreated back inside. Joanie's hand and Crusher's face were both messily smeared with blood, so much blood, in fact, that the small hole was hard to find.

"What the hell have you done to this man?" the cop asked.

Darren realized he was talking to Joanie.

"Me?" she screamed. "He was *licking* me!"

"You okay?" He asked Crusher, who was staring straight ahead, and slowly turned to look at him. "You want to press charges, sir?"

"There was a *worm* coming out of his *head*!" Joanie yelled. "It was *licking* me—"

The cop held up his hand for her to stop, glared at her a moment, and turned back to Crusher, who opened his mouth, and issued a cross between a crow's caw, and a cow's moo.

The cop looked at them.

"He's my cousin," Darren explained. "He has brain damage. Vocal coordination is difficult."

"You're his guardian?"

"Uh, yeah."

"Do *you* want to press charges?"

"Huh? Heck, no!"

The undercover policeman stared at him, then turned to Joanie. "You're coming with me."

"Why?" she exclaimed. "*He's* the one who was assaulting *me*. It was the worm, but—"

"Shut up! It's not about this." He looked at Tony. "You're the shipping supervisor, right?"

Tony glanced off to his car, as though considering making a run for it.

"Look," the cop said, "I know you are. I want you both to follow me." He turned to the rest. "If you're not employees, then you're trespassing, and need to leave.

Minutes later, they were driving away. Darren didn't know what to say. Adelaide hadn't spoken a word since discovering that Tony wasn't the plant manager. Maybe she hadn't seen it. "That was close," Darren finally said. "I wonder if they'll rat us out."

She looked at him, and he couldn't read her face. Was it criticism, concern, or puzzlement? "Rat us out?" she repeated.

"It means if they'll tell on us, if they'll tell the cop why we were there—"

"I know what it means. I just never heard it outside old movies.

Anyway, we didn't do anything. We didn't receive any stolen goods, no money exchanged hands. We're fine."

They drove on. Darren glanced at Crusher sitting in the back alone. His cousin was staring at his knees. His face looked like it had gone through a windshield.

"I saw it," Adelaide said.

She was looking at him levelly. "The worm. I saw it."

They came to a stop sign, and Darren waited for another car to go through before stepping on the gas. He looked at her. "I can explain."

Chapter 3

"So, you're telling me that I didn't actually see it," Adelaide said, looking at Darren skeptically from the passenger seat.

He had offered that it had been a case of suggestive imagination. He'd heard a piece about this on public radio. Growing evidence was showing that eyewitness testimony in murder cases was often worse than useless. People didn't knowingly lie, it was just that the human brain is terrible at remembering details correctly during times of trauma.

"Right," he said. "You heard Joanie screaming that there was a worm, and that's what got planted in your memory."

"You're telling me that you *didn't* see it?"

He looked at her. He really hated to lie to her. "Right now, as you ask me that, yes, I think I saw it. But, like, a minute ago, I probably didn't think that. You see? *Your* suggestion planted the image in my brain."

Adelaide stared at him. She opened her mouth to say something, and then closed it again, changing her mind. She twisted around and leaned close to Crusher, who was still staring at his feet. "There's a hole in his head," she confirmed, turning back. "Am I imagining that now?"

"Right," Darren said. He'd forgotten about the hole. "It's been there all along, though."

"It has not," she said, a statement of fact.

"It's been … covered with makeup."

There. A big fat lie.

"Where did the blood come from? And why is there a hole in

the first place?"

He considered telling her that before Crusher faked a fall from a high-dive, he'd pretended to inadvertently drill a hole in his forehead. Darren decided that was too extreme. "The hole was made by the doctor—part of a new procedure—and Crusher must have knocked it open."

"The doctor's drilling holes in patients' heads?"

"Exactly."

They rode in silence. She turned around to look at Crusher, and then back at Darren. "Why?"

"It's apparently a radical new medical advancement—it could be the next penicillin."

"I see," she said.

Silence.

"I don't know why it came open again so easily," he added.

"Right," she said.

She just looked out the window at the passing urban scene. He hated that she didn't ask more questions. He had no idea what he'd say if she did, but the silence was damning.

ж ж ж

When they arrived back at his apartment, Adelaide said, "Do you want your aunt to see him like that?"

The blood on Crusher's face had dried, and he looked like a bona fide zombie.

"I take it she doesn't know about the radical new medical advancement," she said, managing to subtly place virtual quotes around "medical advancement."

Darren nodded. "I'll maneuver Aunt Melba into the kitchen, and maybe you can get Crusher into the bathroom before she sees him." He reached into the glove compartment and handed her a paper towel. "Give me a few minutes. Clean him up as best you can, first. Use your spit."

"Okay," she said, watching with a hint of a smile, as though waiting for *him* to come clean.

"Right," he said, and got out.

When Darren opened the door to his apartment, he heard voices in the living room. He recognized Melba, and the other voice was … Sharon! When he entered the room, she jumped up and gave him a long hug. "Uh, hi," he said into her hair.

She pulled away and gazed at him. "Tanya confessed," she said.

"She did? Uh, about what?" He remembered. "Oh! The lie about me kissing the floozy."

Sharon's brow furrowed. "Of course! Did you *forget*?"

"No! Of course not."

Now *there* was a lie.

"Anyway," Sharon said, "we can't hold it against Tanya."

"No, I guess not. She just hates me."

"That's not why she lied."

"She doesn't hate me?"

"Yes, she does. But at least she has a good reason."

"Uh, oh. What now?"

"It's nothing you did," she said, giving him a playful little push, "it's what you *are*. Tanya explained that she was just jealous."

"Of *me*?"

That was hard to imagine. It wasn't like he was taking Sharon away from her. Those two spent more time together than married couples.

"She wanted me all for herself," Sharon said.

She was looking at him like the meaning behind this was obvious.

He laughed. "What? Is she *gay*?"

Sharon's raised brow told it all.

"She's *gay*? No way!"

Tanya was even hotter than Sharon, and Sharon was, well, really hot.

"Yes," Sharon said, "she is. And she's one very disappointed LGBT right now."

"Uh, I think she's just one of those."

"What are you talking about? I told you—she's *gay*!"

"Right. Of course."

This was turning out to be one of their normal conversations.

"Anyway," she said, holding up her hand and wiggling it so the engagement ring twinkled, "I guess I'll keep this after all."

"Right," he said. That sounded hollow. "Good," he added, forcing some enthusiasm.

She pouted. "You don't sound very excited."

"Of *course* I am!"

He wasn't. He'd hardly given her a thought ever since the alien commandeered his computer monitor. He mostly just felt guilty about that. He heard rustling in the hallway. Melba sat smiling and watching them have their moment, and now her eyes widened with recognition, and then scrunched together. "What in heaven's name happened to *you*?" she said, jumping up.

Adelaide stood looking sheepish next to Crusher, who's caked blood was now mostly gone, but his face was still smeared as though he'd gone wild with rouge and lipstick. She threw Darren a quick glance. "We had a little accident. He was, um, sort of slapping his face—"

"I know what happened," Melba said, nodding. "He was picking his nose."

Adelaide gave a little shrug, as though she wasn't willing to squeal on him.

Melba tsk-tsk'd. "He was always picking his nose until it bled. I told him that someday his finger was going to poke right into his brain, and then where would he be?" She frowned at what she'd just said.

Adelaide wrapped her arm around Crusher and gave him a little hug. "Well, no harm done. I'll just get him cleaned up a little."

Darren watched as she maneuvered him around towards the bathroom. She was so ... what was the word? Capable. Yes, capable.

The sound of a loud throat-clearing came from behind them, and Adelaide stopped and turned back.

"Oh!" Darren exclaimed. "Right. Adelaide, this is my, um, my—"

"Your fiancée!" Sharon said.

"Right. My, um, fiancée ..."

"Sharon!" she cried. "What's the *matter* with you?" She eyed Adelaide. "What were you doing with *her*?" she asked, like the object was too vile to verbalize.

"We were on a little, uh, errand."

"I'll bet you were. As soon as you thought you were free, you grabbed the first floozy that came along."

"Now that's not fair—"

He saw a blur as her hand flew up, and then pain and stars filled his head. His vision settled, leaving a stinging cheek. Sharon made a dramatic point of removing the engagement ring. She thought a moment, and then put it in her purse, and stalked off, pushing Adelaide roughly aside.

The front door slammed, shaking the whole house.

"That *wasn't* fair," Adelaide said softly.

Darren didn't tell her that he wasn't talking about Sharon's irrational assault. He didn't like that she called Adelaide a floozy.

Crusher opened his mouth and honked.

ж ж ж

"It was a lot easier communicating with you when you were just a freaky little alien hiding behind my monitor," Darren said.

Crusher opened his mouth and bleated.

"Exactly," Darren said.

Aunt Melba and Adelaide had gone off to sign the rental papers on their apartment and run some errands, and Darren was working with Crusher to develop a means to converse. The alien wasn't able to manipulate the larynx and mouth enough to form words, let alone sentences—a daunting amount of coordination that Darren had always taken for granted. Instead, the alien was practicing just saying individual letters—"ahh," for the letter A, "buh," for B, "la," for L, and on and on.

Darren pointed to the letter J on the sheet of paper where he'd written out the entire alphabet. "Huh," Crusher said.

"'Huh?'" Darren said. "No, it's 'juh.'"

"Huh," Crusher repeated.

The alien had learned a lot of his language skills watching television, and there were a number of Spanish channels in southern California. "You're pronouncing it like a Mexican. In English it's 'juh.'"

This time the alien, via Crusher, got it right. Distinguishing between Q and K, and R and L were difficult, but the vowels were the toughest. The letters E and I came out essentially the same, as did U and O. Consonants are launched from distinctive positions of lips and tongue, but the vowels are formed by subtle differences in the shape of the mouth, differences that to the alien were like poking a pole blindly through a curtain to push buttons on a remote.

"Tell you what," Darren said, "hold up your left hand when you want to say E, U, Q and R, and your right hand for I, O, K and L."

The alien would have no problem remembering this—he was an interstellar traveler, after all. Darren wrote it down.

"Okay," Darren said, "let's go through the whole alphabet one more time."

Crusher opened his mouth and let loose with a raucous honk, like the air horns at ball games.

"Hey!" Darren yelled. "What's that for?"

"Nuh!" Crusher breathed, "ooo," he said, flapping his right hand up and down.

Darren consulted his notes. "No? We're done for the day?"

Crusher honked again, this time even louder.

"Okay, already!" Darren exclaimed. "The neighbors will complain. What do you want?"

Crusher flopped his hand onto the table, and slid it so that it bumped the pencil towards Darren.

"You want me to write something?" Darren asked.

"Yeh," Crusher said. They had agreed that this was the shorthand for "yes."

Crusher baby-talked, and Darren transcribed, letter-by-letter until a word formed. "Radio?" he asked, looking at Crusher.

"Yeh," Crusher said.

"I don't understand. You want to listen to the radio?"

"Nah," Crusher mouthed—"no." He lifted his finger and let it fall on the paper.

"Okay," Darren said. "We'll do more."

Four letters later, Darren looked at Crusher. "NASA? You'd like to become an astronaut?"

Crusher opened his mouth—a threat to honk again—and flopped his finger on the paper.

When the next word was done, Darren stared at the paper. "You're out of your mind—and now that makes two of you. I know what SETI stands for. Let me guess—you'd like to get NASA to use the SETI program to contact your people—and I use the term loosely—to come and get you."

"Yeh."

"Let's think about this. You're going to flop yourself down into a chair in the NASA director's office and explain that you've occupied a human and turned him into a space alien zombie."

"Yeh."

"And he's going to shake your zombie hand and say, 'You bet, parasitic alien, I'll get right on it.'"

Crusher honked.

"Alright," Darren said. "I'm sorry for calling you a parasite. Crusher's seeing more action than he could have hoped for. On the other hand, you really are a burden, you know. So I wasn't too far off the mark."

The muffled words of Melba and Adelaide was followed by the sound of the front door opening. "We'll talk about your insane idea later," Darren said quietly. "In the meantime, I assume getting our hands on some rhodium takes priority."

Crusher honked his approval.

Melba walked in. "How's my sweetie doing?" she asked.

"It's like caring for a toddler," Darren said, "but I'm doing okay."

"Well," his aunt said, "you're my sweetie too."

Darren blushed. Crusher was light years removed—almost literally—from the sweetie she'd raised, but she didn't know that.

"What's this?" Adelaide asked, picking up the alphabet sheet.

"Ah, that. I, uh, was thinking we could come up with a method to communicate."

She nodded, looking at the paper. "Sort of like *The Diving Bell and the Butterfly*."

"Where the paralyzed guy wrote a whole book by blinking his eye?" Darren said. "Yeah, sort of like that."

"How is it going?" Adelaide asked.

"Not so good. I'm not sure he even understands."

Darren tried to catch Crusher's eye, but the zombie was staring at his knees. Darren didn't want to let on that there was advanced thinking going on inside the handsome idiot's head.

She pointed to his work sheet. "Why NASA?" she asked. "And SETI?"

"Right." Darren looked at the words. "I thought they might strike a chord with Crusher."

Melba leaned in to look. "I don't think he even knew what they stand for."

"Right." Darren looked up at his aunt. "When we were kids, Crusher once told me he wanted to be an astronaut."

Melba put her hand to her chin. "Hmm, I do remember that."

"You do?" Darren said, surprised. He'd made it up.

"Yes," she said, "he loved the idea that they went wee-wee right in their spacesuits. He lost interest when he found out that the screens on the control panels weren't televisions."

Ж Ж Ж

Darren was cleaning up the chia-seed pudding mess in the kitchen when Adelaide called to him from the living room. He came in wiping his hands.

"I think I found some," she said, pointing to the computer monitor.

"Well, I'll be," he said. Among the random posted Craigslist pictures was a metal bar the size and shape of a *Baby Ruth* with "Rh" impressed on the face. "I take it that means rhodium?"

"Yes. I looked it up. The caption says it weighs one ounce, and the asking price is three-hundred dollars."

"Hmm," he said, mentally calculating his checking balance after the rent, "I could probably swing that much. It looks awfully big for just one ounce."

"Perhaps it looks larger in the picture than it really is."

"Maybe. But why would the guy be selling it at a third the going rate?"

"He needs the money badly?"

"Or it's stolen," he said.

"Is it a crime to receive stolen goods if you don't know it has been stolen?"

"No. They have to prove you knew. So we don't ask?"

"I doubt he'd admit it voluntarily."

"Don't ask, don't tell."

"Americans believe they're the only nation with unbridled free expression, yet you use self-denial whenever convenient."

"I thought you were also American?"

"Only when convenient."

Ж Ж Ж

"You asked for a receipt?" Darren said. They were sitting in a booth in the *Los Pollos* fast-food restaurant where "Joe" had said he'd meet them. "What did he say?"

"I didn't ask for it," Adelaide said. "He offered it when I said we were a little concerned about the rhodium's source."

"What happened to 'Don't ask, don't tell'?"

"I didn't ask. Weren't you listening?"

"Is that him?" Darren said, gesturing out the window at a man walking into the parking lot, hands in pockets.

Adelaide watched him. "I think so. He said he had a full beard, and he'd be wearing a red shirt."

"I guess he considers scraggly whiskers covering half the face a full beard." He turned to Crusher sitting next to him. "Stay!"

Adelaide shook her head in disapproval as they stood up to meet "Joe," who paused just inside the door to look around before walking towards them. He nodded and said, "You Ada?"

"I'm Adelaide," she said. "Are you Joe?"

He stared and nodded. "Yeah, Joe." He looked around again and motioned for them to sit down. "You have the three-hundred bucks?"

Darren guided Adelaide into the seat and sat next to her, leaving Joe with Crusher. Instinct warned against putting a female next to a stranger. "I've got it," Darren said. He left the envelope in his pocket.

Joe nodded again and pulled a small bundle wrapped in brown paper from his pocket. He carefully unwrapped the metal bar for them to see, then wrapped it up again and placed it on the table. It was smaller than Darren had expected, but still obviously at least an ounce. The rhodium symbol looked like it was carved with a knife. "How do we know it's really rhodium?" Darren asked as Adelaide unfolded the paper and delicately picked it up.

Joe reached into another pocket and pulled out a folded piece of paper, which he handed to Darren.

Crusher lifted his hand and then let it fall with a thump on the table. "Crusher!" Darren scolded. "What is it with you? Cut it out!"

Joe nodded knowingly sliding away from Crusher a few inches. "My neighbor's kid's a retard. Always getting in the way. Let's see the money."

"In a minute," Darren said, unfolding the receipt. It looked legitimate, from a company called *Rare Metals Galore* for one ounce of rhodium. The total came to nine hundred, eighty-six dollars with shipping. "Why are you selling?" he said.

"My girlfriend needs an abortion," Joe said looking Darren in the eye. "Now, how 'bout it?"

Adelaide had let Crusher take the bar, and he held it against his forehead.

"Christ," Joe muttered, "what're ya doin?" He tried to take it from Crusher, and they tussled a bit before Joe yelled, "Ouch! The retard *bit* me!"

Other customers had turned to look at them. Darren pulled the envelope from his pocket and handed it to Joe. "Here, sorry. He didn't mean it."

"He sure as hell did," Joe said, taking the bills out to count. "The next guy he bites won't be as easy as me." He pocketed the money and stood up. "Nice doing business," he said, and walked out.

"That's wasn't so bad," Darren said, glancing over the receipt. Crusher lay his hand on the table, palm up and honked. "You want to see it? Here," he said laying the paper in his hand. Crusher stared at the paper lying in his open hand. He opened his mouth and honked three times. "Cool it!" Darren hissed. "You're making a scene."

"Nah! Nah! Nah!" Crusher squawked, letting the receipt fall and bouncing his hand on top of it.

"He seems upset with it," Adelaide said.

Darren glanced around. People were settled in, tablets propped in front of them. The restaurant offered free WiFi. Crusher could have done some web searching. "He thinks *Rare Metals Galore* is a fake."

"How would he know that?" she asked, picking up the bar. "Look, there's scratches."

Darren glanced at Crusher's forehead. Sure enough, the little hole was red with a bit of fresh blood, irritated when the alien had probed through with the tip of a tendril.

Adelaide probed at the scratches with her fingernail. "Uh, oh. It's just a coating."

"Son-of-a-bitch!" Darren exclaimed, jumping up and running out. He didn't have to go far. Just around the corner "Joe" stood talking with his phone to his ear. He had his back to Darren, and didn't see him until Darren grabbed the cheat by an elbow. Joe jerked away, surprised, and Darren snatched his phone from him. It was an act done completely on impulse. The guy had his money, and now Darren had his phone.

"Gimme my phone," Joe said, holding out his hand.

It was as much a plea as a demand, confirmation that he was a con man, at a disadvantage, caught in the act.

"Give me my money," Darren replied, taking a step back.

"That's stealing," Joe said.

"Same as you did to me."

"No, no. We had a deal. Give me my phone."

"You lied. That's fraud." Darren glanced towards the sound of pounding footsteps. Adelaide was running towards them, pulling a stumbling Crusher along by the hand. "Tell you what," Darren said, turning back to Joe. "How about I use your phone to call the police? Let's see who's really in trouble here."

Joe glared at him. "Fine." He took the money from his pocket, but pulled it away when Darren reached for it. "Not 'till I get my bar back."

Adelaide and Crusher had arrived, puffing. "Give him the bar," Darren said.

Crusher honked loudly in protest. Even though it was only a coating, it *was* rhodium.

"Curb the retard," Joe growled.

"He wants something," Adelaide said. The alien zombie pawed clumsily at the bar she was holding. She handed it to Darren, and he fended off Crusher's ineffectual attempts.

"Like Joe said," Darren muttered, "he's a retard."

Darren regretted the words as they spilled from his mouth, and the look Adelaide gave him confirmed his fear.

"That's mean," she said. "He obviously wants the bar."

"I know he does, but it's my three hundred bucks."

"Joe," Adelaide said, "you're sure the coating is rhodium?"

"Yeah, I'm sure."

"You believe him?" Darren said. It was getting difficult to fend off Crusher's determined lunges. The zombie started honking. "Alright, already!" Darren yelled. "Yeah," he confirmed, "it's rhodium."

"How do *you* know?" Adelaide asked.

Crusher had obviously tasted it through the hole in his forehead. "I trust Joe," he said. Now that he actually knew it was rhodium.

Adelaide eyed Darren and then Joe. "How about this," she said to the con man, "you keep fifty dollars, and we keep the bar."

"Fifty dollars!" Darren exclaimed but nodded grudgingly before Crusher broke out in a new blast of honks.

Joe studied Adelaide. "A hundred."

"Call the police," she said to Darren.

"Okay! Okay," Joe said, counting out fifty dollars and handing the rest to Darren. He took his phone and walked away without looking back.

"And let that be a lesson!" Darren called after him.

"What lesson?" Adelaide asked.

"Don't mess with German-American women," he said, but thought, *and don't try to fool an alien zombie.*

She looked at him skeptically, and shook her head.

There was a bus stop bench next to them, and they sat down. "You didn't have to be so generous," Darren said. "He'd probably have taken twenty."

"It was his rhodium," she said, "and the coating is probably worth more than fifty dollars. He did try to cheat us, but two wrongs wouldn't make it right. Besides, we wouldn't have actually called the police."

"We wouldn't?"

She looked at him, surprised, then at Crusher, sitting quietly holding the bar to his forehead.

"You think I was bluffing?" he pressed.

"Weren't you?"

He had been. Was it so obvious?

She glanced at Crusher and then looked Darren in the eye. "Something tells me you don't want Crusher to come to the attention of the authorities."

His head jerked back in surprise. "Why do you say that?" he

asked.

She shrugged. "Call it German-American woman intuition. Am I right? Do you want to keep Crusher under the radar?"

Darren held her gaze. He didn't want to lie to her. Not to her.

"He's special somehow, isn't he?" she said.

Darren glanced at Crusher, and the alien had turned his expressionless gaze on him. Just the fact that he wasn't staring at his knees said it all.

He had to answer her. "Crusher's cortex is essentially dead," he said, "and the doctors know this. They wouldn't believe that his brain is coming back. They would want to do tests."

She was watching him closely, following each word. "And what they found would surprise them?" she said softly.

Darren's breath caught. *Does she suspect?* "They know his cortex isn't working, but they wouldn't expect it to be gone, to be replaced by ..."

"By what?"

He couldn't say it. Even if Crusher didn't care—which he apparently did—he couldn't look her in the eye and tell her that there was a rat-sized alien living inside his cousin's head. "It would be arrogant of us to think we're the only intelligent species," he said, thinking his way through this.

She nodded, encouraging. "Like dolphins, and elephants, and apes."

"Yes—yes, there are those, but I was thinking of ... truly conscious intelligence—species even more intelligent than us."

She grinned. "Species that can factor polynomials before they learn to speak?"

"Exactly." He realized she was joking. "But, seriously, as intelligent as that. It's just that we're separated by such huge gulfs of time and space—" Crusher honked at this, but Adelaide seemed not to notice. "Every now and then, though, one species is able to move through a different dimension—"

She placed her hand on his. It almost took his breath away, the soft touch, the warmth, the womanliness. "A being from another dimension is communicating through Crusher?" she asked. "Is that what you're trying to tell me?"

He stared at her. He tolerated—patronized even—Aunt Melba,

but it was embarrassing sometimes to be with her in public. He looked at the soulless eyes of Crusher watching him, and back to the waiting eyes of Adelaide. "Yes—sort of." It was like jabbing a rusty needle into his arm. "I know—it sounds stupid. I don't want you to get the idea that I believe everything that—"

She squeezed his hand and shook her head. "I understand. I know you're not talking about aboriginal myths. It's a sense you have—a feeling of presence beyond physical explanation."

"Do you … feel it?" he asked hesitantly.

She held his gaze, and then shook her head, smiling ever so slightly. "No. But I understand what you're talking about."

Darren wished that *he* did. What the hell kind of cockamamie nonsense did she think he believed? It was more than he could bear to have her think he was some kind of new age nut. He turned to Crusher. "The square root of thirteen. If it's less than three, raise your left hand, otherwise, raise your right."

Crusher's dead eyes stared. He opened his mouth and honked once.

"Darren," Adelaide, said, grasping his arm, "it's okay. You don't have to prove anything."

He looked at her. "No, I do." To Crusher, he warned, "There's alternatives."

Crusher honked in protest, but raised his right hand.

Darren looked to Adelaide, and she nodded appreciatively, but he had the sense she was now patronizing him. Crusher's success could have been just a coincidence.

"Crusher," he said, "point towards Tijuana, and then towards Chicago."

The alien zombie sat staring at nothing.

"Alternatives," Darren reminded.

Crusher looked up at the sun and pointed south, and then swung his arm around to the north-east.

"Hawaii," Darren said.

Crusher's arm continued the arc and stopped south-west.

Adelaide's supportive nod had paused, and her brow was crinkled.

Crusher reached for the scam rhodium bar, and Darren held it away. "Not here, you dope." He noticed the scratches on the bar's surface, as though a hungry worm had crawled along, eating its way across it. Or the tip of an alien tentacle. As Darren looked at the bar, he heard the pounding of running feet, and the next instant, the bar was snatched from his hand.

Joe ran away down the sidewalk with the bar.

"Son-of-a-bitch!" Darren yelled.

The con man turned once to glance back and didn't see a middle-aged man come around the corner dressed like Jesus, followed by a young woman in a full-length robe and hijab. The man wore a black, close-cropped beard and colorful keffiyeh headdress, and was obviously Muslim accompanying his daughter. Joe ran smack into the man, who deftly plucked the bar from him. The Arab glanced at Darren and handed the bar to his teenage daughter, before grabbing Joe by both shoulders.

Darren was so surprised by the turn of events, that he didn't notice at first that Crusher had staggered off towards the fruckus. "Crusher, no!" Darren called, sprinting off after him, but was too late. The alien had far too little control to use his hand to grab the bar. The best he could manage was to raise both arms and fall onto the girl, wrapping his arms around her neck as she staggered backwards.

The father's eyes flashed with murderous rage.

"I can explain," Darren said.

Chapter 4

"How can you factor polynomials in your sleep, and yet be so utterly stupid?" Darren said. "That Saudi guy was going to *kill* you!"

He would have killed Crusher, the alien corrected.

Adelaide had gone off to see Melba, and Crusher sat with his head on the table next to Darren's computer, allowing the alien to communicate via Bluetooth. "Oh!" Darren exclaimed. "Of course! You're right—there was no consequence at all to groping the daughter of the Crown Prince."

I assume that is sarcasm, and he is only next-in-line to the Deputy Crown Prince.

"The point is that it was stupid. *You* are stupid!"

I got the bar.

"And I had to beg for your life!"

He could have given it back to Joe. You don't understand how critical the rhodium is to me.

"Apparently not! Besides, you didn't even eat it all anyway."

I explained—it's not possible to completely separate the rhodium from the underlying lead of the bar, which is toxic—I overdose if ingested too quickly. Also, I don't eat it. I don't have a stomach.

"Well, excuse me for maligning your anatomy, if you even *have* an anatomy."

You accuse me of being stupid, but you know that I must have an anatomy, since you saw that I am a physical being.

"As opposed to what? A spirit?"

A rhetorical question?

Darren blinked. "What the hell *are* you, anyway?"

An alien from outer space.

"*Now* who's being sarcastic? Are you a mammal or reptile? Male or female? Democrat or Republican?"

All of those uniquely evolved on Earth. You know that.

"Fine. I know what you're *not*. What *are* you?"

A fair question.

The words faded from the screen, leaving darkness.

"Do I get a fair answer?" Darren asked.

Darkness.

"Has the lead overdose knocked you out?"

Words finally formed. *I am an emissary to Earth.*

They faded.

"Good start. So you didn't stumble on Earth by accident. 'Emissary,' implies you came to open relations."

Correct.

"It also implies a peer relationship."

Don't push it.

Darren wasn't sure if this was a joke, but he followed the advice. "So, are you able to carry out your mission? Without your ... colleagues?"

Another fair question. I'm afraid the answer is "Not to completion." My specialty is alien contact.

"Where I presume I am the alien."

Correct. Our mission was to study the life on Earth, and, if appropriate, negotiate a far-portal.

"What's that? Sounds like a door of some kind." The opening sequence to *The Twilight Zone* floated into his imagination.

A good analogy. A far-portal allows two-way passage through extra-dimensional space. The technology of the home portal is advanced—far beyond your comprehension. A far-portal, on the other hand, can be constructed using the industry of emerging species.

"Where 'emerging' means primitive, I suppose."

If you like.

Darren did not like, but he didn't argue. He couldn't factor polynomials without referring to his high school text. "Why can't you complete the mission? Because you don't know how to build a far-portal?"

You are astute Darren.

"Sarcasm?"

You guess. As I indicated, my role is alien communication.

"So, you're stuck here with primitive aliens?"

Unless another exploratory mission is sent through.

"'Unless?' Not until?"

Even had my colleagues not destroyed themselves, and even if I could convince your species to build a far-portal, it would take years. Those waiting at the other end wouldn't expect anything to happen until then.

"They won't know something's gone awry until then."

Most astute.

"Can we resist the sarcasm for awhile? So, you wait a few years. Maybe you can learn how to play tennis using Crusher's body."

It's not that simple. From thousands of light years distance, all we could discern was that Earth hosts life of some sort. If an industrial technology capable of building a far-portal had not evolved, then a second mission would just be dooming yet more explorers.

Darren wondered if he could do it—embark on what was more than likely a one-way journey. "What about our radio and television transmissions?"

You asked me to refrain from sarcasm.

"What—? Oh, I see. Our transmissions won't reach your star for thousands of years. If your civilization is so advanced, what do you get by opening a door to us?"

We are traders. A world rich with life has much to offer. Your own history is replete with more advanced civilizations trading productively with primitive societies. The Dutch East India Company and Indonesia, for example.

"I have some friends who would argue that Europe was no more enlightened than the natives of the far east."

I am referring to the degree of technology, not wisdom.

"Right. Hey, but speaking of human examples, European contact with other people was rarely, if ever, mutually beneficial. In fact, exploitation is a better description than trade. Ask the native Americans—north and south."

Analogies go only so far.

Darren let it go. Arguing the point would probably just devolve into a yes-it-would, no-it-wouldn't debate. "Your method of exploration means that your trading territory only expands as other civilizations develop certain levels of technology."

Unless you only care about propagating your kind.

"Which you don't?" It was a question he wasn't sure he wanted answered.

No. Not us. There is another that does.

"Oh, yeah? Who are they?"

There is no way to write their name using your Latin characters. They punch through extra-dimensional space with no intention of returning. Their only goal is to dominate and propagate on new worlds.

"Sounds like fungus."

Indeed. A good analogy.

"So, uh, where does all this leave you? Wondering the world inside a brain-dead body in search of tidbits of rhodium?"

As I indicated previously, we need to contact NASA.

"What can they do for you? Get you into Earth orbit? You'd still have a thousand light years to go."

If any Earth organization could develop a far-portal using my meager knowledge, it would be NASA.

"Not Russia?"

They are flying with thirty-year-old technology—reliable, but nearly obsolete.

"How about the European Space Agency?"

They have a six billion dollar budget, versus NASA's twenty billion. Plus, my host body happens to be a US citizen.

"I don't get how SETI plays into this. They can't possibly contact your folks."

I understand that.

"So, why ask about it earlier?"

I was being unreasonably hopeful.

That would be a first—the alien making such a blatant mistake. "You were using it for misdirection, weren't you?"

Slightly.

"Slightly? Misdirection either works, or it doesn't."

Were you completely convinced that my only goal was to contact SETI?

The stranded alien had a point, one that Darren hated admitting.

"Who are you talking to?"

Darren jumped. It was Adelaide. "Where did you come from?" he asked.

"Uh, our new apartment, one floor down? I heard you talking, and I didn't want to interrupt." She looked at the monitor. "Who's contacting SETI?"

"Nobody!" Darren replied a little too exuberantly as he elbowed Crusher. The words faded from the screen.

"What's wrong with him?" she asked, pointing at Crusher's head lying on the desk.

"He's tired."

"Why doesn't he go and lie down?"

"He, uh, he likes to listen to the wood."

"He listens to the desk?"

"To the vibrations. My fingers on the keyboard."

She stared at him, and then shrugged. "Melba asked me to invite you and Crusher to join us for spaghetti this evening. She'd like to welcome Crusher's guest to the family."

Darren's jaw dropped. "She ... knows?"

Adelaide nodded, blushing. "I told her. I didn't think you'd mind. Do you?"

He remembered. "The being from another dimension!"

"Of course. What did you think I was talking about?"

"I didn't know." Time to lie. "Maybe one of Crusher's high school friends."

Adelaide looked at him oddly and shrugged again. "Anyway, Melba said you should come down around six." A hint of sly smile appeared. "Don't forget the guest of honor."

Darren watched her walk out and then nudged Crusher. "Don't let it go to your head. If they knew the truth, they'd be throwing the spaghetti at you."

Crusher honked.

"Never mind. You don't even have a head for it to go to."

ж ж ж

"Darren! Honey!" Melba called when he arrived with Crusher in tow. "This is so exciting! I know that Crusher would be happy if he knew."

Darren didn't say anything as his aunt led them to folding lawn chairs set up around the folding table that served as the dining room set. The less he said, the less he'd be admitting he believed in extra-dimensional beings. Extra-terrestrial beings that traversed extra dimensions, sure. Just not the kind that *lived* there.

"I thought we'd do a little channeling before eating," his aunt said, reaching out to each side to hold hands with Adelaide and him. "Crusher's guest may enjoy communing with his friends back home."

Darren took her hand and glanced at Adelaide, but she was looking at Melba with calm acceptance. He admired her nonjudgmental support, at least what showed.

"Darren and Adelaide, sweeties," Melba said. "Take Crusher's hands so we can complete the circle."

Darren and Adelaide lifted Crusher's arms and lay them on the table, while he stared at the far wall, seemingly oblivious. Clasping his cousin's unresponsive hand was like trying to greet someone who was unconscious. Which was in many ways the case.

"Close our eyes," Melba instructed.

Darren closed his, but peeked out. Adelaide sat serenely. Her unkempt hair seemed appealingly natural—what would greet you, after all, in the morning at the beginning of a new day. He pushed the thought away. No use fantasizing. Crusher stared past their channeling leader. Crusher rarely blinked. He'd have to mention that to the alien. That couldn't be good for the corneas.

Melba's voice broke his reverie. "Astral spirits from beyond!" she intoned in a deep, affected voice. "Come to us now, come and commune with spirits of kindred beliefs!"

Darren peeked at her. His aunt sat with ramrod straight posture, as though stretching upward to meet the visiting spirits halfway. With eyes closed tight, she began to hum softly. The tuneless drone hovered over the table, like a lawn mower far off in the distance. The mower moved their way, growing in volume. As it grew in volume, it grew in wavering pitch as well, imparting a sense of suspense, like the music in a horror movie when the clueless girl decides to open the door. Just when Darren imagined a puff of smoke appearing above the table, Crusher let loose with a loud, raucous honk.

Melba's soundtrack broke, and her face scrunched in displeasure, but she recovered quickly, and picked up where the foolish girl slowly, slowly pulls open the door. A second honk let loose, and Melba opened her eyes and sighed, letting go of their hands. "I guess it's time for spaghetti," she said.

ж ж ж

"You have to wash," Darren said. "You have to brush your teeth. You have to relieve yourself, and for God's sake, blink every couple of seconds. You're borrowing Crusher's body, and you have a responsibility to take care of it. Do you understand?"

Crusher sat on the sofa, staring at the carpet. "Yeh," he said.

The alien could tap into only so many of Crusher's nerves, and the sensory feedback associated with basic bodily needs hadn't made the list. Realization of this came when Darren began getting whiffs of odors redolent of garbage meat scraps left too long in August heat.

"That's the extent of your luggage?" he asked, pointing to a paper bag at the zombie's feet.

"Yeh."

"I saw what's in there—my tablet, the charger, and one pair of underwear. Did you even think about a toothbrush?"

"Nah."

"Of course not. All you think about is rhodium and a far-portal."

"Yeh."

"'Yeh,' indeed. Well, lucky for you, I packed extra toiletries in my bag. When Adelaide gets here, for God's sake behave yourself."

"Yeh."

She was taking them to the airport. They were flying to Houston to meet with the director of NASA. Darren could still hardly believe it. After some deep diving on the web, the alien had concluded that the director would be open to the whole idea of aliens on Earth, and Crusher had instructed Darren to call a certain unlisted number and explain that he wanted to talk to the director about SETI. The assistant at the other end initially gave him the brush-off until he reminded the woman that he had called on a number that was supposed to be secret, and—as Crusher had tutored him—that if the director didn't want to talk, then perhaps a certain junior member of the Senate might want to instead. The alien had used his super alien intellect to sidestep online cyber security to discover that the junior member, a former astronaut, was unlikely to retain his seat in the upcoming elections, and was vying to be named the new NASA director. Darren didn't get to speak with the director. Instead, they'd been sent tickets, and told to be at his office at 10:00 the next morning.

Crusher bent forward and plunged both hands into his paper bag.

"No!" Darren admonished. "Adelaide will be here any minute."

The alien wanted to use the tablet to tell him something—their new method of communicating.

"Sah, ooo," Crusher said, reverting to spelling. "Waw, ha, ahh, tah."

"So what? Do you *want* her to catch Crusher doing something other than behaving like a mobile turnip?"

"Nah."

"Because, if you do, please tell me! There's nothing I'd like better than to have her peer up your nose to see you peering back at her. I hate this subterfuge."

"Nah!" he repeated, unusually animated.

A knock on the door was followed by Adelaide's head appearing through the opening. "Am I interrupting something?" she asked.

"No," Darren replied. "Just me arguing with a turnip."

She rolled her eyes. "Are you ready? We should go."

ж ж ж

Darren glanced at his watch for the sixth time. He and Crusher had been sitting in a small waiting area presumably near the NASA director's office for twenty minutes. For the third time, Susanne, the director's assistant—a short, brusque woman with black-rimmed glasses—had come by to tell them that it would be just a few more minutes. Darren was on edge. He felt foolish, or, rather, he was afraid he was about to appear deeply foolish. He'd planned on going over their strategy on the plane, but the flight attendant had made him put away the tablet when she realized he was connected with WiFi. He hadn't paid for the in-flight service, and he couldn't explain that the connection was just a few feet away in his traveling partner's head. By the time they arrived at the hotel, he was dead weary, and planned to pick it up in the morning, but woke up late, and ended up rushing just to get to the NASA complex on time. He'd wanted Crusher to brief him there in the waiting area, but he refused. Crusher had spelled, "T-a-p-p-e-d." The wireless connections were monitored.

So, now he was going to sit down in front of the director of NASA and explain … what?

He was about to find out. Susanne appeared around the corner and beckoned them with a crooked finger. As she led them down the hall, Darren said, "He, uh, knows what we're here to talk about?"

She glanced at him. "You're here to talk about aliens."

Darren did a double-take. "Uh, yeah. Sort of."

She studied him. "You want to talk about the SETI project, of course."

"Yeah. Yes! The SETI project."

She seemed about to say something, but changed her mind and instead said, "I prepared a memo brief for him," and ushered them through a set of doors.

Darren was expecting a plush expanse, and thought at first that they'd been pawned off on an underling until he saw the title resting on the desk. It wasn't a small office, just not the expression of vast power that Hollywood might portray. The director had temporarily moved, along with his staff, to downtown Houston while his office was being renovated. Maybe the plush expanse was in progress.

The director greeted them with a benign smile and motioned for them to sit. His practiced bureaucrat face broke into a quick frown when Crusher accidentally kicked the chair away when trying to turn around, so that Darren had to jump up and help him. The director threw Darren an alarmed look and glanced down at his schedule. He looked back up with a changed expression, one of interest. "Ah," he said, "SETI enthusiasts. What can I do for you?"

"You, uh, flew us here," Darren reminded.

The director's frown returned, and he glanced again at his notes. This time he looked up with caution. "How did you get that telephone number?"

Darren glanced at Crusher, but he was staring at the wall. *What the hell am I supposed to say?* "My friend here," Darren said, gesturing at Crusher, "he, uh—this is going to sound really crazy—he is in contact with, uh, with aliens—space aliens."

Darren gulped.

The director glanced at Crusher, who essentially looked like a dead man propped up in a chair. "Him?" he said.

"Uh, yeah. You see—it's complicated. Crusher—actually my cousin—he seems totally out of it, because his cerebral cortex was damaged—"

"What do these aliens look like?" the director asked. "Their appearance."

The man asked this casually, but Darren sensed true interest. "Well, they, um, they're small," he said, as though he'd managed to hit upon at least one important point. "They're sort of silvery colored. They resemble a squid—but only sometimes. They can change shape—look, I know this sounds nuts—"

"No," the director assured, standing up. "I wouldn't be head of the space programs if I objected to strange ideas. Excuse me a moment—I'll be right back," he said as he walked around them and out. He closed the door behind him, and Darren heard a soft click.

Darren blinked. "Can you lock an office from the outside?" he whispered. It was a rhetorical question and he put his hand over Crusher's mouth to avoid a reply honk. He got up and tried the door. "Damn!" he whispered. "It *is* locked. Is that even legal?"

"Fuh," Crusher said.

"What?" Darren asked, still whispering.

"Fuh!"

Darren at first thought that his alien-occupied cousin was commiserating by using a bad word, before he realized he was spelling something. "The first letter is 'F'?" Darren asked.

Crusher honked. "Fuh, buh, iee," he said.

"F-b-e?" Darren asked. "That doesn't spell anything. 'Fbee?'"

Crusher honked in protest. "Iee! Iee!"

"Oh! You mean 'I'?" Darren noticed that his cousin was holding up his right hand—part of the code. "F-B-I? Holy shit! You're saying that the FBI's here?"

Crusher honked enthusiastically.

"How do you know this?"

"Wuh, iee, fuh, iee."

"WiFi? I thought you couldn't use WiFi—the room's bugged." Crusher just stared at him, or mostly past him. "Oh," Darren said, "I see. Only if you transmit to the tablet—you can listen all you want. Can you tell what the FBI is doing—?"

A click interrupted him, and the door opened. The man that walked in was in many ways the opposite of the NASA director. Where he was graying and almost frail, this man was at least six feet tall and all heft. The conciliatory demeanor of the director verged on patronizing, but this man's face exuded confident dominance. You either bowed to or rebelled against a man like this—you didn't share a chuckle. He closed the door and stood watching them, hands in pockets, as though the two NASA visitors were a task that he'd knock off in a minute or two, and then head off for a whiskey—neat, no ice.

Darren got up to face him, and had to help Crusher out of the chair. His cousin stood, his arms dangling at his side, staring moronically at the man.

The man didn't say anything. He just looked at them.

"I'm, uh, Darren. This is my cousin, Crusher." The man looked at him without reaction. Maybe he was deaf. "He's the one who's in contact with the, uh, the aliens."

The man nodded slightly, appraising Crusher. At least he could hear.

"Where's the director?" Darren asked.

The man gave a nod over his shoulder. "He'll be back in a minute," he said in a deep voice wrapped in a Texas drawl. Having made the point that *they* were at *his* disposal, he reached out and shook Darren's hand. "McKinney," he said.

"Right," Darren said. "Uh, is it *agent* McKinney?"

The man raised one eyebrow a millimeter, holding the handshake a moment so that Darren's hand cried out for release. "What kind of agent do you mean?" McKinney asked, finally letting Darren's vanquished hand go.

"I don't know," Darren stammered, floundering under the glare of dominance. "Maybe FBI?"

McKinney's mouth turned in the slightest smile, and he tilted his head, as though graciously refraining from laughing out loud. "Now what would the FBI be doing at the offices of NASA?"

Darren trusted Crusher—the alien. He resented that McKinney was being disingenuous. Not that he was trying to mislead them, but that he was making sure they knew he was.

"I was hoping *you* would tell *me*." Darren said, his voice warbling in the way he hated.

McKinney looked surprised, again a blatant play-act. "You are assuming I'm with the FBI." He shook his head in faux commiseration. "I'm afraid not."

"What are you doing here, then?" Darren asked. His antagonism was wavering. He wanted McKinney to just leave and let the director back.

"Talking to you."

"That's not an answer."

"It is. This is part of my job—special projects. You called the director's office claiming to be—" here he paused the barest moment "in contact with space aliens."

"Not me," Darren said, reflexively escaping ridicule, "my cousin."

McKinney looked at Crusher, again feigning surprise. "Him?" he said, jabbing a thumb in the alien zombie's direction. "Can he even talk?" he asked, waving a hand in front of Crusher, who's eyes continued to stare, as though blind to the motion. "What's wrong with him?"

"He, um, has a degenerative disease. It affects his speech. And his hands. And feet. Any sort of motor control—but don't be fooled, there's a genius inside that head."

McKinney smiled openly now. "Another Stephen Hawking?"

"Yeah. Exactly."

"Minus the wheelchair and synthesized voice."

"Crusher can still talk. Sort of. He spells out words."

"So, he can spell? A genius indeed."

Crusher came to life. "Fuh! Uuoo! Kuh! Huh! Iee! Muh!—"

"Hey!" Darren exclaimed.

"What's he saying?" McKinney asked.

"Oh, nothing—uh, I think we should maybe talk to the director," he said.

McKinney ignored the suggestion. "Do you believe he's been in contact with aliens?" he asked. His tone was perfunctory now. He wanted to be done with these two boobs.

"Yes. Yes, I do."

In contact? Darren thought. *Oh, boy. If this guy only knew.*

"Can you describe them?"

"Well, like I told the director, they're not very big, maybe the size of a rat—no, not a rat, a chipmunk. They're silvery—sort of. They mostly look like a squid, but that's just mostly. You see, they can change their shape—not like they can appear like, you know, something *else*—they can't, you know, pretend to be a *chipmunk*, for example. They can just change their shape like if they were made of clay, and you were able to squeeze them—"

McKinney was staring at him, and Darren felt goosebumps run up his arm. It was the look your spouse would have, sitting across from you when she sees the tidal wave bearing down behind you.

"They don't look like birds?" McKinney asked, his voice dead serious now.

"Birds? No. I guess it—they—could change their shape to sort of resemble one, but it wouldn't be very convincing—"

Crusher suddenly came alive. He opened his mouth and let loose a barrage of honks like a semi when a wayward car swings into its path. Simultaneously, excited voices began shouting from beyond the door.

McKinney's eyes narrowed, and he took one hard look at Crusher before turning away. "What's going on out there?" he bellowed through the closed door.

A woman's voice shouted back. "A bomb! We're supposed to clear the building!"

From the street outside, the haunting wail of a siren rose in tribute to the mayhem.

McKinney spun back and approached Crusher. He grabbed the human shell by his shoulders. "What kind of contact have you had?" he growled. Darren tried to pull one of his hands away, but McKinney brushed him away like he was an annoying spider web.

The door opened and a woman stuck her head inside. "Sir! We're supposed to evacuate!"

McKinney grunted in anger, gave Crusher a little push, and went to the door. "Do not open this door again!" he yelled.

"But, sir—"

"Leave!" he shouted. "Now!"

Darren had caught Crusher and steadied him. A loose strand of hair fell across his cousin's face, between his eyes. No, it wasn't a strand of hair. The tentacle now reached from the hole in his forehead to his chin, and was continuing to lengthen. "Christ!" Darren hissed. "What the hell?"

McKinney returned, and stopped in his tracks, staring. "My God," he whispered. "You're—you're—"

Crusher leaned forward, and staggered towards him. McKinney took a couple of steps back, but a chair stopped him. He watched in horror as Crusher lifted his hands in Frankenstein imitation and fell on the special projects agent, wrapping his arms around the man's thick neck as though welcoming a long-lost sibling. Darren heard a snap, and McKinney's whole body jerked once, and went limp. The bulky body fell heavily to the floor, followed by Crusher, who made a soft landing on his chest.

Darren ran over, and saw the tentacle withdraw, like a strand of spaghetti sucked up. He looked down at the two bodies, one lifeless, the other nearly so.

"Oh, boy," Darren said. "This can't be good."

Chapter 5

Darren grabbed Crusher's hand and pulled him to his feet, leaving McKinney lying motionless on the floor. His zombie cousin started to fall, so Darren maneuvered him into a chair. "What the hell did you do to him?" Darren asked.

Crusher just sat there, his eyelids drooping, as though half asleep.

Darren knelt next to him and shook his arm. "Hey! You in there?"

The eyelids opened wide, and the eyeballs slowly turned to look at him. His arm raised, and a finger extended.

"What are you pointing at?" Darren asked, but Crusher didn't move, he seemed frozen in that position.

Darren looked around. His bag. Inside was a change of clothes, toiletries, his wallet, and ... "The tablet? Is that it?"

Crusher closed his eyes and opened them again—a slow-motion blink.

"I thought we couldn't use it?" he said, pulling out the touch-screen computer. "You sure?" he asked before turning it on. Crusher slow-motion-blinked again. It took a minute to come up, and then the screen went blank and the alien's message appeared.

I am depleted from that maneuver. Get us out of here immediately. We only have a few minutes.

"But—isn't the room tapped?"

It doesn't matter now. We must go.

Darren felt dizzy. The world was spinning away ahead of him. "What about McKinney? Is he ... dead?"

Probably not.

The words disappeared, and were replaced with:

Maybe. WE MUST LEAVE!

Darren nodded vigorously. "Right. Okay. Uh, can you walk?"

You must help me. Don't talk to anybody. I must shut down now. Watch out for birds.

"Birds? What birds?"

The tablet screen changed, reverting back to the normal icons. The alien had disconnected.

Crusher sat staring, his arm in the same position, still pointing. It wasn't his cousin, the human body, that was depleted, but the alien pilot inside. Darren jumped a little when Crusher suddenly went limp. Darren caught him before he fell out of the chair.

Darren tried to lift him to his feet, but his cousin was 170 pounds of dead meat. He let him slide back into the chair. "I need a little help," he said, not sure if the alien was listening. "I can't drag you out." Darren put his mouth to Crusher's ear. "Hello!" he called.

Okay, that was dumb. He tried another tack. He placed his hands on each side of Crusher's head and shook it, then shook it again.

"Hello? Some help here?"

Crusher's eyes opened.

"Up!" Darren said, pulling his arms.

Crusher leaned into it, and with Darren's help stood up, swaying unsteadily. "You can do it," Darren encouraged. He wrapped Crusher's arm around his neck, and picked up his bag. Supporting Crusher like a wounded combat buddy, Darren staggered to the door. Beyond, the area was empty. Only the forlorn sound of the siren outside broke the silence.

Together, the cousins stumbled and staggered to the stairs. Darren gazed down the abyss. Half a flight down, the stairs made a ninety-degree turn into the building lobby. He heard shouting from behind them—firemen combing the building, making sure everyone had evacuated. "Here we go," he said, and carefully took a step down, and then another. Crusher wasn't following. "Come on!" Darren urged. Crusher stepped out ... and fell forward, pulling Darren along. Darren ran down the stairs, trying to keep ahead of the loose cannon, trying to keep him upright. When they reached the landing, they bounced face-first off the wall, and caromed on down the second flight. At the bottom, momentum carried them into the lobby, where Darren finally lost his footing and fell, letting Crusher come down on top of him. Darren was staring at the ceiling, wondering if he'd broken anything, when a head appeared above him. It was a fireman in full, heavy fireman gear.

"You okay?" he asked. Before Darren could answer, the head disappeared. Darren turned his head. The fireman had knelt down, studying Crusher. "We need help here!" he called, waving to somebody.

"It's okay," Darren said. "I mean, he's okay. If you could just help me up—"

"Don't move, sir," the fireman said, waving again for help. "We'll get to you soon."

Darren pushed at Crusher, rolling him off.

"Sir!" the fireman exclaimed. "Please! This man is hurt!"

"He's not hurt. He's just retarded." That could have been phrased better. "He has a degenerative nerve disease. He's perfectly fine. Just help me get him up, okay?"

Looking deeply skeptical, the fireman waved off the approaching help, and carefully examined Crusher, feeling along his arms and legs, checking for broken bones, then slowly rubbing his thumb along his backbone.

"Thanks," Darren said. "I'll take him from here."

The fireman ignored him as he finished his survey. Finding nothing wrong, he slid his arms under Crusher, lifted all 170 pounds, and strode off towards the exit. Darren ran to catch up. He figured that carrying people to safety was instinctive for firemen.

The parking lot was a sea of milling chaos as NASA staff and visitors roamed about trying to get news. Darren followed the fireman to an emergency vehicle. "He's okay!" Darren called. "Really!"

The EMT personnel took over, accepting the unconscious man and gently laying him on a stretcher as Darren stood by. Darren leaned down over Crusher, and the EMT put his hand up to keep him back. "Crusher!" Darren yelled. "Get up!"

"Please get back," the EMT barked, and turned to the truck to get something.

Darren snatched the opportunity, and knelt next to Crusher. It had worked before. He grabbed his cousin's head and shook it.

"Holy Christ!" the EMT yelled, pushing Darren away. "What's the matter with you?"

"He's okay!" Darren exclaimed. "Crusher, get up! Now!"

Crusher's eyes opened. He tried to roll over, but the EMT held him. Crusher let loose a semi truck honk, which startled the technician, allowing Crusher to complete his roll and get up on hands and knees. Darren helped him to his feet as the stunned EMT watched.

"Thanks," Darren said to the man as they stumbled away. "I'm sure you would have done a bang-up job!" he called over his shoulder, and then winced at what he'd said.

Where to? The airport. Home. He needed to hail a taxi. That meant winding through the chaotic crowd, which was good, since the random ambling of people would provide cover. From what, though? Why was he running from NASA? A "special projects" agent had simply been grilling them, and the alien took him down. If there was any government agency to be trusted, it had to be NASA. Shouldn't he actually be running from the alien?

His gut told him no. McKinney had done nothing to indicate he was dangerous. He was simply the sort of man you ran from after you crossed him. Crusher—the alien—had obviously found something, though. Darren wouldn't have guessed that he would trust Crusher's hijacker, but he did. The alien could travel interstellar space, could tap directly into WiFi. Maybe that was it—maybe the alien had found something.

They arrived at the street, Crusher stumbling along in tow. Their luck was with them—a taxi sat there not fifty feet away. "Come on!" Darren said, and hurried his pace. This unbalanced Crusher, however, and he fell to his knees. "Wake up, will you!" Darren scolded. "You can shut down in the cab!" He yanked his cousin's arm, pulling him roughly to his feet. Darren looked around. A dozen people were watching him, some surprised at his behavior, some visibly angry. "He's my cousin," he explained. "He has a neurological disease."

It was the only thing that came to mind, and it explained nothing about Darren's apparent abuse. "He can't feel anything," he added lamely, which was at least partially true. The part of Crusher's brain that registered pain lacked a conscious mind to register it. Darren put aside the philosophical relevance of this for later, and turned back to the waiting taxi. It was no longer waiting. A man helped a female companion step inside, and was climbing in. "Hey! You!" Darren yelled, giving another yank at Crusher's arm. "That's my cab!" The man threw him a withering look of scorn, and closed the door. A moment later, the taxi pulled away.

"Damn you, Crusher!" Darren exclaimed, ignoring what the people around him thought.

As he scanned for another taxi, his eyes fell on a familiar face. It was the NASA director looking at him in alarm. He was talking on his phone. When he caught Darren's eye, his voice rose, and Darren heard him say, "Hurry! I'll try to hold him." He put his phone away, and strode towards them.

Darren panicked. He would be charged with murder. No jury would believe that poor, retarded Crusher could kill somebody—unless Darren could convince the alien to show a few tentacles. Forget it. They had to get the hell out of there.

There were no taxis. None. A shiny black Chrysler sat right in front of them, though, with a back door wide open. An elderly woman sat in the back seat, and she waved. What the hell, Darren waved back. "You must be Tommy," she said in a thin, wavering voice as he came closer. "And you must be little Johnny!" she added, looking at Crusher.

The driver wore a classy uniform cap, the kind that limo drivers sported. He turned and looked at them. "Ma'am, are you sure these are your nephews?"

"Of course we are!" Darren said, taking the woman's hand. "Auntie, it's so good to see you. Now, let's go," he said, tossing his bag in and practically pushing her away as she scooted to the side. The NASA director was steps away, and Darren pulled Crusher's arm so that he fell forward. Darren kept pulling, and the alien zombie ended up sprawled across both their laps.

"Now hold on, there," the director said, peering into the car.

"Who's this?" the woman asked.

"He's bad," Darren said, his mental gears whirring. "He's a con artist. He claims to be the head of NASA."

"I *am!*" the director exclaimed. "I'm the NASA *Administrator!*"

"You're uncle was a con artist," the woman said. "Terrible man. Wilfred, pull away."

"Now, wait just one minute—" the director sputtered, but the driver glanced around casually, and suddenly the wheels squealed as the car jerked away.

Crusher's feet still stuck out, and the door bounced off them. "Johnny," the woman said, "get inside the car."

Darren tugged at Crusher's knees and reached out and pulled the door closed. Silence filled the car.

"How's your mother?" the woman asked, stroking Crusher's hair.

"She's, uh, she's fine," Darren said, spinning the gears some more, searching for an innocuous response. "She goes to church every Sunday."

The woman's peaceful countenance turned alarmed. "She converted?"

The driver glanced at him in the rearview mirror.

"Um, not really."

"How can she not be a Gentile if she goes to church?"

Gentile. That meant she was Jewish. Wait, Mormons also use the term. But they go to church. "She still goes to synagogue. She, uh, likes the music on Sunday mornings."

The driver held his gaze in the mirror. Darren couldn't see if he was scowling or smiling.

"Tah!" Crusher said. "Aaa! Bah!"

"Good Lord!" the woman said, "what's wrong with Johnny?"

"Oh. He, uh, we just came from the dentist. His mouth is still numb."

The driver shook his head.

"Lah! Ehh! Tah!" Crusher continued.

"Don't drool on your Aunt Sarah, deary," she said, patting Crusher's head.

T-a-b-l-e-t "Got it!" Darren said, unzipping his bag and turning on his tablet.

"Is that one of those smart phones?" Sarah asked, peering curiously.

"Huh? No. It's a, uh, computer."

She gave him a little nudge. "Oh, Tommy. You always were the kidder. I used a computer in my day, you know. Nineteen seventy-six, at IBM. That's where I met your uncle. The computer was in the basement somewhere. I never actually saw it. But, my goodness—your smart phone is a big one, isn't it?"

"Yeah, a big one," Darren said. "A big smart phone."

The driver snorted.

The array of icons gave way to a black screen and white words, and Darren casually leaned against the door, tilting the screen away from Sarah.

There will be birds. We must get away from them at all costs.

"What birds?" Darren asked.

"Are you talking to me, dearest?" Sarah asked.

"No," Darren said. "The, uh, you know—the phone."

New words appeared.

I can explain later. Just know that they are dangerous.

"Okay," Darren said, sighing. "Hey, was there really a bomb?"

No. I hacked into their security system. It appeared to them as though the warning came directly from the FBI.

"Ha! Good thinking. But I guess that's your forte."

"Tommy," Sarah said, grasping his elbow. "I hate to interrupt your phone conversation, but what's this about a bomb?"

"Oh! No, there's no bomb. It's, you know, it's a metaphor. His girlfriend—she just told him that she's pregnant. From another man."

The driver's eyes were watching him.

"Well!" Sarah said. "That is a bomb indeed. Tell your friend that he can do better."

The driver pointed off to the side. A bird flew along beside them, pacing their car, just above the heads of the pedestrians. The size of a large crow, it flew oddly, as though a simplistic animation, pasted into the scene. The body of a bird normally oscillates up and down slightly as the wings flap, but this bird flew straight as an arrow, the wings moving in a blur. Also, where were the feathers? The bird's surface was smooth, like polished stone.

And it was the color of silver.

Darren glanced at Crusher, but his face was hidden in Sarah's lap.

"Another one," the driver said, pointing out the other side. He looked at Darren in the mirror. "Should I be concerned?"

"No," Darren said studying their escorts. "They're not after you."

"They're after *you*?" the driver said.

"Yes. I don't know. Maybe—Crusher, what should we do?"

Get away.

"Oh, thanks. Why didn't I think of that?"

Suddenly the bird on the left closed in until it was barely a foot beyond Sarah's window. The eye was featureless, like a clear marble. The car's windows were tinted, but Darren had the eerie feeling that this creature was absorbing every detail inside the car.

They came to a stop at a red light, and the first bird took up position on the other side.

Where are they?

"Right outside."

Get away. Now.

"How do I get away, for God's sake?"

"You want me to lose them?" the driver asked.

"Can you?" Darren said.

He didn't answer. He tapped his finger on the steering wheel, waiting for the light to turn green. Darren was suddenly pushed back against the seat as the Chrysler's V8 engine launched them forward, tires squealing like captives being tortured.

"Don't get another ticket, Wilfred," Sarah said calmly as she watched the bird slowly catch up and pace them again.

"Yes, ma'am."

Darren was thrown violently sideways against Sarah as the driver fishtailed to the right onto another street. Seconds later, the birds caught up. "It's not working," Darren said, wondering how the strange birds were dangerous. Did they shoot little bullets? Sharp talons to tear at your eyes? Caustic poop?

"We're not there yet," the driver said, twisting them onto a street on the left this time.

"Where's 'there'?"

The driver didn't answer. He pulled into the oncoming lane to speed around another car. Darren was thrown forward. "Here," the driver finally said.

71

They turned into a downward sloping driveway that dived into what appeared to be a marble and stone parking garage. The driver proceeded slowly now, as though unsure what lay ahead. The birds hugged them on each side, little fighter escorts. Barrier arms lifted, and the driver stopped when the front of the car reached the entrance.

Darren avoided the cold, emotionless gaze of the birds. They gave him the willies. "I don't understand what we're—"

He gasped as a deluge of water blasted them, ricocheting off the hood with a deafening sound. The driver rolled the car slowly forward, and the downpour moved along the roof and down the back windshield. The car stopped, leaving the solid sheet of water thumping on the trunk. He turned to them, grinning. "A benefit of affluent living," he explained. "The condo management has to show off something dramatic in return for a thousand dollars a month fee."

"A carwash at the entrance?" Darren said.

The driver shrugged. "Houston is ungodly hot in summer."

"It cools off the car," Darren said, wonderingly.

The driver nodded. "As soon as I pull all the way in, the water will stop, and your stalkers will get through."

"Right," Darren said, stuffing the tablet into his bag. "Come on, retard," he said, slapping Crusher's butt. He glanced at the woman who was watching them serenely. "When I open the door, you might get wet, um, Auntie."

The driver laughed. "She doesn't have any nephews."

Darren looked at her, wide-eyed.

She smiled. "I hope you don't mind."

"Mind? Why would I mind?"

"Why, I fooled you."

"But … we fooled *you*! Actually, I guess not." He looked at the driver. "I don't get it."

"It's a little game we play. A little adventure now and then. She was a field photographer for Time Magazine in her younger days. It's tough growing old and feeble."

Sarah sighed and nodded. "But, tell me. What are those birds?"

Darren looked at her. What the hell. "I'm guessing aliens."

One side of her mouth turned up in a tiny grin. "As in space aliens?"

Crusher had rolled onto his side. He honked.

"There's your answer," Darren said. "In this case, I think that means 'yes.'"

Her grin widened. "There's another garage entrance on the north side. If the birds are indeed space aliens, they'll be figuring that out."

Darren wasn't sure if she believed him. "Bad news for us."

The driver glanced at Sarah. "How about the delivery passage?"

"Ah, yes," she said. "The street-level shops under the condos next door take their deliveries from the basement floor below them. There's an entrance there, off against the right wall, a green door. Space aliens are very smart—they may figure that out as well." Her grin swelled. "On the other hand, their heads are quite small—just bird brains."

She definitely didn't believe him. It didn't matter. He took a deep breath. "Right. Come on, Crusher," he said, and threw open the door. The sound of the thrashing water nearly drowned out his words. "Thanks for the … adventure."

She said something he didn't hear. He shook his head as he pulled Crusher out. She spoke louder. "Give 'em hell!" she yelled.

He smiled and nodded, then swung the door closed. The driver waited as Darren pulled Crusher along towards the green door marked DELIVERIES. The sound of the manmade waterfall echoed through the garage, filling every nook and cranny, but cut off instantly when he closed the metal door behind them. The condo basement was all concrete and black, unwashed floor. It smelled of mold and old garbage. "Something tells me that our adventure is just beginning," Darren mused.

Crusher honked.

Chapter 6

It didn't take long for Darren, with Crusher lagging behind, to find his way up to the ground floor, where the array of shops created a mini-mall for the condo residents, and anyone else wandering in off the street. "So, the birds are aliens," he said, sitting down on a bench next to a fountain. Crusher stopped and stood staring at nothing. Darren waited for the answer to appear on his tablet.

Yes. They are the stellar-capable race we compared to fungus earlier.

"The ones that punch through to other planets with the sole goal of dominating and propagating."

Your memory is good.

"When it comes to space fungus that could invade Earth."

Not could invade. Have invaded.

"Yikes. How many do you think there are?"

The amount at this point is not relevant. The point is that they have chosen Earth as a next target.

"God. This sounds bad."

It is bad.

Darren stared at the words until they faded. "I don't understand. Why would they be working with NASA? I mean, they are, aren't they?"

Having a strictly self-serving approach to existence doesn't mean they are not intelligent. Sarah referred to them as bird-brains, but she was assuming that their mental processing was confined to their heads.

"Fine. So they're really smart birds."

You must remember that they are not birds. They only look like Earth birds. It is a convenient form. Every planet worth invading will have an atmosphere, and flight is most useful in a foreign environment.

"You don't fly."

I don't want to dominate your planet.

"Good point. I mean, that's a damn good point. Okay, they're geniuses—so NASA wants to work with them because it reveres intelligence?"

You asked me earlier to refrain from sarcasm. I ask you—how can NASA verify what the Fungus Birds tell them?

"I see. They're lying."

They have probably told NASA that it is my side that's invading.

"Which you claim isn't true."

You either believe me, or you don't. I see no way to provide evidence for validation.

"Okay, okay. I believe you."

He didn't have much choice.

The Fungus Birds have not given up. They are looking for us.

"How do you know?"

I can hear their communications. I cannot understand them, but the sources are all around us.

"What do they want?"

I think it would be obvious. They want to kill both of us, and probably anybody else you may have spoken to about me.

"Because you—your 'people'—are competitors?"

Because a lie's only enemy is truth.

"Right. Of course. You sound like Gandhi."

I don't think you understand the dire nature of our situation. Escape is imperative.

"You're doing most the talking."

Then I will stop, and let you get us away.

As he packed the tablet back in his bag, Darren muttered about the travails of serving as a nursemaid to a space alien who couldn't even tie his shoes. "Come on, genius," he said.

He led them along the store fronts, waiting for an idea to percolate. He took in the vast array of consumer offerings—jewelry, herbal supplements, sunglasses, phones, sports clothes. Maybe they could disguise themselves. Or maybe assemble some sort of protective gear. He didn't know what to defend against. He should have asked Crusher how the Fungus Birds were dangerous.

Conversations of scattered shoppers caught his attention. A young girl asked, "How do they get in here?" And her mother answered that sometimes they just get in when somebody opens the door—maybe another bird is chasing them.

Another bird?

Crusher bumped into him, flopping one arm ahead of them. Darren stared. He saw it. A Fungus Bird hovered high up near the ceiling, surveying the crowd. It was facing away from them.

Darren grabbed Crusher and pulled him back against the window of a shop. A pillar between the shops half hid them, which was worse than not at all. It just made them conspicuously trying to hide. Books were arrayed on display on the other side of the glass behind them. "Come on," Darren said, pushing Crusher through the open door. Inside, the shop was empty, not even a clerk. The selection was pretty thin—a few dozen books scattered around with the covers facing forward to fill out the shelves. Lots of comfortable chairs for perusing, though. Just no perusers. The theme seemed to be self-help. Multiple covers—quite a few, in fact—included repeated pictures of a dowdy nineteenth-century woman with hair parted tightly down the middle of her crown in the style of Mary Todd Lincoln. She looked familiar. One book included her name, and she was even named Mary—Mary Baker Eddy.

Darren noticed signs on the window: *Can prayer heal the "big" things?*

Ah, ha.

"Welcome gentlemen!"

Darren spun around. The young man must have come in from a back room. A one-word description would have been "thin." His body was thin, limp hair hung flat against his forehead and over his ears, and his voice wouldn't have carried across the room if Crusher knew how to hum a tune.

"Hi," Darren said. "I guess this is a—"

"A reading room," the man said. "I'm the librarian. Feel free to relax and browse the books. They're for sale, but you're welcome to just sit and read if you like. Nobody will bother you." He held out his hand. "I'm Emile," he said.

Darren would have liked to get an affidavit on the nobody-bothering-you part. He shook Emile's hand and introduced himself and Crusher, and then grabbed a book at random and looked for chairs facing away from the door.

"Nah," Crusher said.

"Why?" Darren asked.

The zombie swung his arm back, towards the door.

"Fungus?" Darren said.

"Tah! Tah! Tah!"

"The tablet," Darren guessed, fishing it out of his bag.

Emile pretended to be busy behind his counter, but watched Crusher out of the corner of his eye.

While Darren waited for the computer to boot up, he glanced at the book he'd grabbed. Just as he'd guessed. This was a Christian Science enticement enterprise. They believed that prayer rather than medicine should be used to treat illness—disease was a mental error. Jehovah's Witnesses shoved their propaganda in your face. At least this cult let you make the choice.

The tablet was up.

Both Fungus Bird and government agents are searching the shopping area. They're confident we're here somewhere.

"Shit," Darren breathed, staring at the words as they faded.

They'll find us as soon as they reach this shop.

"I should have grabbed you before you crawled inside that head," he muttered looking at Crusher, who swung his arm towards the door again.

"Nah!" Crusher exclaimed.

"I don't want to seem pushy," Emile said, "but we encourage our guests to put away their computers and phones. We feel that they're distractions from the important thoughts that permeate this room."

Darren looked at him. Fine. He'd go with it. "I agree completely," he said, slipping the tablet back in the bag. "This book," he said, holding it up as though it deserved a place higher than him while he read the title, "*Science and Health with Key to the Scriptures*—I've been looking for this for a long time."

Emile seemed puzzled. "Yes, that was written by Mary Eddy herself—but, well, it's available on Amazon."

Darren held his gaze on the book while he continued thinking. "Yes," he said, finally looking at Emile, "but I was after the gestalt."

"The, uh, gestalt?"

"Of course. These books," Darren said, waving Mary Eddy's tome in an arc, "together, they represent something greater than the sum of their parts."

All he'd done was repeat the definition of the word, but what the hell.

Emile nodded slowly, going with the flow. "They do represent a broad coverage." He glanced again at Crusher, as though keeping an eye on him.

Darren walked along the shelves, picking out a few more books at random. "I'd like to absorb their energy," he said, "but I hate to be interrupted."

"Oh, I won't bother you," Emile said. "I'm only here to help if asked." He paused. "I understand that some people want to discover the truth on their own." He watched Darren, as though waiting for a response.

"Exactly. That's what I'm after … in fact, it's more the, uh, other people wandering in that I'm concerned about. Do you by chance have—oh, you know—a more private reading area?"

The young man held his gaze a moment, and nodded. "Yeah. I do." He glanced around, even though the room was empty except for the three of them. "This way," he said, leading them through a doorway behind the counter.

The door led into a general work area, where boxes of books were stacked, and files lay scattered on a desk. The Christian Science librarian gathered up the files and motioned for Darren to take a seat. Emile pulled a padded chair with a broken, listing backrest next to the desk for Crusher, who promptly fell when trying to sit on it. Darren and Emile helped him up and into it.

Darren laid the books he'd gathered onto the desk and spread them out. He picked one up, pretending to study it. He peeked up at the young man who was standing at the doorway, hesitating. When Darren caught his eye, Emile came back. Again glancing around the otherwise empty room, he said, almost in a whisper, "You said that you like to discover the truth on your own." He seemed to be holding his breath as he watched Darren.

It had actually been Emile who had said this. "Yes. That's right." It was what the guy wanted to hear.

Emile nodded slowly. "You aren't, um, actually a member of the church, are you?"

"You mean Christian Science?" Darren said. "No, why?"

Again the nervous glance around. "I'm not either," he whispered, and then stood back expectantly.

"Okay … uh, what are you trying to tell me?"

He squatted next to Darren, laying his hand on Crusher's knee, and then quickly removing it. "It's a sham," he whispered so quietly Darren wasn't sure he heard correctly.

"A sham? Why do you work here, then?"

"I volunteer. I'm trying to save people. Not everybody—just the ones I think have the potential."

"Potential for what?"

He leaned closer. "The truth. Dianetics."

Darren looked at him, wondering if the guy was pulling his leg. "You're not with the Church of Christian Science—you're with the Church of Scientology?"

He shook his head adamantly. "That's a sham too. No, I'm with the Free Zone."

Darren grinned, but the young man's face remained serious. "I thought Scientology *was* Dianetics," Darren said.

"It is."

"Sorry. It seems like you're contradicting yourself."

"No," he said shaking his head again. "You're right. Scientology *is* Dianetics, but the Church of Scientology has stolen the concept."

"I see. So I guess the Free Zone represents true Scientology."

Now Emile smiled, but then went sour again. "The Church—the Church of Scientology—they hate us."

"Because they hate the truth," Darren said.

The thin man didn't get the sarcasm. "Exactly." Again the furtive glance around. "They've infiltrated the government."

"They have?" Darren said.

"Yes. We're harassed all the time. They killed one of our members."

It was Darren's turn to glance towards the door. He had personal experience with the subject. "How?"

"They made it look like an accident—a car accident."

"And you know it wasn't an accident."

"Of course it wasn't."

"Because the guy wasn't drunk, for example."

"They made it look like he'd been drinking."

"What did the coroner's report say?"

"That's the point! They changed it."

"How do you know?"

He rolled his eyes. "Because he wasn't drunk!"

"Right." It was time to jump off the logic merry-go-round. "What made you think I have ... potential?"

He shrugged. "I can tell. You like to discover the truth for yourself."

Darren wasn't going to point out that the guy had originated the idea.

Emile leaned in again and cocked a thumb at Crusher. "What about him?"

"Crusher? Don't worry about him. He—he has a neurological disease."

The Free Zone Scientologist studied Crusher. "What did you mean about wishing you'd grabbed him before he crawled inside his head?" he asked, turning back to Darren.

"Tah! Tah!" Crusher suddenly squawked.

Emile fell back. "What's that about?"

"Uh, he wants to tell me something. They're getting closer, aren't they?" he said to Crusher.

"Yah! Yah!"

"Could we please close the door?" Darren said.

The Scientology mole shut the door to the inner room. "Who's getting closer?" he asked, coming back.

Darren sighed. What a mess. "People who are after us. Bad people."

Emile looked hard at Darren. "They're after you too, aren't they?"

Darren shrugged and nodded.

"It's because they know the truth about you."

"That I'm after the truth," Darren offered.

"Yes." He gestured towards Crusher. "How does he know?

That they're getting closer?"

Darren took a deep breath. "He—he's special. That's all I can say."

Free Zone Man thought a moment. "I understand." He looked at Darren. "I'd like to try something, if you don't mind. I think it's important."

Darren shrugged.

Their host rummaged through a rucksack and came back with what looked like the hearing tester instrument the school nurse used, except more streamlined. It sported knobs and switches, and a large needle meter. It could have been a prop on the original Star Trek TV series.

"What is it?" Darren asked.

Emile held the plastic device reverently, like a paleontologist returning to camp with a delicate million-year-old fossil. "It's an e-meter. We use them for auditing. This one is an early version. It was used by L. Ron Hubbard himself—"

"Hubbard—he invented Dianetics."

Emile nodded enthusiastically. "I'd like to audit your friend."

"He doesn't have income."

The librarian shook his head, not getting the joke. "Not that kind of audit," he said as he unwound wire from around two metal bars. "It's a procedure we use to find and hopefully eliminate mental aberrations."

You're tackling the granddaddy of all mental aberrations, Darren thought.

"It's too complicated to explain in a short time, but we discover painful past experiences—engrams—and try to clear them from the reactive part of the mind."

"Yeah," Darren said, "it sounds too complicated."

Emile stopped and turned to Darren. In a whisper he said, "I believe that he may have a very strong thetan—possibly even on the verge of an OT."

"His thetan is working overtime?"

Emile looked at him, puzzled. "Maybe. I don't know—oh! I see. No, 'OT' stands for Operating Thetan—where his thetan can transcend his body—all matter, in fact. It's a state very few attain."

"Lucky him."

"You say he has special powers, yet he's working from within an obviously flawed body. I'm guessing his thetan specifically chose this broken shell," Emile said.

Darren blinked. What the hell. *Does he actually know?*

"His thetan searched out a challenge," Emile continued. "Maybe to prove his superior standing with the rest of our thetans."

Nope, Darren thought. *He doesn't know.*

The Free Zone Scientologist tried to hand the metal bars to Crusher, but it wasn't obvious the zombie even saw him. In the end, Emile wrapped Crushers hands around the bars, and laid them on his lap."

"Will it hurt?" Darren asked, again joking.

"Huh? No! Not at all. They're just sensors."

"Electrical sensors? They sense electricity?"

"Yes."

"Well, this should be good."

"Why do you say that?" Emile asked.

Darren just smiled.

Crusher's auditor fiddled with three different dials in turn, watching the needle. Each time he'd have it centered in the meter, he'd pause, and then the meter would drift off, one direction and then the other. "I've never had this problem before," he muttered.

Darren, still smiling, shook his head, but the Scientologist was focused on his task.

Emile finally twisted one knob completely down, and the needle stayed put at last. "Huh," he said.

"What's happening?" Darren asked.

"I had to turn the gain completely off," he answered.

"Maybe his superior thetan energy is overpowering the machine," Darren said seriously.

Emile nodded slowly. "Yeah. That would explain it. Wow."

The needle started to fall slowly down, and Emile's eyes grew large.

"Crusher!" Darren warned, and the needle returned to the center.

Emile took a deep breath. "Well, I guess we should start." He looked at Darren. "We normally do this in private."

"You won't understand his responses."

"Um, I guess it's okay." He slid a folding chair in front of Crusher and sat facing him, e-meter in lap. "Close your eyes, please."

Crusher continued to stare at his toes.

Emile hesitated and looked again at Darren.

"Do it," Darren said, and Crusher closed them.

"I would normally start by asking him about specific incidents in his past," Emile explained.

"Go for it," Darren said.

Emile nodded and turned back to Crusher. "Can you recall an incident in your life where you felt a sense of unease for days afterwards?"

Crusher just sat, eyes closed, possibly dead.

"Do it," Darren said.

"Ieee. Ahh. Rah. Rah," he went on, raising one clenched hand a few inches or the other as he delineated vowels. Darren followed the spelling—"I a-r-r-i-v-e-d o-n E-a-r-t-h."

"What'd he say?" Emile asked.

Darren looked at him. *What the hell.* He told him.

He thought the thin man's eyes were going to pop right out of their sockets. "He *said* that?" he asked in a squeak.

Darren pointed at the instrument, where the needle wiggled its way back and forth across the full span of the meter.

Emile stared, mesmerized. "Lord!" he whispered. He looked at Darren. "He arrived from Venus."

"From Venus," Darren repeated. "He must have been sweating." Emile just sat staring at him. "It's, like, really hot there," Darren said. "I read that lead melts on the surface—"

"Thetans don't ever remember their return," Emile said.

"Their return?"

"From Venus," he replied getting a little agitated. "That's where our thetans go after they abandon our bodies—what we call death. They go to a landing station until it's time for them to come back."

"Kind of like an airport terminal," Darren joked.

"Yes. The point is, *thetans don't normally remember their return!*"

Darren nodded knowingly. "He's definitely special, eh?"

They were interrupted by a voice calling from the front, and Darren jumped, his heart catching in his throat.

"Damn," Emile muttered. "I'll be right back." He carefully closed the door behind him as he left.

"No squawks!" Darren hissed to Crusher as he padded over to the door. He opened it a crack and peered through. His heart moved from his throat to the back of his mouth. McKinney's hunk form was unmistakable, even from behind. "Nobody's come in for the last half-hour?" he asked.

Darren was relieved that Crusher hadn't killed the agent, but also disappointed.

Emile was facing Darren, and his eyebrows bounced in surprise when he saw Darren's eye peering through the crack. McKinney started to turn around as Darren jerked the door closed.

He heard Emile through the door. "Just normal browsing traffic. Nothing unusual."

"What's behind that door?" McKinney said, and Darren heard his footsteps coming closer. Darren gripped the doorknob. Maybe Crusher's electric jolt had weakened the muscular man. Maybe a lot.

"Supplies," Emile said. "A desk. Customers aren't allowed back there."

"I'm not a customer," McKinney replied.

Darren felt the doorknob turn inexorably, as though powered by an electric motor. At the same time, he heard a faint call from a distance. "What?" McKinney called.

The voice shouted back indistinctly.

The door knob went loose, and McKinney said, "Stay right where you are. I'll be back."

Darren waited, and then jerked back when the door opened. It was Emile. "That's one of the bad people after you?" he asked.

"Yeah, bad. Real bad. And angry."

"He's probably been implanted by a rogue thetan—he would be under a hypnotic spell."

Darren wasn't really listening. He was looking around for some kind of exit. "Where does that go?" he asked, pointing to a metal door at the back.

"A hallway. All the shops have access. It's for deliveries." He cupped his chin in his hand. "Maybe he *is* the rogue thetan. If so, then he knows exactly what we're doing right now—"

"Is this the only way out?" Darren asked, putting his ear to the metal door. He heard commanding voices beyond, clearly other agents.

Emile was looking at him, brow crunched in thought. He chewed his lip, considering. "No. It's not." He walked over to Darren and put his face close. "I want you to look me in the eye and tell me *you* are not a rogue thetan."

"Oh, Christ," Darren said. "I don't have time for this—"

"Tell me!" Emile insisted, staring at Darren's every move.

"I am not a rogue thetan," he said through gritted teeth.

Emile had moved so close, Darren could feel his breath on his face. It smelled like baloney. The Free Zone Scientologist said something that sounded like "Bixbe—krugth—franell," and watched Darren's reaction closely. Darren's reaction was to roll his eyes and say, "Is there another way out, or not?"

The thin man took a breath and nodded. "Here, help me move the desk," he said.

They slid Crusher's chair aside, with Crusher still in it, then lifted the desk away. Underneath was a cheap short-pile carpet. Emile flung it back to reveal a plywood floor. Somebody had used a saber-saw to cut a two-foot square outline. "You did this?" Darren asked.

Emile stared at the homemade hatch. Darren couldn't tell if the poignant expression of the Scientology devotee was regret at giving up his secret, or the burden that came with knowing the Truth about the universe. "Yes. The Church would kill me if they knew I'd infiltrated. Hand me those scissors," he said as he knelt on the floor. He pried up the plywood panel and pushed it aside, revealing a dark square, dimly lit from below. Darren peered down into the lower level where they'd escaped from the garage.

"You have somewhere to go?" Emile asked.

Good question. He had return flight tickets to New Orleans, but NASA had purchased them. Black suits would surely be waiting at the gate. "I'll call a friend. She'll come and get us."

"You have a phone?"

"Sure," Darren said, reaching for his bag.

Emile caught his wrist. "They'll be listening." He rummaged through his rucksack and handed Darren a cheap phone. "It's got two-hundred pre-paid minutes. No contract."

Darren held the little device in his hand. Rogue thetans wouldn't be tapping his phone, but whatever agency was working with—or on top of—NASA just might. "How much do I owe you?"

Emile shook his head. "It's for the cause. Just pay it forward."

They helped Crusher up and led him to the hole. Grasping each of his armpits, they lowered him until just his head protruded, staring and expressionless, like a very realistic manikin. At the count of three, they let him drop the remaining five feet. The alien zombie lay in a crumpled heap on the dirty floor. One arm flopped to the side, and he rolled away. He looked barely sentient, but, as the citizens of Troy discovered after moving their war trophy inside, appearances are just that.

The doorknob suddenly rattled, and McKinney's voice bellowed, "Open this door!"

"Crap!" Darren hissed as he eased himself as far as he could, and then dropped down, falling unto the grime. When he looked up, Emile was already replacing the plywood panel. Before he closed it all the way, he looked down and called softly, "Good luck!"

"You're the one that's going to need it," Darren said.

He shook his head. "We're not important. We'll have our turn. Right now you have to take care of him," he said, pointing at the motionless pile of human flesh. "He's a keeper of the Truth."

Before Darren could respond, the escape hatch closed.

Crusher's staring eyes swiveled up and looked at him.

"The Truth may set you free," Darren said, "but it's going to cause mass panic for the people of Earth."

For once, he didn't honk.

Chapter 7

"I *know* you need rhodium," Darren said. Crusher sat next to him on the bench, but his words came out soundlessly on Darren's lap.

I don't think you understand the urgency.

"What do you want me to do? Find an alchemist?"

Alchemy is not a science, and I suspect you meant it as hyperbole. There's a precious metal shop eight blocks from us.

"And you know they have rhodium?"

I do not. I could query, but I expect your government is monitoring all internet traffic.

"*All* traffic? That's, like, billions of megabytes, or whatever."

Not quite, but a good guess. Approximately one hundred million megabytes every second. You're off by just a factor of ten. They would be monitoring just the traffic terminating in Houston.

"They can do that? Email too?"

Of course.

"I thought that was illegal."

It's your government, not mine.

"Hey, wait a second. You're transmitting right now!"

At this power level, my transmission falls below background noise within thirty feet.

"Well, eight blocks is as good as a thousand. Adelaide will be here any minute. We're staying put. Why didn't you think of this five hours ago when we called her?"

I was inactive, recovering. And then I was busy assessing the situation— you don't realize how much information passes continuously through your body in the form of radio frequencies. And then you fell asleep. I tried to wake you, but it was clear that people passing by were going to call the police.

"Because you probably sounded like a walrus being stuck with a fork."

If you're trying to insult me, you should know that I don't take offense.

"Therefore, I'm wasting my breath. Let me guess—you don't take offense in the same way that I wouldn't be offended if a hamster tried to goad me."

Do you want me to answer that?

"No. Please, no." Darren chuckled. "It must really frustrate you that you're completely dependent on me, a virtual hamster."

I don't get frustrated.

"Ha! I remember a few times you came close—wait a second, are you a machine or something?"

The response came back in less than three seconds, but that was at least two seconds longer than usual.

It's complicated.

"What? You *are* a machine?"

As I indicated, it's complicated. Adelaide is approaching.

Darren looked up and down the street. "I don't see her—ah! There she is."

He stood up and waved, and she pulled up to the curb. He walked around and met her as she got out. It was so good to see a familiar face. Without thinking, he reached out and gave her a hug. She hesitated, but returned the gesture, if not quite as enthusiastically as he.

"So, what happened?" she asked.

He'd kept the call short, concerned that it would be picked up and traced. He'd told her only that they needed a ride back to New Orleans, that he'd explain later. "We ran into some trouble at NASA," he said. "We had a disagreement."

"And they took back the return flight tickets?"

"In a manner of speaking."

She handed him the keys and he climbed into the driver's seat. "Since last night, she said, "your 'manner of speaking' has been to hardly speak at all." She helped Crusher into the back and slid in the passenger side. "I think you owe me some explanations."

Before their flight, he'd only told her that the rhodium client had arranged the meeting—to approach NASA about a support contract. Assuming that Crusher's alien was the unnamed client, it was basically true.

"You're right," he said. "I do owe you explanations. Uh, can we put it on hold for now, though?"

She gave him a hard look, and said, "Yes. But I have to tell you, I hope I'm not being used."

Darren winced. Damn! He *was* using her. And probably putting her in danger as well. Damn. "Listen, Adelaide, I have a confession. I can't tell you everything, but … well, we're in a bit of trouble."

"That's putting it mildly."

"What do you mean?" he asked.

"Oh, come on. NASA doesn't pay to fly you here on less than one day's notice, and then take back the return tickets. You never talked to NASA. This probably has something to do with acquiring rhodium. The whole story about your scientist client sounded flimsy from the beginning."

"You're wrong about NASA. We did talk to them—it just didn't turn out so well. Listen, you yourself said that Crusher was somehow special." He tensed, waiting for a honk protest from Crusher, but the zombie sat staring, from all appearances, not even listening.

"You mean that nonsense about how he's channeling a spiritual voice from another dimension?"

Nonsense. It felt like a slap in the face.

"I'm sorry," she said, laying her hand on his arm. "It was a long five-hour drive."

"You do think that it's nonsense, though," he said, unable to let it go.

She didn't answer at first. "Yes, I'm afraid I do," she said.

"Well it is nonsense," he said, surprising himself. "But the truth is even harder to believe."

He glanced back at Crusher, ready for the protest squawk. The eyes swiveled to look at him. "Yah," he said.

"Yes?" Darren repeated. "Tell her?"

"Yah."

"Tell me what?" Adelaide asked.

Darren looked at Crusher and then at her. "This isn't good."

"Darren, what are you talking about?"

"He wants me to tell you. I guess it really drives home how important—how dangerous—the change of events is."

"Tell me *what*? What change? What *events*!"

He sighed. "You really aren't going to believe it—" He glanced again at Crusher. "Not without the alien's cooperation."

"Alien?" she repeated.

"Space alien."

Suddenly, Crusher honked.

"Dammit, Crusher!" Darren exclaimed. "Do you want me to tell her or not?"

He lifted one arm and extended one finger. He honked.

Darren looked off in that direction. "What? What am I supposed to see? Oh shit."

It was a Fungus Bird, cruising along on the other side of the street, passing them. Darren slouched down, trying to melt into the seat. He peeked sideways. Was it really a Fungus Bird? Instead of bright silver, the color was more like pewter, and the formerly smooth surface now traced the outlines of feathers.

No, it was definitely Fungus—the too-straight flight, the blurred beating of wings, and the feather outlines were just that, outlines. Maybe they were adapting, slowly taking on the appearance of Earth birds—the same morphing ability as Crusher's alien, only in slow motion.

"What do you see?" Adelaide said, leaning over Darren and peering out the side window.

"Don't be so obvious!" Darren whispered, pulling her down.

She pushed his hands away and looked again. "There's nothing there," she said.

"It's another alien. It's flying."

She threw him a worried look. "Darren, it's just a bird."

"Look closer. It's not."

It had passed them, and was gaining distance.

"It's an odd bird, for sure," she admitted. She looked at him skeptically, like she'd caught him pulling her leg. "Wouldn't it be quite a coincidence that an alien creature would have evolved to look just like our birds?"

"Air is common to all inhabited planets, and flight might result in a common form—"

"Convergent evolution," she said, eying him carefully.

"Uh, yeah—that. Plus, I think they can actually change to look more like our birds. Is that right, Crusher?"

He honked agreement.

She watched Darren with a wry smile, waiting for him to dig himself deeper into fantasy do-do.

"Tah! Tah!" Crusher called.

Darren sighed, and took out the tablet. There was one word. *Rhodium.*

"Where did that come from?" Adelaide asked, pointing at the screen.

Darren looked at her, trying to convey seriousness. "From Crusher," he said, gesturing towards the back seat. "From the alien inside his head, actually."

She held his gaze, her face frozen in skeptical reservation. "Right," she said.

"You don't believe me."

"Are you asking me?"

"Sure."

"I don't believe you."

He glanced back at Crusher, but his former cousin's eyes looked past him, unmoving. "You sure about this?" he asked.

Yes. She should know.

Adelaide was watching him, and he pointed down at the screen. Her expression turned puzzled. "How did you do that?"

He lifted his shoulders. "It wasn't me."

"Let me hold it," she said, taking it from him. "Okay," she said. "Change it."

Darren nodded at the screen in her lap. She looked down, and her puzzlement deepened.

It's not Darren, Adelaide.

She looked at him, and he shrugged. The message changed.

We don't have time for this. We must get the rhodium and then escape from Houston. Every minute counts.

"Welcome to the alien support squad," Darren said, putting the car in gear and pulling away.

They passed another Fungus Bird, scanning pedestrians. It

swooped down, and examined a taxi as the passenger pointed, tickled at the inquisitive avian. Darren turned quickly off at the next street, lengthening their route to the precious-metal shop. Adelaide was a continuous stream of questions, and Darren tried his best to keep up, but he was distracted watching for gray birds. "Ask Crusher," he finally said. "He has all the answers anyway."

As Darren finally pulled into the curb near the shop, Adelaide gave a little squeal. "Oh, my," she said. "That gives me the chills."

Darren glanced back. The alien had stuck out an inch of tentacle from the hole in Crusher's head, and was wiggling it seductively. "Quit messing around," Darren said. "Do you want rhodium, or not?"

Of course. It's important that Adelaide be secure in the truth.

He took the tablet from her and put it in his bag. "Well?" he said to her. "Do you believe there's a space alien living in Crusher's head?"

She took a breath, letting her emotions catch up to reality. "If there's not, it would be the most elaborate prank ever pulled."

Darren studied the surroundings, up and down the street, and said, "You two stay here." He opened the door, glanced around a second time, and got out.

The sign above the shop read *Lone Star Antiques and Consignment*. In smaller letters underneath was *Loans, Bail Bonds,* and almost an afterthought, *Jewelry.* Darren looked at the other shops. On one side was a garage. Inside, a blinding point of light and a spray of sparks confirmed its purpose. On the other, was a flower shop. This had to be it. An electronic beep announced his entry, where he found a dim cave filled with junk. People brought in property in exchange for a "temporary" loan, and the property never left. After a decade or two, the status changed from possibly-useful appliance, to antique.

A pudgy old man with white flying hair, white bristly mustache, and white stubble of week-old beard shuffled out from a back room and took up station behind a dusty glass counter piled high with more junk. "Lookin' to buy, or just lookin'?" he asked gruffly. "If you're just lookin', I don't have it."

Darren peered down into the counter, hoping to see a labeled tray or box, but found just a small arsenal of hand guns and knives.

Even there, the dust had managed to layer every surface, like a fine blanket of gray snow. "I was led to believe that you deal in precious metals," Darren said.

"You were, were you?" the man grouched. "You hear this from some preacher?"

"Uh, no—online."

"So, the internet's your church?"

"No—ah, I get it. I was led to believe. So, you don't sell precious metals?"

"I didn't say that."

Darren counted to three. This guy probably kept the shop just for a chance to harass customers. "I'm looking for rhodium," Darren said. "You know what rhodium is?"

"What? Do I *look* like an imbecile? Of course I know what it is. I got some. How much money have you got?"

The question tripped Darren. It put things backwards. "Enough for what I need," he said, parrying the swipe. "How much rhodium do you have?"

The old man eyed him. Darren could be with the IRS, or intent on robbing him. "Enough for what you need," he said.

This was getting nowhere. "How much for, say, a quarter ounce?"

If he asks me again how much money I have, I'm going to punch him in the nose, Darren thought. The old fart didn't say anything. He shuffled away into the back room, and returned and lay a tiny glass vial on the counter. It was no bigger than a pencil stub. "Two hundred," he said.

"Dollars?" Darren said.

"No, ducks. Of course dollars, you numbskull."

Darren picked up the tiny container. "This can't be more than a couple of grams," he said, putting it back down. "Do you have a scale?"

"Broke," the man said.

"This is worth maybe fifty dollars," Darren said. "Seventy at the most."

The man shrugged, but left the vial on the counter. The negotiations weren't over.

They both turned at an electronic beep. "I told you to stay in the car!" Darren said.

Adelaide held up her palms. "Can *you* tell him what to do?" she said.

The shop owner watched warily as Crusher toddled to the counter. "What's up with Frankenstein?" the man asked.

"Neurological disease," Darren replied. "I'll give you eighty bucks, but that's it."

The owner shook his head. This guy spent his life negotiating items of questionable worth.

"I happen to know that an ounce of rhodium is going for less than a thousand dollars," Darren said, distracted by Crusher, who had flopped both hands onto the counter.

"You happen to know, do you?" the old man said. "Well, I happen to know that this rhodium is going for two hundred dollars—hey!" he barked as Crusher picked up the vial. "Watch the merchandise!"

"A quarter ounce might be worth two hundred," Darren said, "and there's maybe a quarter of *that* there. A hundred dollars is more than twice what it's worth. That's my final offer—"

"Hey!" the owner yelled. "Put it down already!"

Crusher had picked up the vial, and was holding it against his forehead. *Shit.* "Put it down, Crusher," Darren said.

"What the hell—?" the owner started to say, but froze, staring. Crusher held the vial against his skin as a thin tentacle emerged from the tiny hole in his forehead. The little worm deftly removed the cap, dropped it on the floor, and dove into the glass container.

"What in Judas name …?" the old man muttered as he took a step back. He stood speechless as the particles of rhodium danced up the tentacle and into the hole, like a miniature conveyor belt. A moment later, Crusher let the vial fall, and is hands dropped to his sides.

"You—owe—me—two-hundred—dollars," the man said tonelessly as he stared, wide-eyed, at the tiny hole where his rhodium had disappeared.

Bang!

Something had slammed into the glass at the front of the shop.

The old man was torn from his trance. "Goddamn pigeons!" he growled as he picked up a youth-size baseball bat and headed for the front.

Adelaide grabbed Darren's arm and pointed. A Fungus Bird hovered at the front door, as though it didn't realize there was glass in the way. The beak withdrew into the head, and another concussion set Darren's ears ringing—this time creating a spider-web of cracks that spanned the width of the door. The alien was hammering the glass, using its beak as a pneumatic ram bolt.

"Judas!" the owner bellowed, and opened the door, one hand holding the bat cocked. The pseudo bird flew past him as he swung and missed.

Darren pushed Adelaide behind him. Instinct. It was all there was time for before the alien invader was hanging before them, it's featureless eyes staring in all directions at once. Darren felt a waft of air from the blurred movement of the wings. Incongruently, it felt pleasant.

Darren debated whether to get the two of them away, leaving Crusher to deal with the predator, or stay and help his zombie cousin. He compromised. "Walk away," he said to Adelaide quietly. He'd do what he could to defend the alien emissary.

The white-haired owner appeared behind the Fungus Bird. The alien started to turn, but the bat caught it square, and it disappeared off to the side.

"Dah!" Crusher called, and waddled off. Darren pushed Adelaide off after him towards the front of the store.

"What the hell …?" the shop owner muttered, staring at the crippled intruder lying on the floor. Darren took a quick look as they hurried out. The creature flopped back and forth. One of the wings was bent. Not broken—bent. Like metal. Fine lines traced the outline of feathers, as though a master artist had embossed the thin material. Sharp talons scrapped across the floor, failing to get a purchase on the smooth linoleum. Intrigued by the sight, Darren glanced back before leaving. He could have sworn that the wing was now straighter.

Outside the shop, Crusher stood staring through the window. He turned to Darren and pointed at him. "Tah! Tah!"

"He wants to use the tablet," Adelaide said breathlessly, keeping an eye on the shop door.

"I know," Darren said, already pulling it out. Luckily he'd left it on.

Destroy the Fungus Bird.

Darren looked at him. "You want me to go back *inside?*"

Yes. Destroy it.

"We can get away in the car. It won't catch us."

Given time, it would follow. It was fixing itself. Darren was convinced of that.

You must destroy it. Now.

"If I try, that could just give it more time to—"

Crusher's steamer honk echoed among the rundown shops. People on the sidewalks stopped short and stared.

"Okay!" Darren said. He took a breath before opening the damaged door.

Inside, the shop owner still stood, staring down, entranced, the bat hanging from his fist at his side. A buzzing like a hive of angry bees filled the shop, and then stopped. It began again, but now the tone was more even. It was fixing itself.

Darren glanced around for a weapon, and picked up a table lamp. Stupid choice. He put it down and picked up a frying pan, a classic weapon.

The determined whirring swelled, and the creature rose into view, swaying slightly, a bit unsteady. Darren started forward as the owner cursed, stepped back, and cocked the little bat. The faux bird rose, gaining altitude, tilted forward, and dove. Darren was barely an arm's length away when the creature clutched the front of the man's shirt in its talons and poked his forehead with its beak. A crack, like a firecracker, rang out. The bat rattled to the floor as the man jerked, and fell, dragging the Fungus Bird along.

The bat banged Darren's shin. He dropped the frying pan for the bat. The alien creature twisted its head to look at him. The featureless eyes seemed to bore into his brain. The wings blurred, and the murderous bird rose as Darren cocked his weapon. It seemed to hesitate, deciding whether to come in for another kill, or back off. Darren didn't let it finish the thought. He'd batted .38 in Little League. The impact was like whacking a grapefruit. The alien fell against shelves, and then to the floor, where it thrashed madly.

Darren approached slowly. It was difficult to see with all the flailing about, but he could tell that one wing was bent completely in half, and the body visibly dented. The ineffectual wing caused it to turn in a slow circle on the floor as it struggled. As the head swung around towards him, another crack rang out, and he felt a stabbing pain envelope his whole foot. He cried out and staggered back. The pain was intense, bringing tears to his eyes and rage to his brain. Howling, he stepped forward and swung down at the beast. He missed the body, but caught the good wing, bending it as well. As he pulled the bat away for another blow, it resisted. The alien had grasped the end with its talons. Pain and panic overwhelmed Darren, and he yanked the bat back. The beast hung on, swinging along with it, the centripetal force keeping it beyond the bat's tip. The Fungus Bird slammed into an old sewing machine and released the bat. It hung there, impaled on the long spool pin.

Darren hammered it with the bat, and it fell to the ground. He slammed it again. And again. He didn't stop until Adelaide took his arm. "I think it's dead," she said.

Darren stood up, gasping for air. He was shaking. The alien creature lay, mangled and twisted. One wing had torn off. Darren didn't trust it. He prodded it with the bat, but it showed no signs of life.

"Look," Adelaide said, pointing to the tablet in her hand.

It is destroyed. We should leave.

Crusher stood staring expressionlessly at the floor. The alien carcass began to smoke. It smelled acrid, like burning plastic.

We must leave, now.

Darren hesitated, not wanting to look. He had to. To make sure. He knelt next to the shop owner, expecting to see a smashed skull, but there was only a broad red blotch, as though the alien had merely smacked him. The man was clearly dead, however. His eyes were wide open, staring at infinity.

Darren stood up and limped along, following the others out. The pain had eased, but his foot felt numb, sluggish to commands.

At the shop entrance, Darren stopped and ran his fingers along the surface of the glass door, feeling the outlines of the cracks made by the Fungus Bird's hammer beak. "It could have killed me," he said.

Adelaide held the tablet for him to see.

I know.

"You *knew?* And you sent me in anyway?"

It was important. We need to get away. Now!

"As important as my *life?*"

The tablet was blank.

Darren looked at Adelaide, who was watching him intently, as though imagining him lying in there on the floor next to the dead shop owner. "I think I don't like aliens," he said.

She pursed her lips and glanced at Crusher, making sure he wasn't looking. She gave a little conspiratorial nod.

As Darren pulled the car into traffic, the buildings were suddenly brighter, as though a cloud had moved from in front of the already blinding sun. Within seconds, the light faded back to normal Texan blaze. Adelaide gasped. "Oh my God!"

Darren felt a thump, and then heard shattering glass. He turned to look back. The shop was glowing with an angry ruddy light from within. A flame licked out one of the broken windows.

Adelaide held out the tablet.

The energy contained in a Fungus Bird equals several tons of TNT.

"Right," Darren said, as he stepped on the gas pedal and moved into the opposite lane to pass the car in front of him.

Chapter 8

"I don't understand why it was so important to kill *that* Fungus Bird," Darren said, as he swerved around another slow car. "We didn't go out of our way to risk my life when we saw them in the shopping mall."

Adelaide held up the tablet.

That would have revealed our presence. This time, it already knew we were there.

"So, I'm supposed to risk a thunderbolt to the head every time a bird finds us? I assume that's what it was—an electric shock."

Indeed. Fungus Birds are capable of generating electric fields of hundreds of volts.

"Like an electric eel?"

An electric eel's discharge lasts for just a few milliseconds. A Fungus Bird can sustain it for far longer.

"Like you did to McKinney."

The tablet was blank for a moment.

I did not kill him.

"A difference in scale?"

Again blank.

Yes. Among other differences.

"Electrocution is, like, a common trait of space aliens? Somehow evolution dropped the ball with humans?"

It's complicated. But the reason it was so important to destroy this Fungus Bird was that it would have communicated our location. McKinney's agency has focused its activities on finding us.

"How do you know that bird didn't already tell them?"

It tried, but the welding next door interfered with its transmissions.

"Well, I hope you're happy. You finally got your rhodium."

It is welcomed. This relieves the immediate dire need.

"So, you need more."

Of course. That was barely two grams.

"I knew it! That son-of-a-bitch was trying to rip me off."

The car was silent.

"He's dead," Adelaide said.

"That's true," Darren agreed.

"And you didn't pay him anything."

"That's also true. But he tried."

"He did try," Adelaide said, nodding.

"You're patronizing me, aren't you?"

"Some questions are best left unasked."

"Fair enough."

Darren took the entrance onto the 610 inner beltway. "Did you know that the Fungus Bird was going to kill the old guy?" he said, glancing in the rear mirror. "I'm talking to you, tentacle-head."

Adelaide sighed and held up the tablet.

Of course not.

"Yet you showed him your tentacle. That sort of gives you away, you know."

There is no reason to hide my existence now. In fact, your government—specifically McKinney's agency—very much wants to keep me secret.

"Hmm. Because you might spill the beans about the Fungus Birds?"

My existence would provide incontrovertible evidence to support the inevitable rumors of space aliens on Earth.

"And the government obviously wants to keep Fungus Birds secret."

Secrecy as a rule is the natural tendency of governments everywhere, but in this case, it's also at the urging of the Fungus Birds.

"Why would they care? They're already flying around Houston like it's one big aviary park."

The Fungus invasion has only just begun. It occurs in three phases. The first phase consists of just a handful of scouts. Their role is to quickly evaluate the new planet, and prepare for the second phase—the advance squad. The first phase is mostly about maximizing the effectiveness of the advance squad. In this case, it means convincing the American government to work with them when they come through.

"And they've already convinced NASA and McKinney," Darren said. "If the public found out, the resulting media circus would spawn congressional hearings and political battles that would bring the whole plan to its knees."

Correct.

"And on top of that, an alien of a different species that knows their real intention is a metaphorical fly in the preparation ointment for the bruised knees."

So to speak.

"What does the advance squad do?"

It consists of dozens of invaders. They assess the possibility of ultimate success, and if considered positive, then their job is to make way for the safe passage of the hundreds of thousands that comprise the mass invasion. They will coordinate with the unsuspecting natives—humans, in this case—if they can, and if that's not possible, they seal off and protect the point of entry.

"And if the assessment is negative?"

This is unlikely, but if the native population is sufficiently advanced and savvy enough to pose a real threat, then the advance squad will attempt to communicate the fact back. They can only attempt this as the mass invasion begins, when the portal is pushed open from the far end.

"So far, though, the US government thinks the bird aliens have nothing but peaceful intentions."

Indeed.

"Won't a dead shop owner sort of break the pretty bubble?"

They will undoubtedly blame it on me. After all, one of their own lies destroyed next to him.

"They'll frame you?"

I believe that is the right expression.

"NASA will at least get to do an autopsy on the smoking remains of one of them."

Almost certainly not. The others will do what they have to in order to prevent that.

"Why?"

After a moment,

It's complicated. In any case, it would require sophisticated forensics just to detect remnants of the Fungus Bird.

Darren had been privy to his own private adrenaline-soaked autopsy. "There was no blood," he said.

The screen was blank.

"In fact, there were no guts—nothing that looked like internal organs. It was more like a bowl full of snakes and spaghetti that had all melted together."

The screen remained blank.

"Yo! Squid brain! You there?"

It's complicated.

"Come on! anytime we start to talk about what's inside them—or you, for that matter—it gets 'complicated.'"

It is complicated.

Adelaide put down the tablet and nudged him. "Are those aliens?" she asked, pointing out her side window.

Darren studied the forms flying along as he maneuvered among the frantic highway traffic. They were too far away to tell. Then they stopped. They were still flying, they'd just stopped.

"Hey, friendly alien," Darren said to the back seat. "Can the Fungus Birds hover, like a hummingbird?"

Adelaide held up the tablet as she continued to watch them.

They can. How many are there?

"Uh, I see three—no, four. They're spread out."

"There's a fifth one," Adelaide said, pointing.

This is very bad news.

"Why?"

This many on patrol indicates that the advance squad—the second phase—has already arrived.

"Yikes! That means that the mass invasion is next?"

Correct. That will be the end.

"The end of what?"

I should say the beginning of the end. The end of humanity.

"Oh, shit!" Darren exclaimed, glancing in the rear mirror.

Adelaide looked at the tablet. "Oh, shit, indeed," she said.

"No! I mean, there's a police car behind us. He's got his cherry light on."

At that moment, a siren wailed loudly.

"What'll I do?" Darren said.

"I don't think you have a choice," Adelaide said. "You can't outrun it."

Mumbling curses, Darren moved to the right lane, and then off the highway onto the wide shoulder. The police car followed him closely, and turned off the siren when they stopped, but left the cherry light flashing.

"Were you speeding?" Adelaide asked.

In the rear mirror, Darren saw the cop talking on his radio. "A little, but there were other cars passing me. Why'd he pick me?"

Adelaide looked back. "I guess we're about to find out."

In the mirror, Darren watched the cop get out and walk up to them, his hand resting on his holstered pistol. Darren lowered his window and said, "What's the problem, officer?" He remembered to keep his hands on the steering wheel, visible.

The policeman quickly scanned the three of them, and then leaned down. "Are you Darren Jackson?"

"Neh!" Crusher wailed. "Neh!"

"No," Darren said. It was out before his brain processed it.

"You're not Darren Jackson?" the cop repeated.

"Neh!" Crusher yelled.

The cop leaned down farther and looked angrily at the zombie.

"He has a neurological disease," Darren said.

"Neh!" Crusher yelled.

The cop's jaw muscles worked. "Driver's license and registration, please," he said stonily.

Adelaide opened the glove compartment and handed him the registration as Darren pulled his license from his wallet. "Um, when I said I wasn't me, I, uh, wasn't thinking," he mumbled as he handed them out the window.

The cop took one glance and stood up straight, his eyes alert now. "Step out of the car, please," he said. It wasn't a request. His hand was back on the butt of his pistol.

"Neh!" Crusher yelled.

"Will you shut up!" Darren exclaimed. "You've gotten me in enough trouble already."

"Out of the car," the cop commanded. "Now."

As soon as Darren was out, the cop said, "Turn around," as he grabbed his arm and spun him. "Hands on the car," he said, giving Darren a little push to help. As Darren stared at the gravel, the cop frisked him up and down.

"What have I done?" Darren asked.

The cop ignored him, his hands moving to probe along his legs. His hands froze. "Back in the car, sir!" the cop called, standing up.

Darren looked up and saw Crusher staggering around the back of the car before the cop pushed his head back down. "Get back in the car!" the cop yelled. "Immediately!"

"He doesn't understand," Darren lied. "He's a retard."

"Dammit!" the cop exclaimed. "Tell him to get back in the car!"

Darren peeked under his armpit and saw the officer pull his gun from the holster.

"Hey!" the cop called. "Put that camera away!"

Darren peeked under his other armpit and saw Adelaide holding her phone out the window.

"I don't think so," she said. "In fact, this is now streaming live."

"You!" the cop yelled. "Get away from my car!"

Crusher had stumbled to the police car, and was lying across the hood, his head resting sideways on the windshield.

The cop glanced back at Adelaide, and, cursing vehemently, put the gun back in the holster and pulled a taser from his belt instead. "This is your last warning!" the cop said, as he ran to Crusher. He stood over him, as though deciding what to do, and then jabbed the taser into Crusher's back. The response was instantaneous and dramatic. Crusher jerked and flailed his arms, hitting the cop in the head and sending him staggering back.

The cop recovered and came back, but Crusher's spasms had already stopped. The commandeered body lay back on the hood, staring at the sky. The cop jabbed him again for good measure, and this time jumped back to avoid the swinging limbs. He glanced at Adelaide and her phone, and his brow furrowed. Crusher had fallen to the ground, and the cop squatted down and lifting him by his armpits. "You're okay, buddy," he said, stepping carefully back as Crusher stood swaying slightly. "Now get back in your car." The cop watched as Crusher staggered away.

Darren heard the crunch of gravel as the cop came back to him. "Up," he said, pulling Darren upright by his shoulder. "Hands behind your back." Darren heard the tinkling of metal and then the cold touch of the handcuffs on his wrists.

"Tah! Tah!" Crusher said from the other side of the car.

"Sir!" the cop called. "Please get back in the car!"

"Tah! Tah!"

Still holding the phone in position, Adelaide reached down and picked up the tablet. She held it for Darren to see.

Ask to see the warrant.

The cop glanced at the tablet, frowned, and looked at Adelaide. He seemed confused, but then said, "Come on," and pulled Darren by his elbow towards the police car.

"Officer, what's the offense?" Darren asked.

The cop ignored him, and worked tonelessly through his Miranda Rights instead.

"Officer, don't you have to tell me?" Darren asked.

"No," the man said, opening the back door of the police car. "Actually, I don't." Then he said, "There's a warrant for your arrest."

He placed his hand on the top of Darren's head as he guided him into the open doorway. Darren had never been handcuffed before. It was really uncomfortable sitting in a car seat with your hands twisted behind you, and the metal cuffs digging into your back. All the times he'd see this on TV, he'd never thought about that. Of course, for those people, discomfort was probably the last thing on their minds. They had actually done something bad. The cop got into the driver's seat, and was calling for backup, which meant, what? They were going to haul Adelaide and Crusher in as well?

Darren leaned forward and said through the metal grate dividing the interior, "Can't you at least tell me who issued the warrant?"

The cop sighed and poked at the screen on his dash. "It came from the FBI. All it says is that you are wanted for questioning—" He paused, staring at the screen. "What the hell?" He leaned forward, making sure he was seeing correctly. "God *damn* it!" he exclaimed, throwing his door open. "Son-of-a-bitch!" he growled as he opened the rear door. "Come on," he said to Darren motioning with his hand. "Out."

"What's going on?" Darren asked, scooting sideways and letting the cop help him to stand up.

"Turn around," the cop said. Darren felt the handcuffs coming off. "The big boys have made an ass out of me, that's what's going on."

The police officer escorted Darren back to his car where Adelaide was standing, still holding her phone up. The cop then addressed Darren, enunciating his words for his cyber audience. "There's been a mistake, and the city of Houston apologizes." He glanced at the phone camera. "For the record, though, it wasn't the city's mistake, but the FBI." He turned and started to walk away, but stopped and turned. "Enjoy your stay in Texas."

They got Crusher into the back seat, and Darren wasted no time getting back on the freeway before the cop had a chance to change his mind. "You did that, didn't you?" Darren said, glancing in the rear mirror out of habit. The zombie never turned his eyes unless he had to. "While you were sprawled across his hood."

Adelaide held the tablet for him to see.

Of course.

"You pretended to be the FBI and removed the warrant."

I didn't have to pretend to be the FBI, just a digital transmission containing a new message.

"Whatever. They're going to figure out the mistake sooner or later—we need to be far away when they do. I'm thinking that we should take smaller highways—maybe the 190 to Baton Rouge. They know we're from New Orleans, and they'll be watching Route 10 east—"

"Nah!" Crusher called.

"What do you mean, 'no'? It'll be faster if we stay on the interstate, sure, but—"

Adelaide nudged him and showed him the tablet.

We have to go back.

"What?" Darren exclaimed, looking back at the comatose face. "They're after us! We won't be able to fool them a second time. I won't hold up under torture. Excruciating pain is my Achilles heel."

Your comfort is not the issue.

"My comfort? My *comfort*! You don't know what it's like. You're not connected to pain nerves. I'll bet the only thing that happened to you when you got tasered was that you lost control for a couple of seconds—"

"Nah!" Crusher honked.

Adelaide held up the tablet.

What I mean is that there's more at stake than our fate—you, Adelaide, me. You saw five Fungus Birds back there. The logical conclusion is that the second phase of the invasion has already arrived, which further means that we don't know when the mass invasion will begin. It could be any time, and once that starts, there's no stopping. That will be the end.

"All this because we saw five birds?"

The first phase consists of perhaps twice that many. It is virtually impossible that half of that population would be scouting together over the city.

"What are we supposed to do? Convince McKinney that we're the good guys? I don't want to come within fist-punching distance. Maybe we could just call him. After we're a hundred miles away."

The Fungus Birds have surely set an elaborate stage depicting my kind as the danger to be fought.

"What are you saying? We need to go back and perform a few angelic deeds of goodness in front of them?"

What I'm saying is that it would be wasted effort to try to convince them. In any case, we may not have time. We need to go back to find out where the Fungus Birds came through from hyperspace, and when.

"All the phases come through at the same place?"

Naturally. Each phase needs to be ready at the point of entry of the next.

"What's so important about knowing when they came through?"

Take a guess.

"I thought we were short on time."

We can't turn around until the next exit. Until then, there's nothing to expedite.

"Okay. I'll bite. Hmm—ah! You'll know approximately when the mass invasion will begin?"

Not approximately—precisely. Fungus Birds follow exact schedules.

"You know a lot about them."

The tablet was blank.

They came to the next exit, and Darren pulled off. "If McKinney punches me, I'm going to punch you," he said into the rear mirror.

Ж Ж Ж

"This is nuts," Darren said as they sat down on a park bench a hundred yards from the temporary NASA offices. They'd left Darren's car parked on a residential street, and brought a taxi into town. "Why don't you just crawl out of Crusher and, like, go through the air ducts or something?"

The tablet lay on his lap.

Firstly, I don't think Crusher's body would survive very long now if I left. Secondly, and more importantly, I still wouldn't have access to the information. I can't dig into the files. They'll have the firewalls locked down tight by now. I can only intercept the information if someone with access and passwords actually pulls up the files.

"So we have no choice? Adelaide has to walk right into the snake pit?"

"If it was a snake pit," she said, "I'd be climbing down, not walking in."

"Whose side are you on?"

"Humanity's, I guess," she said. "Look, how much danger can there be? What crime would I be committing? Lying?"

"They won't bother to arrest you. They'll just take you right back to the water-boarding room, then they'll hang you on a wall by your wrists, assuming you survive."

"Your dramatics are impressive, but heavy on exaggerations."

"You're used to Germany, where the government hasn't molested its citizens since WWII. You're not in Kansas anymore, sister. This is the U-S-of-Abusing the Constitution."

Crusher honked.

We must proceed. In twenty minutes, the NASA offices will begin shutting down for the day. Adelaide, do you remember the name of the deputy?

"General Francis Farnham," she said. "His parents must have hated having a child. I'll meet you back here." She looked at Darren. "Assuming I survive the torture."

She strode away towards the NASA entrance without looking back.

"Okay, klutz," Darren said, standing up and offering Crusher a hand, "let's find a hole to hide in."

They'd picked the building on the east side of the NASA office complex. Within its residential apartments, Darren guessed that they'd have an easier time slipping in and finding a location along the west side, where Crusher could monitor the myriad wireless transmissions of NASA, the FBI, and whatever other clandestine government agencies huddled next door.

They hit the first snag when they came to the street entrance. They stood twenty feet away, trying to look casual—or, at least as casual as Crusher could look, standing like a statue, staring at nothing. A woman walked to the door, moved her package to the other arm, and, glancing once at them, punched in the entry code, hidden from view by an inset keypad. The door buzzed, and she went in. "Did you get it?" Darren asked.

No. There was no radio transmission associated with the entry. It must be a wired system.

"Oh, geez. Is that what you thought? That it was wireless?"

Car entries are wireless.

"Cars are cars, buildings are buildings. Besides, this one must be fifty years old. I don't think they even had remote garage door openers back then. What'll we do?"

I obviously am not qualified to offer a suggestion.

"I thought we were going to avoid sarcasm."

True. That was actually passive aggression.

"I don't think it can be when the aggressor declares it. It's sort of a paradox."

We don't have time for this. How do we get in?

"Leave it up to the primitive Earthling," Darren muttered as he walked over to the doorway. A list of residents with associated call numbers was visible behind a Plexiglas display. Darren picked one at random and waited. Soon, an elderly woman came up, and Darren pretended to push a call code, and then wait, shaking his head in frustration.

"What's the problem?" she asked.

Darren sighed dramatically. "I guess Karl must be in the bathroom."

"Karl?" she said.

"Karl Peckham. I'm his cousin."

"Oh! Mr. Peckham. Nice gentleman. Always holds the elevator for me, even when the other—not so neighborly—residents tap their toes impatiently. Are you in town visiting?"

"Yeah. Just for a couple of days. Listen," he said, lowering his voice and gesturing secretively towards the immoveable figure of

Crusher, "that guy over there. Does he always hang out here?"

She looked at the alien zombie and frowned. "No. Not at all. He looks …"

"Suspicious," Darren said.

She nodded. "Come. Let's get inside." She punched in a code, and they were through. He stood at the door as she walked down the hall. She turned. "Aren't you going up?"

"Uh, no. I … I think I'll wait a couple minutes to make sure that creepy guy doesn't do anything." He peered out the glass door and waited.

"Maybe we should call the police," she said.

"No! I mean, he hasn't actually done anything illegal. If he tries something funny, I'll call the police."

She frowned again. "Very well. You be careful. Don't be a hero."

"Me? I'm not the hero type."

He waited until the elevator took her away, then opened the door and called to Crusher. They took the elevator to the third floor, the same as the NASA director's office in the adjacent building. As they rode up, Emile's phone beeped. He tapped the answer button. "Are you ready?" Adelaide asked. "I'm in the lobby, and there's a guard starting to give me looks."

"Give us a couple of minutes. We're almost there."

The elevator door opened, and Darren stepped out and turned left.

"Nah!" Crusher honked. He flopped his arm in the other direction.

Darren thought about it. "You're right. I got turned around."

He wondered if he'd made the best choice, picking this building. The hall stretched away on both sides, identical apartment doors marking the distance. They turned west. That end terminated in a blank wall, broken only by a fire extinguisher nook. Darren sat down, his back against the wall, and the tablet resting on his bent knees. Crusher sat too, his legs spread out before him, as though he'd been shot. A dark red smear down the wall would have completed the picture.

"Shall I call her?" Darren asked.

"Yah!" Crusher answered, his eyes not straying from a spot on the far wall.

Darren dialed Adelaide, and when she answered, he said, "We're 'go' to proceed."

"Roger, Mission Control," she replied with feigned gravity.

"No need to get snarky. You're going to keep your earpiece in, right?"

"Gee, I hadn't thought about that."

"Okay, I get it. I didn't mean to insult you." To Crusher, he said, "You've got the video tap?"

The tablet changed to a monochrome view of the area outside the NASA director's office. At the far corner of the image they could see Susanne, his assistant, working away at her laptop.

"You didn't consider that the monitor cameras might be wired, did you?" Darren said.

"Nah," Crusher replied.

"If they were, you wouldn't be able to tap in, would you?"

"Nah."

"Uh, 'no' you wouldn't have been able to tap in, or 'no' my statement was not correct?"

Words appeared superimposed on the video image.

I would not have been able to tap. You could phrase your questions with less ambiguity.

Darren snorted. "Man, I'm getting stung on all sides."

Down the hall, the elevator door opened, and a middle-aged man in cargo pants and a *Led Zeppelin* T-shirt stepped out. He glanced at them as he walked to his door and inserted a key, but then he paused and looked at them again. Leaving the keys hanging in the door, he approached them. "Do you live here?" he asked in a tone that didn't indicate he was looking for new buddies to hang out with.

"No," Darren said, keeping an eye on the tablet. "Just visiting."

The man took a few steps closer. "Who you visiting?"

"Look," Darren said, "we'll be gone in a few minutes."

Mr. Zeppelin gestured at the tablet, giving Crusher a suspicious side glance. "What're you doing?"

Darren looked at him. *Oh hell.* Tipping his thumb at Crusher, he said, "There's a space alien living in his head, and we're tapping into NASA's video surveillance."

The man glared, debating his next move against impudent trouble makers, and then his eyes went wide. He leaned back as though avoiding a swinging fist, turned, stumbling, and ran to his door, where he frantically jiggled the keys and pushed open the door. A second later, it slammed shut with a loud thud.

Darren looked at Crusher. A foot-long silver tentacle was waving like a loose jib sheet in a gale around his head. "He's gone," Darren said. "You can pull back into your shell."

He glanced down at the tablet. A woman's head had appeared. It was Adelaide, walking towards Susanne with her phone tucked into her jeans pocket. Darren set his phone down on the floor so they could both hear what it picked up.

Susanne looked up. "You're here to see the director?"

"That's right. My name is Adelaide—"

"I know," Susanne interrupted. "They called up." The director's assistant studied her. "You're here on behalf of General Farnham, is that correct?"

"Yes, that's correct."

Susanne nodded, but didn't say anything. Adelaide waited patiently. Darren was impressed with her cool composure. They'd taken their best guess based on Crusher's internet diving as to which sub-branch of the military would be pulled in for support in securing the alien entry point. But it was only a guess.

"The director's in a meeting," Susanne said. "Perhaps I could help you?"

"Perhaps," Adelaide replied without skipping a beat. "The general would like information about possibly dangerous radiation at the entry point. Specifically, whether his men should have special gear."

"I thought the General was on his way?" Susanne said. "He'll be here within the hour."

"I know," Adelaide lied. "He wants to be prepared to talk about that when he arrives."

"Why didn't he just call me?"

"Frankly? I'm afraid he doesn't trust anybody but me."

Susanne held her gaze. A tiny grin formed. "That will require me to access top-secret files."

"I realize that," Adelaide said.

Susanne nodded, still suppressing a grin. She tapped away at the keyboard, looked at the screen, then up at Adelaide. "Some amount of radiation is expected, but not enough to warrant—"

The director's door flew open, and McKinney's head appeared. He looked mad. He strode out, glanced at the screen, and slammed the laptop shut. "What the hell do you think you're doing?" he bellowed. He spun around, but Adelaide had already disappeared around the corner.

Darren nudged Crusher with his elbow. "Did you get what you need?"

"Yah."

"Hot damn! Is that gal one cool cucumber, or what?"

"Yah."

Darren nudged him again. "Is that unambiguous enough for you?"

"Yah."

"Hot *damn!*" Darren said again.

Crusher stared at the wall.

Chapter 9

"Anza Borrego?" Darren said. "It sounds like a Mexican dish."

"It's the second largest state park in the country," Adelaide read off the tablet in her lap. "It's between San Diego and the Salton Sea, and includes 600,000 acres of undeveloped land."

"Why haven't I ever heard of it?"

She waited for Crusher's reply. "It's a desert, and there's other deserts closer to LA for people who like that sort of thing."

"Well, it sounds conveniently remote when hoards of alien Fungus Birds pop through from hyperspace."

Adelaide watched the words appear. "He says to remember that the government doesn't know that there's a mass of aliens on the way. The Fungus Birds just got lucky with the remote location—they can't tell from the other end where they'll come through."

"*He* says to remember? Since when did the alien become male?"

"You're right. I guess I just associate him with your cousin."

"Let's ask him—squid-brain, are you male or female?"

Adelaide grinned at the tablet. "He writes that it's complicated."

"I could have guessed."

"Here's one," Adelaide said, pointing.

Darren pulled over to the side of the street. They'd brought a taxi back to Darren's car and had been patrolling the residential streets looking for another one from Louisiana. Adelaide stood watch while Darren used a screwdriver to remove the license plates in exchange for his own. The theory was that the other owner wouldn't notice that his plates had been changed, at least not until half a dozen squad cars came down on him, at which point their new plates would become hot.

"So, we drive to San Diego?" Adelaide asked as Darren pulled back onto the street.

"Yah!" Crusher called from the back seat.

"It must be at least a thousand miles!" She glanced at the tablet. "Oh, dear. Crusher says it's fifteen hundred miles. It'll take us days to get there!"

"We can't fly. That's for sure. What's today?"

"The fifth."

Darren shrugged. "We have three days. It'll take us—uh, let's see …"

"Crusher says about twenty hours driving time," Adelaide said.

"I was just going to say that—twenty hours. We'll drive straight through. We can take turns."

"Twenty hours straight? That seems … aggressive."

"You're in America now, the land of wide-open spaces. Driving cross-country marathons is a way of life. Sort of like the second amendment—an inalienable right."

"Okay," she said, sighing and staring out the window.

ж ж ж

"Well, at least we almost made it to New Mexico," Darren said as he pulled into the motel parking lot.

"Alive," she noted. "Which wasn't an obvious outcome."

He'd fallen asleep, and had woken to Adelaide's scream as the car tilted off the shoulder onto the sand and gravel of the desert that was west Texas.

They sat in the darkness now, listening to the struggling electric buzzing, their faces flashing with random shades of red as the neon sign above them alternated between MOTE and MOTEL. "They'll be watching for my credit card," Darren said.

"I know," Adelaide said. "I'll use mine."

"I'll pay you back," he said. They were talking in the 2:00 AM monotones of exhaustion.

"Thanks," she said.

They sat there.

"We should check in," he said.

"Yes," she said.

He opened the door, but it seemed too much effort to do more.

Maybe they could just sleep in the car. Adelaide got out the other side, ruining his plan. He pushed himself out and stood up.

The line of motel doors facing the main street of the tiny town of Tornillo seemed as tired as Darren felt, most of them scuffed and gouged at the bottom from decades of angry kicks—long past recoverable with a simple coat of paint. Just four exits from El Paso, there was no good reason for travelers to stop in Tornillo, short of avoiding metropolitan authorities. The motel probably served the locals, in all the ways motels have always served locals, like the abandoned sheds that teenagers find where they can be the teenagers their parents worry about.

As Darren and Adelaide walked to the office, one of the battered doors opened a crack, and a slice of unshaven face peered out. There's a fine line between a stylish stubble and mere laziness, and these cactus whiskers had gained distance from that line. The visible eye followed them until they entered the office, where magazines and old newspapers dominated the decor. The room was empty. Darren tapped the bell on the counter, and it went *klunk* instead of *ding*. "Hello?" he called.

He heard a groan from a back room, and a rustle, and a stout, middle-aged woman shuffled out, squinting and rubbing her eyes. She wore a faded, flowered tent dress, and smelled of old sweat. "Thirty bucks," she said, hardly looking at them.

Darren glanced at Adelaide. "Did you say thirty dollars?" he said. "For a room?"

She looked him in the eye. "No. For that chair. Of course for a room. Wa'dya think?"

Darren got it. "Uh, we'd like it for the night—the whole night."

The bleary-eyed woman looked at Adelaide and back at him. "Suit yourself. That's seventy dollars. Plus tax." She disappeared into the back room and returned with an armful of folded sheets. "Seventy bucks buys you clean linens," she said, plopping the pile on the counter.

The woman was finally waking up, and she stood smirking at him while Adelaide handed over her credit card. Darren itched to explain that they weren't here for a surreptitious bounce on the mattress, but in fact were on their way to save the Earth. The woman swiped the card, waited, then handed it back, saying, "Hope it's worth it." Darren's itch turned to a fantasy where he was strangling her while Crusher stood by, a tentacle waving goodbye.

Their room was two doors down from stubble-face, who had retreated back into his cave. Only one of the two lamps next to each of the single beds worked, but they'd come to sleep, so Darren let Adelaide strip the beds while he went back to the car to retrieve Crusher. "Come on," he said, leaning into the open back window, "you can sleep on my bed, as long as you don't twitch too much."

"Nah," the alien zombie said without looking at him.

Darren sighed, and reached in for the tablet.

The lower layers of this brain—effectively all that's left—are already asleep. There's no need for me to disturb you and Adelaide.

Darren looked at Crusher. "What's with everybody? Just because I'm a man and she's a fine looking woman, doesn't automatically mean we're bump partners."

His cousin's eyes were closed. He was talking to the sleeping body of his cousin.

I don't understand that, but time is precious. You should sleep so that we can continue to San Diego. You can explain later.

"Fine," Darren said. "Don't worry—we're not going to waste time on anything except sleeping."

He didn't bother to look at the tablet for a response.

Adelaide was putting the clean sheets on the beds, and he helped her, and then plugged in the charger for the tablet.

"Can I borrow your toothbrush?" she asked.

She'd left New Orleans eighteen hours earlier expecting to be back home in her own bed by now. She didn't even have a change of underwear. He dug the toothbrush out of his bag and handed it to her along with a tube of toothpaste. She looked weary but still a fine looking woman. Heck, with some makeup, hair styling, heels, and a dress, she could be a model. Or at least a TV anchor.

When he returned after washing and brushing, she was already asleep. He quietly reached over and turned off the lamp, then crawled into his own bed. The sheets smelled clean but the odor of old cigarette smoke, dust, and other things indefinable that he wanted left undefined forced an odorous background that he couldn't ignore. He turned over. He waited, then turned the other way. This was ridiculous. Not a half hour before, he couldn't stay awake, even though all their lives had depended on it.

He must have fallen asleep, because he woke with a start to the bed bouncing. An instant later, a heavy body was on top of him. He cried out in pain as a knee smashed his left arm, and a strong, sinewy hand held down his right wrist. "Make a move, and you're dead," a whiskey-soaked voice said as something cold and sharp pressed into his Adam's apple.

Somebody turned on the light, and he was looking into the face of stubble-beard. He heard a woman's voice say, "Take it easy, gal. Try anything, and your boyfriend will be losing blood by the gallon."

The man threw a quick glance sideways. "Get anything?" he asked as he turned his hot whiskey breath back on Darren.

"Shit. Just thirty—no, forty in cash."

"How about the purse?"

The sounds of rummaging. "A wallet. Ah—here we go. Shee-it! A pile of twenties. Must be a couple hundred."

The man looked off to the side, pressing the knife harder into Darren's neck for good measure. "She's not bad. Not bad at all."

"Ah, Jesus, Carl. Your dick's insatiable."

Terror burned Darren's ears, and yet he wondered at the fact that a drug-hungry lowlife would wield a word like "insatiable."

The stubbled face lowered to within inches. "So help me, one move, and you're dead. You understand?"

Darren couldn't nod his head. He'd be cutting his own throat.

"*Understand?*" Carl repeated.

"Yes!" Darren said, the vibration of the word working the knife edge into his skin.

"Alright, then," Carl said, pivoting sideways while holding the knife at his neck. "Up," he said, pulling Darren by his shoulder into a sitting position. He could now see the other woman. She looked ancient, her face a weathered mass of wrinkles. He guessed that she was probably only forty, but the Texas sun and a scrabbled life had accelerated the onslaught of age. She jammed their money into her pants pockets and walked around behind him. He sat on the bed, a knife to his throat, looking at Adelaide. She was huddled at the head of the bed, holding the sheet desperately around her shoulders. He'd expected her to look as terrified as he felt, but she seemed angry, furious, in fact.

"Got it?" Carl said, and Darren felt hands exchanging the knife.

"You're a swine," Adelaide said as she watched the man come towards her. She squinted her eyes and her nose turned up in scorn. "I have AIDS, you idiot."

He chuckled. "Well, ain't that a coincidence," he said.

The woman laughed. "Oh, now ain't that pretty? AIDS all around!"

Adelaide's fury turned to fear. She looked at Darren, as though she'd forgotten he was there. "Don't make them watch," she pleaded as the man unbuckled his belt.

"What's the matter?" he said. "They gonna ruin the mood?"

He dropped his pants, but before he could kick them off, a loud thump sounded behind Darren. The man spun and his brow furrowed. "Who the fuck are *you*?"

"Nah!" honked Crusher's voice.

The woman turned to look, and the knife pressed harder. Darren cried out in pain. "Christ!" she yelled, and the next instant she was thrown sideways. The knife was gone, and Darren turned to find Crusher sprawled on top of the woman, who lay under him, pressed against the bed stand.

"What the *fuck*!" Carl exclaimed, diving across the bed next to Darren. Too late, Darren saw that the woman had dropped the knife right next to him. He reached for it, but Carl was quicker. The rapist stood up, kicked off his pants, and walked around the bed. Cursing, the woman pushed Crusher off of her, and he rolled over onto his back. She scrambled to her feet and moved off, behind Carl. Darren reached down and pulled Crusher up. His brain-dead cousin stood, swaying a little back and forth.

Carl shook his head in disbelief. "You just committed suicide, you fucking prick," he said to Crusher, who stared unblinking at the man's chest. Carl's brow drew together. "What the fuck's wrong with him?"

"He's retarded," Darren said.

Carl hesitated, and then snorted. "That don't matter. I'll be doing the world a favor," he said as he held the knife, point forward, and stepped towards Crusher, but then stopped, frozen. "What the—!"

The alien's tentacle had appeared, wiggling out from Crusher's forehead. It extended outwards, as though searching for Carl's face.

"Good fucking *God!*" the man uttered as Crusher staggered forward, arms spread wide as though greeting a loved one. Carl stepped backwards until he was up against the dresser, and Crusher fell unto him as a sharp snap, like a stick breaking, caused Carl to yelp. Crusher backed away, falling onto Darren's bed. Carl blinked and shook his head. He put his palm to his temple and moaned, clearly dazed.

The woman went to him and grabbed him by his shoulders. "What'd he do to you?" she asked, throwing a cautious glance back at Crusher, but the zombie lay staring at the ceiling. The tentacle was gone.

The woman took the stunned man by the hand and led him out of the room. At the doorway, she turned and looked at them. "Y'all are going to rot in hell," she said, and they were gone.

A cricket outside chirped once, twice, and took up a song of beckoning.

"Wow," Darren said to the empty doorway. "Talk about irony."

"She has all our money," Adelaide said.

"Shit," Darren said quietly. He turned to her. "I'd go after them, but they have a knife—"

Adelaide was looking at Crusher, her eyes wide with horror. She pointed at him. "No they don't."

A deep red splotch had formed on the sheet under Crusher's right shoulder. The handle of the knife protruded up from his bicep.

"Oh, Lord, Crusher," Adelaide whispered, going to him and placing her hand gently on his chest.

"He can't feel it," Darren said, coming over to stand beside her.

She looked at him. "But ..."

"He can make contact with only so many neurons. He can barely control Crusher's body movement, let alone tap into pain connections."

"I was talking about ... Crusher, your cousin."

"I see. Adelaide, you have to understand that my cousin—he just doesn't exist anymore. Look at him—does it look like there's a Crusher in there feeling pain?"

The body of Crusher lay there as though truly dead. The eyelids snapped open, and the eyes slowly rotated towards them. "Nah!" he honked.

"Listen!" Adelaide whispered.

"That's all he does—honk out one-syllable words—"

"No! Sirens!"

She was right. They were still off in the distance, but coming closer.

"The motel manager must have called the police," she said. "Maybe we can get our money back."

"Nah!" Crusher called. "Tah!"

"Uh, oh," Darren said, picking the tablet up off the dresser. "That doesn't sound good." He looked at Adelaide. "He says they're coming for us."

"For *us*? How could they know that we're here—?"

"We have to get out," Darren said, throwing his things into his bag. Adelaide stood staring at him. "Now!" he exclaimed, yanking the charger from the wall.

"But Crusher! We have to get him to a hospital!"

"Nah!" his zombied cousin honked. Crusher pulled his elbows back in preparation to push himself upright into a sitting position, but only his left arm did any pushing, and he rolled over instead, falling to the floor.

"Oh Christ!" Darren muttered, bending over him. "Help me lift him up," he said to Adelaide.

"He's in pain!" she insisted, stepping around him.

"Nah!" he honked, his face buried in the dirty carpet. "Gah!"

"See?" Darren said. "He's telling us we have to go."

Her face screwed up tight in anguish, Adelaide squatted down and helped Darren lift Crusher to his feet. His whole right side was wet with blood.

"Oh, Lord!" Adelaide whimpered, gingerly touching the handle of the knife still protruding from his arm. She ran to the bathroom and returned with two towels. "Pull it out," she said.

"We don't have time!" Darren argued. "We have to get away from here—"

Adelaide's mouth drew tight with resolve. She grasped the bloody handle between thumb and forefinger, threw Darren an accusing glance that withered his heart, and, whimpering, slowly withdrew the blade. Crusher's body twitched once, and again. Some amount of the pain storm raging among billions of neurons must have reached the deep animal core of Crusher's cerebellum. She tossed the knife onto the bed as though it might twist around and bite her, then lifted Crusher's arm. "Hold it up," she ordered, and tried, unsuccessfully, to rip the towel with her teeth. "Damn it!" she hissed, and, wincing in horror, grabbed the knife and attacked the towel as though it was responsible.

"Give it to me," Darren said, taking the knife and handing her Crusher's lifeless arm. The handle was slippery with blood, but he managed to shred the towel into strips, which Adelaide wrapped around Crusher's upper arm. Darren looked around, and settled on the tablet charger. He wound the cord around the makeshift bandage and tied it. He grabbed his bag, and they led their wounded comrade out, the plastic charger device dangling like a rappelling mountain climber who'd lost his hold on the cliff face.

The sirens were closer, and Darren got Crusher part way through the back door of his car, and then pushed him the rest of the way in with his foot.

"He's not a piece of luggage," Adelaide scolded, getting in the front passenger side.

"In a way, he is," Darren said, starting the car as tires suddenly squealed across the parking lot and out onto the street. He looked just in time to see the tail end of a nineties-era Camaro fishtail away.

"That was them," Adelaide said wonderingly. "The ones who robbed us."

Just then a screech drew Darren's attention back towards the motel office. The stout woman who'd checked them in was hoofing it across the parking lot, holding a tire iron over her head with both hands, a rampaging Viking she-warrior. "Jesus!" he said, putting the car into gear. "What kind of nut hole is this place?"

"You sons-of-bitches!" the woman screamed. The Corolla's 130 horsepower carried them away, but not quite fast enough. A pop, like a watermelon dropped from fifteen feet, was followed by a swish as a cascade of rear windshield glass pebbles fell, covering the prone body of Crusher like snow. "Rot in hell, you asshole freaks!" the woman screeched as they pulled out into the street.

"What's with this town?" Darren said. "Everybody's determined to get us into hell to start rotting. Sounds like a contradiction, actually. Hell would be too hot for the microorganisms that cause rot—"

"She let them in," Adelaide said.

"Huh?"

"I woke up to the sound of jiggling at the door. They didn't break in. They used a key."

"Huh. No kidding? You think she, like, takes a cut of what they get?"

"Could be. They thought that we'd called the police. Where are we going?"

Darren drove past the interstate entrance sign. "We definitely don't want to get back on the freeway. I'll go into town. We'll have to ditch my car for another one."

"We sound like bank robbers."

"Except in reverse. We got robbed."

That reminder kept them quiet for a few blocks. "Back there ..." Darren finally started.

"Yes?" Adelaide said.

"You told him that you had ..."

"AIDS?" She laughed. "It might have worked if it hadn't back-fired."

Darren sighed.

"You're relieved," she said, surprised.

"Well ... sure!" he said, feeling his face grow hot. "I mean, geez, that would be terrible if you ... had aids—for you, I mean."

"For me," she confirmed, smiling.

The tiny sprawling town of Tornillo consisted of little cinder block bungalows and prefab houses next to tin-roofed agricultural warehouses spread out across large dirt lots. There were no sidewalks, just wide sandy shoulders. Darren took a couple of turns and pulled off into the dirt. "What'll we do now?" Adelaide asked.

Darren shrugged. "Steal a car."

"How? Can you hot-wire one?"

"Sure. I can also make it fly."

"I didn't think so. We'll have to find one with the keys still in it."

Darren looked up and down the expanse of empty street. All the cars sat parked in dirt driveways next to the humble houses. "Walking around peering into car windows is going to get me shot when the dogs started barking."

"Tah!" Crusher called from under his blanket of glass pebbles.

"He lives," Darren muttered as he pulled the tablet from his bag.

Many cars are keyless.

"So?" Darren said.

They use radio transmission.

"Ah! Of course. You're a genius, squid-brain."

The police have searched the motel, and are broadening their hunt. We don't have much time.

"Always the logical one."

Minutes later, Darren crouched in the bushes fifty feet from a house with a new-model Ford parked in the driveway. Crusher lay in the dirt next to him. Pieces of windshield glass still decorated his hair like faerie dew. Places where blood had soaked through the towel were caked with dirt.

"Here goes," Darren said. He took a breath and ran to the car. He gave it a nudge, and it beeped. He shoved it, and the alarm came to life as Darren scuttled back into the bushes. He was breathing hard as a window in the house came alive with light and then the door opened and a man emerged carrying a shotgun. He glanced around, then walked to the car and looked around again. He pressed something in his hand and the alarm stopped. He pressed it again, and the tail lights flashed. He opened the door and peered inside. Satisfied that nothing was disturbed, he turned and went back inside. A minute later the light went out. "Did you get it?" Darren asked.

"Yah," Crusher honked, sending a little geyser of dirt where his mouth lay. "Nah," he added.

"Damn. I'm going to get shot for sure," Darren muttered.

The alien had explained that keyless entry cars used encrypted transmissions. It was impossible to determine the code by observing a single instance of use, but it was mathematically possible—in theory—to deduce it from subsequent observations. The more cases, the fewer the calculations. Crusher had caught just one transmission.

Darren crept quietly back to the car. He waited, watching the house and thinking. It shouldn't take much. He grabbed handfuls of dirt, and sprinkled them on the hood, and then took off one shoe and impressed random patterns with it. He tip-toed up to the window, and, holding both hands over his mouth for muffling, he uttered, "Help!"

He waited.

Nothing. He called into his hands again, louder.

He thought he heard sounds from inside, but the window remained dark. He gasped as a blazing light illuminated the area from near the peak of the roof. The front door burst open, and he only had time to drop flat onto the ground.

The man reappeared, shotgun held ready. Darren didn't breath. An attic vent cover had come loose and hung partially open, casting a mottled shadow down the wall, and he huddled inside the foot-deep patterned darkness. The man peered around, but the spotlight was now in his eyes. He saw the dirt on his car, and he muttered curses about "fesskins," probably referring to Mexican immigrants. Tornillo's southern border was Mexico. The man stood looking at the footprints. He glanced around, trying to understand what had happened. *Come on!* Darren thought, willing the man to be curious about what might be inside. Cradling the shotgun in one arm, he reached into his pocket and took out his keychain. He pressed it, and the car beeped and flashed its lights. He opened a door, glanced around again, and then bent over to look inside. Satisfied, he slammed it shut, the car beeped and flashed one last time, and he went inside.

Darren waited. The light stayed on. He waited some more. The man was obviously going to leave it burning, maybe scare away marauding fesskins. Darren snake-crawled to the corner of the house, and then scuttled off into the bushes. He circled around, keeping low until he found Crusher, still lying in the exact same face-down position. Before Darren even asked, the alien zombie honked, "Yah" into the dirt.

"Shh!" Darren scolded, but he was relieved.

Minutes later, Darren backed out of the driveway, stopped to let Adelaide jump in, and then drove away, flipping on the headlights a block later. Before heading west on Route 20 towards El Paso, they stopped and exchanged plates with a random car.

Their remote entry fob sat in the back seat staring at nothing.

Chapter 10

The fesskin foe had not only lost his car, but also a full tank of gas, which carried the Earth defenders across the southwest corner of New Mexico and into Arizona. Just thirty miles shy of Tucson, Darren left the interstate and pulled into a gas station as the sun peeked above the horizon behind them. The fuel display bar had disappeared miles back. Darren unclenching his hands from the steering wheel and massaged his cramped fingers. Running out of gas on the interstate was a guarantee that a highway patrolman's face would appear in your window.

Adelaide sat up, rubbing her eyes. "Where are we?"

"The end of the line," he said.

She blinked, still waking up. She looked out the window at the scattered trees and Saguaro Mountains to the north. "San Diego?"

Darren laughed. "Almost. Just four hundred miles to go."

She looked at the gas pumps and frowned. "We have no money for gas." She sighed. "Time to steal another car?"

"That's like buying a pearl necklace so that you can use the case to hold loose coins."

She shrugged. "What choice do we have?"

"I've had some time to think."

She glanced at her watch and sighed again. "I've been asleep for three hours. Sorry about that."

"No. I'm glad you did. You can drive the next stretch."

"Without gas?"

"We just need to get to Tucson. A gallon or two would do it."

They rummaged through their bags. Darren found a crumpled dollar in one of his pants pockets, and Adelaide pulled eighty cents in change from the glove compartment. "This'll get us to the next exit," he said. He tallied their possessions—his tablet and charger, his spare clothes and toiletries, the pants, shirts, and shoes they were wearing, and one wounded and comatose body.

And a car.

"What else is in the glove compartment?" he asked.

Adelaide extracted the car's manual, a rag, and a flashlight.

Darren took the flashlight and popped the trunk. Inside, he found jumper cables and a bag of empty beer cans. He tossed these on the ground and pulled up the flooring. Underneath was a spare tire, and jack. He felt around the front of the tire. "Bingo!" he called.

Adelaide came around. "More money?"

"Maybe." He held up a metal box the size of a book, and a plastic case.

She shook her head, not understanding.

"A socket wrench set," he said holding up the metal box, "and a portable air compressor."

She furrowed her brow. "You think you can sell them?"

"What do we need? Five dollars? Together, these would cost at least forty or fifty dollars new. Somebody working at a gas station would surely appreciate their value."

The person working at the gas station was a teenage girl who rolled her eyes. Just then a man with a weathered face under a clean cowboy hat pulled up in a beat-up pickup. Darren got his five dollars, but had to throw in the spare tire. The man didn't ask why they were scrounging for money, but he did glance in at Crusher slouched in the back seat. The blood soaking the towel had turned black. "You trying to get this guy to a hospital?" he asked.

Darren nodded. To admit otherwise was to confess that he was either a heartless son-of-a-bitch, or there was something bigger than a man's life was at stake, like the Earth.

The man looked at Crusher again, and then pulled another five from his wallet and handed it to Darren. "The tire's brand new," he said in explanation.

ж ж ж

Twenty minutes later, Darren pulled into a Starbucks, and five minutes after that he'd connected the tablet to the internet and found what he needed. Forty-five minutes after leaving the gas station, he stood at a public phone with Adelaide. He wasn't sure they would even find one, but apparently the city of Tucson wasn't quite ready to assume that every last person had their own.

Darren picked up the handset, and paused. The only parking spot he could find was half a block away. "Maybe you should go to the car," he said to Adelaide. "Wait a couple of minutes, and then come and pick me up."

"You think they can trace the call that quickly?"

He lifted his shoulders. "Who knows what they can do now?"

She nodded and walked away.

He waited until he saw her disappear near the car, then dialed. They would obviously be monitoring Aunt Melba's calls, where "they" would be whatever secret government agencies did such things. That they could do it, he had no doubt. That they *would* do it, he'd bet money. He slipped the precious coins into the slot, dialed, and waited. "Hello!" his aunt's voice said. "Who are you, and how did you get this number?"

"Aunt Melba, it's me."

"Darren, honey? Is that you? Why are you calling from a different number? I've been worried about you."

"I don't have time to explain, but I need a favor—a big favor."

"Of course, sweetie. Some men came by asking about you. Are you in trouble?"

He sighed. "A little," he lied. "Listen, I need you to go to a certain place. I don't want to say the name, but—"

"Darren, honey—are you in trouble with the system?"

To Aunt Melba, the "system" was anything or anybody of authority, or culturally conservative. "Yes," he said.

"Okay, what should I do?"

Good ol' Aunt Melba. "Do you remember the restaurant where we ate the last time you came to visit?"

"Of course. It was called—let's see—"

"Don't say it! I need you to go there. Now! Can you do that?"

"Is somebody listening to our call?"

A horn tooted. It was Adelaide, double parked next to him.

"Almost certainly. Can you go now? I mean *now?*"

"Of course. I have to pee first."

"Pee, then go!"

"What should I do when I get there?"

"You'll find out. Bye—and thanks!"

He hung up the handset and ran to the waiting car. "Let's go!" he said, as he jumped in.

Adelaide pulled away. "How'd it go?"

"Okay," he said, looking back at the pay phone. "I think she'll be there." He watched until he couldn't see it anymore. When he turned around there was a police car racing towards them, lights flashing. "Oh shit," he said, and slouched down. It zoomed past, however.

"You think it's coming already?" Adelaide asked skeptically.

"I don't want to find out," he said, picking up the tablet to study the city map. He looked up at the street signs. "Take a left at the light—three blocks, then find a place to park."

Adelaide found a spot with ten minutes left on the meter, but they had to hoof it a block away to find another pay phone. They left Crusher in the car. He could act as a guard—not that he could do much if somebody tried to break in, but one look at him, and nobody would try. "You'd think they'd have more phones in the downtown area," Darren said, checking his watch and tapping his thigh nervously.

"The one place the city would expect everybody to own a cell phone might be the business district," she said.

"Sounds like class bias."

"In favor of the less well-to-do."

"True—how long do you think it'll take Melba to get to the restaurant?"

Adelaide was grinning. "I was in New Orleans exactly four days, minus the last twenty-one hours. I don't even know where this restaurant is."

"Right. It seems like I've known you a lot longer. I haven't slept in over a day. Let's see—it's maybe two miles, but she'll hit some morning commuter traffic—"

"And pee-time. Don't forget that."

"Yeah—oh hell, I'm going to call."

He dumped the last of his change into the slot and dialed. "Darren, sweetie, is that you?" came his aunt's voice.

"It's me—where are you?"

"I'm almost there. I'll have to find a parking space. I shouldn't be talking and driving—not because it's the law, but because I understand that to do so is dangerous—"

"Aunt Melba, you're not going to the restaurant. I just wanted to get you near the real destination. Find a parking space, and go around the corner. There's a Western Union office. Aunt Melba, we need money—as much as you can spare. I think you need to use either cash or a debit card."

"Hold it. Here's a parking space. Darn, the sign says no parking 6:00 AM to 9:00 AM."

"Auntie, I'll pay the ticket. Please, just grab it."

"Okay. I guess this is sort of an emergency."

"No, it's a genuine emergency."

"Okay, I'm parked. Oops! Almost got my door taken off. People in New Orleans drive like maniacs." She was huffing and puffing. Darren could hear the sound of her sandals flapping on the sidewalk. "I see it. Oh, no! It's not open ... oops. Yes it is. They sure keep it dark inside. That's good. It saves energy—"

"Aunt Melba, you're going to need to know where to send it. Remember the place where you spent the best week of your life? I think you said it was with the drummer in Jackson Browne's band."

"Oh! You mean—"

"Don't say it!"

"You think 'they' are still listening?"

"We have to assume so. Send the money to that town. It's the office on Broadway."

"Okay, but isn't that sort of giving it away?"

"Auntie, every city has a street named Broadway."

"Won't 'they' just ask the Western Union clerk at this end?" Her voice fell to a whisper. "Should I bribe the clerk?"

"That's not necessary. By the time they figure it all out, we'll be long gone."

"Okay, honey. Please be careful. Where are you headed?"

Their destination would be completely obvious to 'them,' but Darren hated to simply hand it over. "The city where you spent what I would guess was the worst week of your life."

"You mean with Paul? The equipment manager for Jefferson Starship?"

"You got it."

"What a dick he was. Did I ever tell you that he told his wife that I was just the cleaning maid? He stood there naked, talking on the phone with me right there in bed. If I'd had somewhere else to go, I tell you I wouldn't have spent another—"

"Aunt Melba! Sorry, but my time is up. I have no more change. And … thanks. I'll make it up somehow—"

"Poo," she said. "I'm just glad to help. Anything to poke the system."

"Okay. Bye, auntie."

"Bye, honey. And it was the drummer of *The Starland Vocal Band.*"

"Huh?"

"They were the warm-up band for Jackson Browne."

"Oh. Right—"

The phone beeped for the third time and went dead.

"Let's go!" Darren said to Adelaide as he sprinted off.

Inside the Western Union office at their end, the clerk shook her head. "Sorry," she said. "Nothing pending from New Orleans." She glanced at the screen and nodded. "Here it is." One eyebrow went up, and she looked up at him. "This amount requires both an ID and a security check."

"How much is it?"

"Over a thousand dollars," she replied, watching him.

Darren's heart beat a pounding alarm in his chest. Security check? Christ. If he'd known this, he would have had Melba just send a couple of hundred. He handed over his driver's license. "What's the, uh, security check consist of?"

She read the screen, and smiled. "You should be able to answer a question," she said, looking at him.

"What … question?" he asked cautiously.

She grinned. "The question is, 'What was the worst song of 1976?'"

Darren returned her grin. "That's easy. 'Afternoon Delight,' by *The Starland Vocal Band*."

Still grinning, the clerk began counting out twenty dollar bills.

ж ж ж

Darren woke when Adelaide turned off the interstate. "Where are we?" he asked, sitting up and blinking away the blur from his eyes. The sun was high overheard, blazing off a flat landscape dotted with hardy looking shrubs and trees. They could have been back in El Paso.

"El Centro," Adelaide said, frowning as she sat at a stop sign, looking back and forth in both directions.

"Where's that?"

"About an hour from San Diego."

"How long did I sleep?"

"Four hours." She glanced at him. "Your shirt was wet with your drool."

"There's a gas station," he said pointing.

"I know," she said. "That's not what I'm looking for."

A car pulled up behind them, and she waved it to come around, then held out her hand to stop it.

"Need help?" a man called through his open window.

"Is there an urgent care center nearby?"

"Yeah. It's near the mall. You know where that is?"

Darren waited while the man gave her directions. "We don't have time," Darren said when she pulled away.

"I can't go on with him like that," she said, gesturing towards the back seat. "It's criminal."

Crusher sat in exactly the same position as four hours before. The bloodstains were the same size. His mouth opened. "Nah!" he honked.

"See?" Darren said. "Even he doesn't want to stop."

She looked at Darren, and her eyes were not patient. "Who exactly are you talking about?"

"Right. I understand your point. He's just a passenger, but he's the only sentient part. I've tried to explain that Crusher's body—"

"You mean Crusher. There is only one Crusher. Crusher's body is Crusher. The other thing, the thing that honks and—transcribes—is *not* Crusher. It has hijacked Crusher."

"That's true in a way—"

"Not in some way. It—has—hijacked—Crusher."

"Okay, conceded. But the alien was very careful to make sure his human host was brain-dead, nobody home anymore. Not even any lights on."

"And you know that for sure? Whatever chance Crusher had has been destroyed. You know there's no room in that skull for a cerebral cortex *and* an alien the size of a squid."

"I know. Believe me, it really creeped me out when he crawled inside—"

"You were *there* when it took over?"

"Well, sure. I—"

"And you didn't try to stop it?"

Darren stared at her. The accusing eyes made him want to melt. Why didn't he stop the alien? "It was inside Crusher before I knew what was happening."

He had been thinking of the alien as "him." Was he back to "it"?

She seemed to accept this. "Crusher is still a human being, though," she said.

"Hey," Darren said, "what's gotten into you? Why does the alien bother you so much all of a sudden?"

She took a breath. "It's been a long four hours. I've had a lot of time to think. When you're sitting a few feet from an alien hidden away inside somebody's head … maybe it's a mistake to think at all."

Darren smiled. "I understand." He waited a moment. "If we take him to a hospital, or even an urgent care center, they're going to ask questions. There's probably rules requiring they call the police."

She nodded glumly. She didn't seem convinced.

"Maybe we compromise," Darren said. "How about we go to a drug store and buy what we need to clean his wound and bandage it properly? That's all the urgent care center would do anyway."

That wasn't quite true. There was the added point about antibiotics, but he decided to keep the argument streamlined.

Adelaide nodded dully. She'd given up.

Crusher—the alien—honked his one-word protest all the way

to the drug store, and didn't give up until they'd taken off the caked towels and wiped away the dried blood with alcohol. Cleaned up, the knife puncture appeared much less fearsome, but began oozing fresh blood as they pressed and dabbed with the cotton swabs. The surrounding skin was a bright, angry red. Darren wondered if streamlining antibiotics away wasn't perhaps a critical mistake. He quickly wrapped the wound with fresh bandages, pushing the problem out of sight and mind.

ж ж ж

Back on the interstate, Darren drove. Mountains rose before them—the Peninsular Range that stretches a thousand miles from the southern tip of the Baja Peninsula in Mexico, to Los Angeles. Some thirty miles north of where their stolen car now cruised westward along the highway lay the inland Salton Sea—the shallow manmade expanse of water accidentally created in 1905 when engineers working for a private development company goofed while mucking around with the Colorado River, spilling the entire flow into the valley. Somewhere to the west of that was the Anza-Borrego Dessert, where, in less than two days, massive hoards of invading aliens would arrive.

But for now, their path lay directly west, to San Diego, paradise of North America.

Next only to New Orleans, of course.

An hour later, they topped the mountains, and followed the long western slope down into the green, sprawling expanse of San Diego suburbs. Far off, almost mistaking it for a mirage, Darren saw the glint of Pacific Ocean on the horizon. This really did seem like a paradise. Possibly better even than his Louisiana home. He could happily live here. What a shame if malevolent invading aliens wiped away humans from the Garden of Eden that was Earth.

He shuddered. It didn't have to happen. Three of them against an advance squad of lethal airborne aliens allied with the most powerful government on Earth—a government convinced that it was they, the three of them, that posed the threat.

Confidence, that's all they needed. It was, at least, a good start. It couldn't hurt.

The first business was to find another car. The Tornillo man would have reported his missing by now, and the "agency" would be broadcasting the car's description. Darren had the money to rent a car, but that wasn't possible with cash alone. The System forced you to abide by its self-serving rules.

He frowned. Life as a fugitive was bending his perspective, moving him towards Aunt Melba's mindset. He understood what must have gone through Bonnie and Clyde's minds. Of course, he and Adelaide had been on the road less than a day. And they hadn't robbed a bank. Or killed a sheriff.

Darren pulled off the interstate once they were immersed in the green suburbs, and found the nearest shopping plaza. They chose a likely suburban mom, and surreptitiously tailed her as she hop-scotched a hundred yards from one store to another, locking and unlocking her car with each stop. After the third leg, she entered a nail salon, and their universal remote car entry fob uttered, "Yah."

Adelaide helped Crusher out of their old wheels and into their new, while Darren gathered their meager possessions. He was sitting with them collected together in his arms when Adelaide came back. "What's wrong?" she asked.

"The tags on this car may never get reported to the authorities. It might sit here in this parking lot forever."

She shrugged.

"I'm thinking I should leave a note or something," he said.

"So it could eventually get back to the Tornillo owner?"

"Yeah."

"Do you know where the term 'fesskin' came from?"

He shook his head.

"I looked it up," she said. "It's a contraction of 'fucking Mexican.'"

She opened the door and held out her arms. He handed her the pile and crawled out. "Well, that takes care of that dilemma," he said.

They exchanged license tags with a random car and headed off to the San Diego downtown area nestled above the protected harbor. The tablet's battery had been low since El Paso, and Darren found a cafe with WiFi where they could get a charge and connect with Crusher. Conversations were nearly impossible when one party could only answer yes or no, or laboriously spell out words.

When the three of them entered the cafe, customers glanced at them as they walked by. They all needed a bath, and he and Crusher had been crawling around in the Texas dirt. Somebody whispered about the smell, and Darren realized that he'd gotten used to it. Crusher—the alien—could keep track of only so much of his host body's functions, and there had obviously been some … leakage.

Once they were settled into a table off in the corner, and the tablet adapter plugged in, Darren asked, "So, what's the plan?"

To stop the Fungus Bird invasion.

"Oh, gee!" Darren said. "What a surprise! I wouldn't have thought of that."

Are we allowing sarcasm again?

"Sorry. But your answer was totally obvious."

In a real sense, that is the extent of the plan so far. The problem is that we know what we want to do, but not how.

"You're saying you don't *have* a plan? What have you been thinking about the last eight hours?"

Thinking without data can progress only so far. The Anza Borrego Desert is one thousand square miles, and we don't know even the approximate point of entry for the invasion. Further, we don't know what tools we have to stop it. Finally, we have no idea how the Fungus Bird aliens and your government are positioned to stop us.

"Fine. How do we get the data you need?"

I'm attempting to do it now. This is the first internet connection I've had since Houston.

"You need WiFi? People connect to the internet all the time, all over the place."

They've contracted data services with their cellular providers.

"You can hack a sophisticated car entry system, and you can't hack a cell connection?"

Of course I could. It would be trivial. The trouble is that unlike a public WiFi link, where internet access is unfiltered, access via the cellular network requires a subscriber ID to connect. I could, of course, fake an existing ID, but the call would comprise a small anomaly in the subscriber's call patterns, and the NSA is adept at detecting and tracking these. Your government knows that we were heading to San Diego, and would focus their attention on our route.

"Okay, okay. I get it. When you set us off to San Diego, you must have had *some* idea how to stop a hoard of flying aliens coming through from hyperspace. Otherwise, we should have been running in the opposite direction."

There is no running, not unless you have access to interstellar transportation, which you don't. We either stop them, or that is the end of humans. Once the invasion begins, there is no stopping it, short of disrupting the hyperspace portal with a nuclear explosion.

Darren swallowed. "A nuclear bomb?"

A big one.

Chapter 11

"That's the plan?" Darren said. "Set off a hydrogen bomb at the entry site?"

Darren's mind spun with the consequences. *A big one.* Even though the Borrego Desert was thirty miles from developed areas, setting one off would mean the instant death of thousands. Detonation at ground level would result in massive amounts of fallout, which the westerly winds would carry over Phoenix and Tucson. Also, they'd have to warn the military, otherwise the explosion might be mistaken for first strike from Russia, or even North Korea. Of course, warning them would mean that they'd try to intervene—

He noticed that the alien had responded.

I had considered setting off a nuclear bomb, but I concluded that this isn't feasible. It will be difficult enough just getting ourselves to the portal entry site, let alone carry along a stolen nuclear warhead. No, we need another plan.

Darren breathed. "I'm relieved, but maybe I shouldn't be. As bad as a nuclear explosion would be, at least there'd be some people left."

There is one other possibility. I explained earlier that one task of the Fungus Bird advance squad is to assess danger from native life—whether the natives are advanced enough to pose a threat. Had your government been less gullible, they might have solved the problem already—convinced the advance squad that they were capable of destroying a significant quantity of invaders as they came through.

"We try to turn that around?"

You've already tried that.

"We did. McKinney definitely wanted nothing to do with it. Besides, the invasion starts tomorrow—the Fungus Birds would know that there's not enough time to set up a defense. So, we really don't have a plan?"

You're not considering the problem broadly enough. The essential point is that a signal that is sent back to the waiting hoard could stop the invasion.

"Okay ... ha! So, instead of impersonating a remote entry car fob, you'll pretend to be an advance squad Fungus Bird!"

I wish it were that simple.

A loud rattling and scraping of chairs disrupted Darren's thoughts. Adelaide nudged him and pointed. Three people at the nearest table noisily moved to a table farther away. One woman said something to her friend, and then held her nose and glanced back to make sure Darren saw her.

"So, you can't impersonate a Fungus Bird?" Darren said to the comatose Crusher.

I could, but that's not relevant. Punching through hyperspace without a far-portal is one-way by nature. There's no way to send coherent messages back.

"You got me, parasite head. I could have sworn you just told me that sending a message back could stop the invasion."

I indicated a signal, not a message. There's a subtle difference. A message implies information of variable substance, a signal could be just a single bit—a yes or a no. In this case, an absence of any signal is interpreted as "Yes—proceed with the invasion."

"So we send a 'no,' back. We make a big circle with a line through it?"

You are either demonstrating deficient intelligence, or being sarcastic, and since we agreed to forgo the latter, I will assume that I need to explain in simple terms for you.

"Ho, ho."

Although electromagnetic energy—radio waves and light, for example—cannot traverse the reverse direction of the opened one-way portal, the Fungus Birds at the sending side can detect fluctuations of the energy they are pumping into hyperspace to keep the tunnel open. These fluctuations in turn can be induced by distortions of space-time at the far end—at our end.

"So we need to bend space-time. That's a bit outside my league. You picked the wrong cousin to inhabit."

It's not as complicated as it sounds. Space time is warped by mass, of course—manifesting as gravity. But it is also warped by energy. As Einstein deduced, mass and energy have equivalence.

"Hold on, bit-brain. This much I do know—it takes a whole lot of energy to equal mass."

Of course. Modulations of mass quantity would produce greater amplitudes of space-time fluctuation, but there's a frequency component, and it turns out that this is more important than amplitude.

"Um, let's see if I've got this. Changing the quantity of mass at the portal opening—shooting cannon balls at it, for example—is relatively slow. But changing energy levels can be done almost instantaneously."

In simple terms, yes. The problem is that opening a one-way portal through hyperspace requires tremendous energy, and detection of fluctuations requires a commensurate amount of impulse energy at our end.

"Commensurate to the tune of …?"

A small nuclear explosion would work—smaller than what would be needed to actually shut down the portal.

"Are you kidding? No way!"

There may be other methods. It depends on what the government has set up on the site in preparation.

"Which brings us full circle. We need to find out the details—where and how in the desert the arrival is staged."

I've been fishing the internet since we arrived here, and it's sparse. The military is apparently reasonably good at keeping major operations secret. There does seem to be equipment movements east on Route 78—this borders the southern boundary of the Anza-Borrego Desert.

"Can't you go deeper? Like, hack into their data bases or something?"

Of course. Attempting to do so will likely be detected. I am prepared to begin, but once I start, we will have limited time before they trace the attack back to here.

"In other words, we need to be ready to run. How long?"

I can only guess, but I'd estimate perhaps thirty minutes for them to trace my cyber probes, and then however long it would take to send authorities to this cafe—one hour total would be a good assumption.

Darren looked at Adelaide. She'd been following along quietly. "What do you think?" he asked. "Ready to make a run for it in a half hour?"

"Sure," she said. "I'll use the bathroom and get some sandwiches to go."

They turned when a middle-aged man wearing a polo shirt emblazoned with the cafe's logo appeared before them. "Excuse me," the apparent manager said, "but if you're done, we'd like to turn the table."

Darren looked around. "There's other empty tables," he said.

The man's face was pinched. He wrinkled his nose. Crusher really did smell bad. "I'm sorry, but I have to ask you to leave."

"Why?"

The manager winced. He gestured towards Crusher.

"Because of my cousin?" Darren asked.

The man gave a quick nod. His pained face turned hard. "Come on," he said, pointing towards the door. "Out."

"Wait a second," Darren said. "Let me get this straight. Your restaurant is too good for my poor, retarded cousin?" Bad habit. "My mentally challenged cousin?" he corrected.

"Now, come on," the manager objected, controlling his voice. "The fact that he's ... disabled has nothing to do with it."

"Then why are you kicking us out?"

"Because he *smells!*" the manager exclaimed, closing his eyes in anguish for a moment at what he'd been forced to admit.

Just then shouts from excited children came from the front of the cafe. A bird had gotten inside, and was darting back and forth, apparently confused at its predicament. Darren caught his breath, but realized that this agile creature was nothing like the stiff, mechanical Fungus Birds they'd encountered. Its predicament must have caused the creature distress, addling its instincts, since it flitted from one person to the next, hovering in front of each, as though searching for a window out.

The frantic bird caused mayhem among the customers. Chairs banged as people scampered out of the way, grabbing children and covering their heads. "Oh, Christ," the beleaguered manager muttered, then called out to an employee who appeared and handed him a broom.

"Nah!" Crusher suddenly honked as the manager went forward brandishing the broom like a battle axe. "Nah! Nah!"

Darren glanced down at the tablet. There was one word in huge font: *FUNGUS!*

The bird had risen above the scrambling crowd, and turned to face the back of the cafe, its wings a beating blur. It had heard Crusher's calls. It flew towards them, but the manager held up the broom to intercept it, calling to the employee to hold the door open. With the acquired agility of a real bird, the Fungus alien could have simply flitted around the ponderous broom, but it chose instead to hover a moment before the man, who watched with surprise at the unusual fearless behavior. Crusher honked a loud "Nah!" just as the alien creature darted forward and pecked once at the manager's arm, then pulled away. The manager yelped and dropped the broom. He looked at the red wound, wiped it with his finger, which came away smeared with blood, and then looked in amazement at his attacker.

Darren jumped up. If this was a Fungus bird, it obviously lacked the ability to inflict electric shocks. Maybe he could bring it down and destroy it before it had a chance to broadcast their presence. Crusher spewed a continuous repetition of warning bleats behind him. Darren guessed he was urging him on.

He bent down to pick up the broom, and the manager gave him a solid push, knocking him sideways, sending a chair clattering away. "What're you doing—?"

The manager hadn't pushed him—he'd fallen against him, and now lay motionless on the floor. Darren looked up, directly into the beady eyes of the bird. With a yelp, he crab-walked backwards, but the bird followed, a foot above his head. He crashed into another chair, and fell to his elbows. The bird dove towards his chest, and the next instant, Darren screamed in agony, except that the scream never made it to his mouth. He was stunned, lying on the floor, staring at the ceiling as bolts of pure pain shot back and forth across his chest, circling his body so that his entire skin was a tight shell of raw fire.

Through the curtain of torture, he was dimly aware that Crusher had come into view, staggering forward, arms swinging wide. He heard shouts, the excited calls from Adelaide, and screams of people rushing for the doors. The fire that enveloped him was slowly easing, and he was able to piece together snippets of thought. It looked like he wasn't going to die, although that had seemed certain just seconds before. He was lying on his back. He watched fearfully for the bird to appear above him. He turned his head ... or tried to. The will was there, but the motive power was not. In fact, he couldn't move anything. He was paralyzed. Panic overwhelmed him and again he screamed. Silently.

The raging inferno faded to a mere scalding. His thoughts now formed a coherent stream. The ceiling seemed to be ablaze with a searing bright light, causing him to want to squint. But he couldn't. Adelaide's face suddenly appeared, huge above him, her features cut sharp by the same knife-sharp light. "Can you get up?" she asked urgently.

He tried to answer, but all he managed was a little shake of his head. This in itself was a victory, a huge relief.

She turned and called for help. *How the hell was Crusher going to help?* he wondered. It wasn't Crusher that appeared above him, but some man he didn't recognize. "Ready?" Adelaide said, and then he was being lifted. In fact, there were four of them, and they were carrying him, bumping into chairs, kicking them out of their way as they made for the door. If anything, the light seemed to be even brighter. It hurt his eyes. He could turn his head now. The room behind him was filling with smoke. In the distance came the sound of sirens. Now he was outside, swaying up and down as the ad hoc brigade carried him across the parking lot.

"In here," Adelaide said.

"Shouldn't we call for an ambulance?" one of the men said.

"No," she replied. "This will be faster."

The open car door slid into view next to him, and he was shaken and bumped as they manhandled him into the back seat.

"Thank you!" he heard Adelaide say. "Thank you so much. I'll get him to the hospital."

By the time Adelaide made the first turn, Darren had recovered enough to croak hoarse words. "What happened?" he asked.

"Oh! Darren! The alien shocked you," she said. "Crusher says that it didn't kill you because they want to question you."

"What happened to the manager?"

"He's ... dead."

"*Dead?*"

"Crusher says that the bird injected him with poison—"

"When it pecked him."

"Right. The aliens are learning more about humans—how to make deadly toxins. Also, how to shock like a taser without killing—as you found out."

The sirens grew suddenly ear-piercing loud, and a fire truck whooshed past them, shaking the car, followed by a second one. "It's burning?" he said.

"The restaurant? Yes. Crusher knocked the bird down and I stepped on it. Actually, I stomped on it until it stopped moving. After that it …"

"Started smoking."

"Yes. Like the one in the pawn shop in Houston. After we were out, it sort of exploded, but without any sound. A few seconds later, though, the whole restaurant just burst out in flames. All at once. It was as though—wait, Crusher is writing something. Ah, he says that the stored energy is released almost entirely in the ultraviolet range. Objects absorb these wavelengths, which either result in breaking chemical bonds, or re-emission in the infrared range. The secondary infrared is what causes everything around it to start burning."

"Stored energy?" Darren said. He remembered that Crusher had mentioned that a Fungus Bird contains the equivalent of tons of TNT.

"Uh, Crusher says that it's—"

"Complicated. I know." He lifted his hand. It still felt tingly and weak, but control was returning quickly. "I don't think I need to go to the hospital."

"We aren't going to the hospital."

"We're not?"

"Crusher said that you would either recover on your own, or, if not, there wasn't anything they could do for you."

Darren held both hands up and clenched and unclenched them. "It wouldn't have hurt," he said, "to go to the hospital. Just in case."

"Yes," she said. "You're right."

He made fists and punched the air experimentally. "You're patronizing me, aren't you?"

She didn't answer at first. "If it was up to me, I would have taken you. Definitely."

"We're taking directions from squid-head now?"

"He understands the aliens."

"And he wants to save the Earth as much as we do."

Darren didn't mean it as sarcastic. It came out that way, though. And now he wondered about it.

"I asked him whether the arrival of the alien bird was a coincidence," Adelaide said. She was trying to break the uncomfortable silence—uncomfortable for the humans, in any case.

"It wasn't, was it?" Darren said. Clenching his jaw, he heaved himself into a sitting position. It wasn't as bad as he'd expected. He was dizzy for a second, but it passed.

"No. How did you guess?" she asked.

"I don't know. Too unlikely. I think they just detected Crusher's public web searches. Not the Fungus Birds—the NSA. Hell, what do I know? Maybe it was the evil avian bastards themselves."

Adelaide glanced at him in the mirror. She seemed impressed. "You were right the first time. At least, that's what Crusher said— or, wrote."

"Well, that's bad news."

"Crusher wrote that now we'll have to go dark—internet-wise. He says we'll need to go in stealth mode now."

"I thought we already were. You two have been sharing a regular old gab session. Where was I?"

She glanced again in the mirror. Her brow was scrunched. "Out."

"What do you mean, 'out'?"

"Out. Unconscious. I thought you were … gone."

"How long was I 'gone'?"

She shrugged. "Maybe five minutes."

"Five minutes? We just passed the fire trucks."

She shrugged again. "It's a big fire. Those are the second batch."

"We passed fire trucks, and I didn't even know?"

"You were *really* out."

"Hmm. I'm glad I came back."

She smiled. "So am I."

It was a smile he could have framed and hung above his bed. His neck tingled.

It wasn't from the Fungus taser.

Chapter 12

"Are you *ever* going to be satiated?" Darren asked "What are you *doing* with all that rhodium?"

It's complicated.

"If you say that one more time, I'm going to stick my fingers up your nose, find your real neck and then wring it, or whatever serves as your neck."

We have acquired less than four grams. That's not very much.

"Fine. Fine. How are we going to find it, now that you're self-exiled from the internet?"

We'll have to ask someone who lives here.

"'We?' I'd like to see you ask someone."

If you're reminding me that I need you, I would remind you that you equally need me.

"Oh, really? What if Adelaide and I just walk away and leave you here?"

Then Earth will belong to the Fungus Birds.

Darren stared at the tablet, then moved his gaze to the waves, ending their thousand-mile march by smashing against the rocks below. They were in a park above the cliffs of La Jolla, the upscale neighborhood ten miles north of downtown San Diego. Crusher lay flat on his back, eyes closed. His host body's blinking reflex had fizzled, and it was easier for the alien to just keep them closed when not in use. Adelaide had gone to buy sandwiches.

A wayward breeze washed Darren's nose with the acrid odor of bird droppings. This was an intractable problem, an enduring embarrassment for the affluent community. Seagulls nested so thickly upon the bluffs surrounding this little peninsula that the cliff faces were whitewashed with a solid coat of excremental paint. Darren watched three gulls soar up and over them, riding the unflagging westerly wind blowing in from the Pacific.

"The Fungus Bird that attacked us was different," he said.

The tablet displayed a lone question mark.

"It looked real—I didn't even know it *was* a Fungus Bird at first."

It was the same as the others. They are all part of the advance squad. They adapt to the local environment. Mimicking the process of natural convergent evolution, they tend towards a form similar to the indigenous fauna, which has been molded over millions of years to an optimal structure through natural selection.

"It doesn't hurt that they get to blend in with Earth birds. Except for their color. That Fungus Bird was the same color as the others—like pewter."

Fungus Birds never developed the ability to modify their color.

"Why? Seems just as useful as changing your form."

It's complicated, but it ultimately stems from the fact that they originated in an environment where color was not important.

Crusher's alien had proved himself—itself—adept at English. Darren wondered at its choice of words—that the Fungus Birds had "originated" from somewhere, not "evolved." At least he'd gotten something beyond the "It's complicated" brush-off. Maybe his threat to stick his fingers up his host's nose had hit home.

Adelaide called from across the grassy expanse, carrying two white paper bags. They hadn't eaten much before the cafe was torched, and Crusher nothing at all. She handed one bag to Darren, and nudged Crusher with her toe. "You have to eat," she said.

Darren glanced at the tablet. "He says he doesn't want to."

"It's not your body," she said. "You're just borrowing it. You have to take care of it." She looked at Darren. "What did he write?"

Darren looked at the tablet and sighed. "He says that Crusher's body won't be needed much longer. The Fungus invasion is twenty-four hours away."

Adelaide furrowed her brow and looked at Crusher. She might was well have been looking at a rock. "What's that supposed to mean?" she said. "I thought that the idea was to *stop* the invasion.

Is he giving up?"

Darren looked at the tablet. He decided not to repeat what he saw. Instead, he said, "No. Of course. We're going to try to stop it. But we can't be certain how it's going to turn out, and if we're successful—as we surely will be—there'll be plenty of time for recuperating then."

Her brow remained scrunched. "Is that what he wrote?"

Darren glanced at the tablet again. Now it read, *Why did you say that?* "Sure," he lied. "Hey, while you're up, could you get us some water?" he asked, handing her his empty coffee cup.

She walked off to the water fountain, and he waited until she was out of earshot. "You can't just tell her that you'll be done with Crusher's body," he whispered.

Why not?

"Why not? Because … because it's insensitive."

Adelaide has no previous relationship with your cousin. She has always known him as my non-sentient host. Surely she must know that the hosting was only temporary.

"She probably hasn't thought about that part at all. *I* haven't thought about it. I don't *want* to think about it. Let's just drop it for now—here she comes."

She handed Darren the cup, and toed Crusher again. "Up," she said. "You have to eat something."

Darren held his breath, but Crusher pushed himself upright, or at least tried to. His left arm remained immobile. "Here," Adelaide said, lifting his shoulders from behind, "let me help you."

She managed to heave him up, and Crusher sat in the grass, legs spread wide, arms dangling in his lap. Darren noticed that his left hand was larger than his right. In fact, his whole left arm looked like it belonged to somebody else—a big man, a really obese man.

"Open up," Adelaide said, holding a sandwich in front of his face. "You're not a baby."

Darren looked at the tablet. "He says that he can't chew."

"What do you mean?" she said, as though Crusher had actually spoken the words. "You have teeth, don't you?"

"He says that the human tongue has more muscular control than any other part of the body. People take it for granted. His inability to manipulate his tongue is the main reason he can't talk. If he tries to chew a sandwich, he'll likely choke."

"He ate before," she said.

"Cream of wheat. Maybe if you break off tiny pieces of the sandwich—wait, he says it isn't worth risking killing Crusher."

Adelaide glared at the difficult patient. "Well then, we'll get him a milkshake, or maybe one of those protein shakes."

"Sure," Darren said. "Sounds good." He was patronizing her.

"What in the world ... ?" she started, staring at Crusher's bloated hand.

"I noticed that. Weird, huh?"

"You noticed it? Why didn't you *say* something," she said, taking the swollen hand in hers and examining it.

Because it won't matter after tomorrow, he thought.

She unbuttoned his sleeve, and rolled it up. It was like pulling the casing off a fat sausage. "My God!" she said. "Will you look at this? What in the world *happened?*"

Darren looked at the tablet. "Ah. He says that the Fungus Bird nicked his wrist. It wasn't enough toxin to kill him, but it's causing some localized inflammation. It's exasperating the infection."

"What infection?"

"Uh, he says from the knife wound."

Determined now, she took the edge of his sleeve in her teeth and ripped the cloth, then unwound the makeshift bandage, revealing the rest of the beleaguered arm. It looked like a crime photo after a bludgeoning. The fat blue wrist and elbow morphed into an angry red swelling around the puncture. "Oh, Lord," she said pointing to purple streaks emanating from the wound, like a giant blood-shot eye. "That's a serious sign—a dangerous bacterial infection is spreading fast."

"Huh," Darren said, staring at the frightful sight. "How long do you think he has to—you know—live?"

Twenty-four hours was all they needed.

She threw him an angry glance. "You make it sound like it's inevitable. We have to get him to a hospital."

"Come on. You know that's not possible."

She fumed. Her face contorted. She was trying not to cry. "We can't just let him die. We can at least get antibiotics."

"You're in America now. You can't get antibiotics without a

prescription. Maybe we could rob a pharmacy."

She looked at him with renewed hope.

"I was kidding," he said.

Crusher honked, and Darren looked at the tablet, then picked it up as though studying it so that Adelaide wouldn't see.

At this point, even with intravenous delivery of antibiotics, it's not certain that Crusher's body would ultimately survive. Without it, he will certainly die from septic shock, but the question, of course, is whether this will occur before the scheduled invasion. Considering the irreparable damage done by the Fungus Bird toxin, it seems the only recourse is amputation.

"No way!" Darren blurted.

Adelaide was studying Crusher's arm, gently touching the swelling, and she looked up. "What does he say?"

Darren looked from the tablet to her. "Uh, you're not going to like it. He says we need to amputate the arm."

Her eyes ballooned. "So we *do* have to go to the hospital!"

He glanced at the tablet, but it had gone blank. "No," he said, shaking his head. "The hospital means we don't stop the invasion."

She sputtered and waved her hand up and down, struggling to keep from crying. "We're going to believe …" she gestured towards Crusher's head, "… that?"

"Well, the wound does look like it's infected, and I've read that those purple streaks mean—"

"No! I mean, are we going to believe … that thing," she said, gesturing again, "about some Fungus invasion."

"It's not really Fungus. That's just a name we came up with—"

"I *know!* This whole invasion could be some fabrication, but that infection is unquestionably *real!* We can't let him die on some supposition."

Darren nodded. In any case, they couldn't let him die in the next twenty-four hours. "We'll do it ourselves."

Her eyes expanded even wider, and he thought she was going to slap him. "Our-*selves?*" she squeaked. "Are you crazy?"

"How hard can it be? It's not like we're trying to fix anything."

She glared at him, and he waited for the slap. "*Verdammte Scheisse!*" she growled, jumping up and storming off. She stopped, put her fists to the side of her head, turned, stormed back, and said, "Fine! But *I'm* going to do it!"

ж ж ж

Darren knocked, then opened the weathered door and walked in. Once again they'd taken up camp in a cheesy motel, this time in Pacific Beach, south of La Jolla. He could hear the waves through the open window.

"What have you got?" Adelaide said.

He dumped the contents of the plastic bag on the bed. He'd bought a pocket knife, a small hobby knife, a needle and thread kit, four bottles of rubbing alcohol, a small wood clamp, a large bag of bandages, and … a hack saw.

"What about the suture clamp?" Adelaide asked. She picked up the spring-loaded wood clamp. "You expect to use *this*?"

"No. I expect *you* to use it."

She pursed her lips and fiddled with the goods. She looked at him. "You're going to do exactly what I tell you. Is that understood? Once we begin, time is everything."

He nodded. Her half-sister—a half far removed from Darren's line—was an EMT in Germany, and had explained over the motel phone how an amputation was done. Darren had asked how an EMT would know about amputations, and her response had been that perhaps German EMTs took their professions seriously.

"He's … ?" Darren said, tilting his thumb at the bathroom.

"I've taken his clothes off, and scrubbed his upper body."

"Why take off his clothes?"

She looked at him under her brow. "There's going to be a lot of blood."

"Ah, right. He only has one set of clothes, although at this point, they probably should be burned. So … shall we do it?"

She nodded, disgusted.

Crusher lay in the bathtub, staring at the wall, his overstuffed arm resting on the side of the tub. Adelaide set Darren to wiping all the tools with copious amounts of alcohol—this after wiping every accessible surface, including his hands and arms. She came in and handed him the plastic tray, the companion to the motel ice bucket. "Wipe it down," she said. Darren looked at it. He got it. They would position this under Crusher's arm to keep the blood flowing into the tub. Adelaide came in and squatted next to him. It was a tight fit next to the toilet, which she used as her tool tray. She had taken off her blouse. Her bra was black, with frills along the bottom. He tried not to stare.

"You're sure he's not going to feel anything?" she asked, balancing the pocket knife in her hand.

"You know how people say, 'This is going to hurt me more than you'? Well, in this case it's true."

She grabbed Crusher's elbow, swollen to the point that her hand didn't even span half the circumference. Her other hand poised a moment with the knife, and then she hacked away as though she was butchering a lamb.

Darren's job was to hold one end of the plastic tray up so that the blood flowed into the tub. With his other hand, he handed her tools as she called for them. He was Hot Lips to her Hawkeye, except that Hot Lips never retched. Adelaide's face was set in complete concentration. Darren guessed that he could have started amputating her arm, and she wouldn't have noticed.

She first made an incision through his skin in a circle all around his arm, and then peeled it back, using the knife to free the skin from underlying muscle and fascia. When she was done, it looked like she'd rolled up his shirt sleeve—a pink and bloody shirt sleeve. Then, muttering and cursing in German, she probed the underside of the exposed muscle with her finger, occasionally cutting away tissue in her way.

"Looking for the artery?" Darren asked.

"Yes," she said. "Here! No, that's not it."

"It looks like an artery," he said, suppressing a gag.

"No. It's blue. That's a vein—here it is!" she exclaimed, then proceeded to pull out a red flexible tube as though it was a rubber band that she was going to snap back into place as a joke. "The clamp," she said, and used it to pinch off the flow. She thought a moment, and then moved the clamp as far up his arm as it would go. "We must move quickly, now" she said. "Have the needle ready."

Darren carefully picked up the pre-threaded needle as she sawed away at the artery with the hobby knife. It was as tough as Teflon. She finally folded the artery in half, slipped the knife inside, and pulled with all her might until the artery snapped in two with a slapping sound. Cursing her blood-slippery fingers, she folded the loose end of the cut artery over, and began sewing it together, pulling the thread though again and again, wrapping the thread tightly around a few times, than back to pull after pull. Just when Darren thought she was finally done, she folded it again and started over. Finally, she undid the clamp and observed the sewed end as it distended with the pressure of pumped blood. Satisfied, she held out her blood-encased hand and said, "Saw."

Darren knew that an amputation was going to be disturbing, but he hadn't expected that he would faint, and he would have if he'd allowed himself. The smell of blood reminded him of raw hamburger, and the sound of the hacksaw on bone was something beyond acceptable realities of nature. Each rasp as she bent her elbow and pushed was like a blade forcing into Darren's own skull. When Crusher's arm finally fell away, dangling by strands of muscle and fascia that Adelaide set to with the knife, Darren fell back on his butt with a gasp. "Not yet," Adelaide barked. "We must finish."

She pulled the rolled up skin back into place, and he handed her a new threaded needle. As she sewed the flapping skin of the new stump end together, Darren couldn't shake the thought that it looked like the end of a sausage, a type of food which he was sure he would never again eat.

Adelaide finally sat back, leaning against Darren's shins. She was bloody up to her elbows. She sat quietly a moment, then heaved herself up, motioned for Darren to move out of the way, and puked into the sink. She paused, gasped a deep breath, and puked some more. "I *never* want to *ever* do that again," she said, gagging on remnant vomit that she continued to spit out.

She turned on the faucet and washed her hands, her arms, her mouth, and then her whole face. "Bring the plastic bag," she said leaning into the sink.

Darren retrieved the bag he'd carried the purchases in. Still leaning into the sink, she pointed at the tub where Crusher lay staring at the same spot on the wall. "Get rid of it," she said.

"What?" he asked, but he knew.

She looked sideways at him, and her eyes burned with weary anger.

"Right," he said. "I got it."

The severed arm lay there, nestled up against Crusher's butt.

Darren wasn't sure he could actually do this. He tried to pick it up by the elbow, but the distended swelling made it difficult to get a grip, and the thick coating of blood rendered it too slippery to hold. He considered picking it up by the dangling muscle tissue and tendons, but he felt the bile rising at just the thought. In the end, he grabbed Crusher's detached limb by its hand. Hand clasping hand, he lifted the body part and jostled it into the flimsy, uncooperative plastic bag.

Adelaide was still camped in the sink, and Darren thought to-hell-with-it, and wiped his bloody hand on one of the motel towels.

"What should I do with it?" he asked, holding the bag up and observing how the contours of the arm and hand were clearly visible.

"Flush it down the toilet," she said, resting her forehead against the faucet.

Darren looked at the bag, heavy with bloated flesh and bone, and then at the toilet. "I, uh, don't think it will fit down—"

"I wasn't serious," she said. "Do you think I'm an idiot?"

He figured it was a rhetorical question and squeezed around behind her, but she reached out and caught his arm. "I'm sorry," she said. "I'm not at my best right now."

Darren smiled. "You just did something that not one person in a thousand could even consider. You've earned a month's worth of grumpiness." He thought about that. "How about a week's worth?"

"I'll keep it to just a week," she said. She smiled. "Thanks, Darren. Thank you."

As he carried the bag at arm's length through the motel room, he decided that she was one cool gal. No, she was one cool super-gal.

He opened the room door and considered. What does one do with a severed human arm? The police would say to bring it to them, but they're all obsessed with proper protocol. He eyed the waves reaching hopefully up the sand, only to fall back, again. Things thrown in the ocean always ended up on a beach somewhere for kids to find. He finally just carried it to the dumpster and gave it a heave. By the time anybody found it, if they even did, the Earth would either be well on the way to belonging to alien Fungus Birds, or they'd be heroes. Or maybe in the custody of the CIA, who could care less about severed arms. Or they might be dead. In any case, the point was that they could forget about Crusher's severed arm.

When Darren returned to the room, he heard Adelaide's imperious voice in the bathroom. She was dressing Crusher, and lecturing him. "If there's actually no alien Fungus invasion tomorrow," she said, "I'm going to rip your other arm off."

"Yah!" Crusher honked.

The stump was still oozing some blood, and she wrapped bandages around it before pulling on his shirt and pinning the empty sleeve up. "If there is an invasion, and you don't save the Earth, then I'm going to rip off your head."

"Yah!" Crusher agreed.

Darren decided that she was one cool super-gal that you wanted to avoid pissing off.

Chapter 13

"It should be somewhere along here—ah, there it is," Darren said, pulling over. The motel manager had been helpful—he told them about a shop right there in Pacific Beach that bought and sold precious metals. Darren felt bad about the towels. He and Adelaide had cleaned up the bathroom, but had to use the motel towels to do it. They couldn't very well leave a bunch of bloody towels behind, so they'd ditched them in the dumpster as well. He'd left a twenty dollar tip for the cleaning help, sort of a bribe to keep their theft from the manager.

Adelaide glanced at him and chuckled.

"What's so funny?" he asked.

"Your face. I can't get used to it."

"Well, you're not exactly miss pearly-white yourself, sister."

The ultraviolet burst from the destroyed Fungus Bird had given them sunburns. Darren's face and hands were tender. They'd probably peel in a few days.

Assuming they would be in a position to even notice.

They helped Crusher out of the back seat. He was even more clumsy now that he had one less limb to flail around. Darren winced every time Crusher bumped the freshly exposed stump, but whatever storm of pain information surged into his brain, apparently ended up in the sensory trash bin.

Inside the small, cluttered shop, they found a teenage girl behind the counter. Her T-shirt read, *Your ad could be here.* She looked at them and smirked.

"Is something funny?" Adelaide asked. She was cashing in her week's supply of grumpiness.

The girl suppressed her grin and shook her head. "Canadians, right?"

Darren glanced at Adelaide. "Why do you say that?"

She shrugged. "Canadians don't understand how strong the sun is down here."

They needed her relaxed and chatty. "You nailed us," Darren said. "One day on the beach, and we look like lobsters—we eat lobster up there in the cold country, you know."

She shrugged again. She wasn't starved for conversation with random tourists, particularly when they were so much older than her—five years at least.

"Hey, I like your ring," Darren said. "It sets off the tattoo on the side of your nose—ah, I see that the ring is supposed to be the tail of the seahorse. Very clever."

He figured it was buttering up time.

She shrugged, her universal response, but turned her head so he could see it better. "What are you shopping for?" she asked.

"Oh, mostly just looking around. We might buy some gold coins if you have any."

Crusher had warned that their pursuers would be on the lookout for anybody buying rare metals. They had to proceed with caution.

"You know that you're in a shop called *As Good As Gold*, right?" she said, reverting back to snarky mode.

Darren smothered the knee-jerk retort. "Well, I bet that's no coincidence, eh?" he pandered instead, mimicking a stereotypical Canadian. He held out his hand, "Darren," he said. "Really nice to meet you."

She shook his hand, exaggerating the gesture with wide pumps as she grinned at his bumpkiness. "Zoey," she said, imitating his enthusiasm.

Time to dig for gold. "I understand there's some excitement going on east of here," he said.

Zoey lifted one shoulder. "Dunno. If you're talking about Sea World, that's south."

"No. Out in the desert, there—what's it called? Anzo's Burrito?"

She laughed. "You mean Anza Borrego. Yeah, my boyfriend's in the Army—Camp Pendleton, up the coast. They have him driving a truck out there where they're doing a lot of construction. He says it's really bizarre—this completely screws up his training schedule. He thinks it must be super important, because they told him that he's not allowed to tell anyone, or he'll be court marshaled."

Darren looked at her. She apparently didn't realize the contradiction she'd just performed. "Whereabouts out there?" he asked. "In the desert?"

A shrug. "I don't know. Somewhere off of Route 78." Her transgression must have finally dawned on her. "You can't go out there. You're not supposed to know about it."

Darren let it go. They still had the rhodium to address. "Oh, don't worry about us. We came down from Canada for the beach, not the desert. Hey, as long as we're here, I remembered that my nephew has a science project, and he's looking for a variety of metals."

"I don't know," she said skeptically. "It's mostly investors that buy our stuff—it's all pretty expensive."

"Like what?"

A shrug. "Palladium, iridium, even platinum." She stopped and eyed him. "We don't keep the stuff here in the shop. You order it, and pick it up later." Gesturing up towards the corner, she said, "We have a video camera, you know."

He forced a pretend laugh. "Oh, you don't have to worry about us. We're Canadians, eh? I sure would like to see some of those precious metals, though—you know, something to tell the folks back home about."

A sigh and a shrug. She reached under the counter and pulled out a large, flat wooden box, which she lay on the counter in front of him. "There you go," she said. The glass cover provided a view into a matrix of little cubby holes, each marked with the name of the metal within. The sample box looked like it might be as old as the shop. Some of the locations were empty.

"Well, wadda-ya know?" Darren said, tracing his finger along the top of the glass. "Hey, I see some of the spots are missing samples."

One hole in particular was empty, marked with *Rh*.

She chuckled. "Those are the sucker slots."

"Sucker slots? You'd have to be a sucker to want those?"

"No. The sucker already bought them. A guy came in a couple of days ago and bought out the whole stock of those—including the display samples in the box."

Darren glanced at Adelaide. Her raised eyebrow indicated that she was wondering the same thing. "A real serious collector, eh?" He glanced again at Adelaide. "I imagine a dapper little guy with thick glasses, eh?"

She took the bait. "Oh, no. This guy could have been a linebacker. A real looker."

"Handsome, eh?" he said, drawing her out.

"Oh, yeah. And he knew it, too. Arrogant."

Darren considered his next gambit. "Probably Italian, eh?"

She shook her head. "Wrong end of Europe."

"How so?"

"He's Irish. Or, maybe Scottish. I never get the names straight. Which one is 'Mac,' and which one is 'Mc'?"

"Um, 'Mc,' is usually Irish."

"I guess he'd be Irish, then."

"Oh, yeah? His name, uh, started with that?"

"Yep. McKinney."

Silence.

"Hello?" she said, waving her hand in front of him.

"Oh, sorry," Darren said. "Must be jet lag."

"From Canada?"

"Yeah. We live in the, you know, the far eastern part."

"French Canadians?" she said. "Who speak French?"

"Right. We, uh, emigrated there. From Toronto. So, this guy was a real precious metal aficionado, eh?"

She snorted. "Aficionado, my ass—excuse my French," she said, smiling at her own joke. "This guy had no clue about market prices. Gary—the owner of the shop—started at fifty percent over market—he always does—and the guy just fell for it. Paid in cash. He was insistent that he buy all that Gary had."

Darren sighed. Crusher was going to be impossible to live with. "Well, your boss made quite a haul."

She was smiling impishly, tapping her fingernails on the glass counter.

"He *didn't* make a haul?" Darren said.

"Not as much as he could have. Gary's maybe a little too wily for his own good."

"How so?"

Her mischievous smile broadened, and she reached under the counter. She pulled out three bottles of metal powder, perhaps an ounce each, and laid them on the glass.

"What's this?" Darren asked.

"Gary figured that maybe—just maybe—this guy knew something. Maybe rare metals were about to spike. So he held back some of his stock."

Darren nodded. "I guess you don't get into this business if you're not a gambler at heart," he said.

He could see that one of the bottles was marked "Rh."

"Tah!" Crusher honked.

Darren figured he knew what Crusher wanted, so he ignored him. "Gary's probably figured out by now that this guy—McKinney was his name?—was just a nut, and that metals aren't about to spike. Tell you what, I'd like to—"

"Tah!" Crusher honked. "Tah! Tah!"

"Jesus!" Darren said, turning to the alien zombie. "Will you stuff it, already?"

"Hey!" Zoey said. "Easy on the guy." She looked from Crusher to Darren. "He has feelings, you know."

"He's an idiot. Just ignore him."

Adelaide rolled her eyes.

"He's doing the best he can," Zoey said, waving her hand a little at him, but then putting it down, embarrassed, when he continued to stare at nothing. "Hey!" she said, suddenly concerned, "his arm it's ..."

"I know," Darren said, peeling off five twenties from his roll of money and laying them on the counter. "He lost it when it became infected."

"That's, like, totally obvious," Zoey said. "No, I mean, his ... uh, stump ..."

"What about it?" Darren asked.

Zoey looked at him like he was the idiot. "Can't you see? It's …
leaking."

Indeed. The sleeve, where it was folded back, was wet. With
something dark. "Oh, that. It's nothing."

"Nothing?" she said leaning over to get a better look. "I think
it's … blood!"

"Forget it! Look, I'd like to buy this bottle of Rhodium. How's
a hundred dollars sound?"

"I'm supposed to report anybody asking about rhodium, you
know," she said distractedly, staring at Crusher's bleeding stump.

"Fine. Can you report it after you sell me this bottle? Oh shit!"

One of the alien's tentacles was easing out Crusher's forehead.

"Tah!" he honked. "Tah! Tah! Tah!"

"What's he all excited about?" Zoey said, and then froze as she
too saw the alien's seductive dance. She threw Darren a wide-eyed
glance and then locked again on the tentacle. "How's he *do* that?"
she asked, intrigued.

Something bumped his elbow. Adelaide was handing him the
tablet.

*The video feed is likely being monitored. It has now been eight minutes since
we came into view.*

"Oh, crap. Look, here's a hundred dollars. Will you please sell
us the rhodium—?"

Bang!

Their heads snapped towards the front of the shop, where the
cracks in the door glass formed a radiating spider-web. A silver bird
was pulling back for another run. "Here we go again," Adelaide said
as she picked up a ruler off the counter.

"Hey," Zoey said, "according to McKinney, silver birds mean
that thieves are probably nearby."

This time the Fungus Bird broke through amid a shower of
flying glass. When the glittering rain settled, the Fungus alien was
gone.

"Now, that was freakin' bizarre," Zoey said.

The sound of thrashing came from the front, and then the
wounded bird scrabbled into view across the floor, scuttling around
on its two feet and one good wing. The other wing was twisted in
half, obviously having gotten caught on some glass as the bird

broke through.

"Dah!" Crusher called.

"I know," Darren said. "I've got this one."

He picked up a ceramic vase as he went forward, an improvised barrel bomb.

Ten feet from the stricken alien, he stopped. The creature had ceased its struggle and was watching him. Something in those cold, alien eyes gripped Darren. Maybe it was the knowledge of what lay behind them—pitiless disregard for human life coupled with multiple lethal weapons. Or maybe it was something more, an indefinable awe at confronting an intelligence whose journey had begun uncountable trillions of miles distant.

Darren's pause spelled his lost chance. As the bird held his mesmerized gaze, the twisted wing had slowly straightened. By the time Crusher's frantic honking broke Darren free of the hypnotic spell, the Fungus Bird's wings whipped into action, flinging bits of sparkling glass slivers, and it rose into the air.

Darren fell back. He threw the vase, but his aim was wide and it smashed into a metal chair. Adelaide had pulled Crusher away, and Darren joined them where they had retreated into a corner formed by the far wall and another counter piled high with boxes. Adelaide handed him the ruler, the only club available.

The Fungus Bird's flight was unsteady. The repair to its wing wasn't yet complete. It hovered before them, waiting to recover full agility before coming in for the kills.

Something bumped Darren from behind. "Hey!" he said. Adelaide was tugging at Crusher, maneuvering him behind the two of them. "If anybody should be out front, it's him!" Darren said.

"He can't defend himself," she replied.

"Can't you get it through your skull? There *is* no Crusher. Just an alien going for a ride."

She gave him a hateful stare as she finished repositioning the zombie. With her chin, she gestured for him to do his duty with the ruler.

Suddenly, behind the bird, Zoey appeared, wielding a metal pipe. The Fungus alien saw her, and spun around. "Arrogance is totally unattractive," she said.

Darren raised the ruler, but it felt like waving a flower at a tiger.

"Oh, hell," he muttered, tossing away the stick. He clasped his hands together and stepped forward. The bird saw him, and turned back, but not it time. Darren swung, and connected solidly. It felt like punching a softball—light, but solid. The bird was thrashing around at the bottom of the counter, and Darren stomped on it. The next instant, he was on the floor himself, his entire right leg numb. The alien had zapped him.

As he lay there, feeling the tingling of a million pricking needles turn into the pain of a million stabbing needles, he was aware of Adelaide grunting and working at something. She was stomping, finishing the job.

"What the heck *is* that thing?" Zoey said, watching Adelaide pulverize it.

"The bad guys," Darren said from the floor. This zap wasn't as bad as the last one, maybe not as effective coming through his shoe. "Don't touch it. There's incredibly lethal poison mixed in there."

"Don't worry," Zoey said, "you couldn't pay me—hey, it's steaming."

"Gah!" Crusher honked.

"Yeah," Darren agreed. "We need to get out of here."

Adelaide's face was tight with determination. She grabbed one of Darren's wrists, roughly in her haste. "Take the other one," she said to Zoey, and they started dragging him out.

"Ow!" Darren yelped when his hip collided with a wooden crate.

"Maybe we should go slower," Zoey said.

"No," Adelaide replied. "Ignore him."

She's really worried about getting caught inside, Darren thought.

"Hang on," Adelaide said. She dropped Darren and ran back. He tilted his head and saw her grab the bottle of rhodium and start back. She stopped, turned back, and snatched his money and the other two bottles off the counter. When she gripped his wrist and yanked him forward again, Darren cried out. "Shut up," she said.

Outside on the sidewalk, Zoey stopped, but Adelaide kept dragging him. "I think I can walk," he said.

"Shut up," Adelaide said.

It felt like she was trying to rip off his arm.

Zoey sprang forward and picked up his other arm. "Where are

we going?" she asked.

"Farther away," Adelaide relied.

"Why?"

"This isn't the first time we've been through this—"

Just then, Darren saw the flash of blinding blue light reflected on the buildings across the street, followed by a *whump!* and the crash of glass exploding outwards. An instant later another soft thump announced that all the flammable surfaces in the shop had simultaneously erupting in fire.

Adelaide dropped Darren's wrist, and Crusher wobbled up next to them.

"That's the third one," Adelaide said.

Zoey watched the growing flames as Darren rolled over, got up on his hands and knees, and then used Crusher as a ladder to pull himself to his feet. He let go and stood, swaying, but in control.

"Third what?" Zoey asked.

"The third shop that we've destroyed," Adelaide said.

"It wasn't us," Darren said. "It's the Fungus Birds."

Adelaide threw him a cold look, and turned back to the growing flames.

"What's a Fungus Bird?" Zoey asked. "Sounds like a mutant monster cockroach."

"Close," Darren said.

"Here," Adelaide said, handing Zoey the money and two of the jars she'd grabbed from the counter. "It's trivial compensation, I know."

Crusher held the jar of rhodium against his forehead, cupped in his remaining hand.

"I wouldn't bust my head over it," Zoey said. "Gary's got insurance, and the metal's all stored in a fire-proof safe. He'll just wade through the ashes after it's cool, grab the safe, and start over."

"I thought you said you don't keep the rare metals there at the shop?" Darren said.

"Yeah, I did, didn't I? Would *you* advertise that you had a million dollars worth of goods in a safe?"

"You are now."

She gestured towards the burning shop. "Help yourself." She shrugged. "Besides, Canadians wouldn't do anything wrong." As she said this, she cocked a knowing eye at him.

They had gotten their rhodium, and destroyed her job in the process. "We're not Canadian," he said.

"I know."

"How'd you know?"

"For one thing, I don't think Canadians have worms crawling out of their heads. Between exploding poison birds, and one-armed idiot savants that eat metal," she said, gesturing toward the empty bottle that Crusher was holding, "I'd say you're about as Canadian as I am a—" She thought a moment. "As I am a space alien."

She wrinkled her brow at this, and shot Darren a piercing look.

What the hell. "He's the space alien," he said, tilting his thumb at Crusher. "At least, the thing inside his head is."

Darren expected the alien to protest, but he honked, "Yah!"

Zoey took a step back, watching Crusher. "There's something … inside his *head*?"

"Don't worry. Crusher—the guy you see—is just a human shell." Adelaide snorted and turned away. "His brain was toast before the alien crawled inside," Darren said.

Adelaide mumbled a curse.

Zoey was beginning to take the whole thing seriously. "That worm I saw—"

"A tentacle. Sort of."

"The tentacle—that's the … alien? Like, a space alien?"

"A good space alien. He can travel interstellar space. His ship got chewed up by the jet airliner that made the emergency landing last week. The Fungus Birds, those are the bad aliens."

Zoey took another step backwards, never taking her eyes off of Crusher. "A good space alien, huh? One that turns a human into a walking zombie?"

She got it. Darren was impressed. "Trust me, Crusher didn't need his brain anymore," he said.

Adelaide snorted again, louder, and shook her head.

"Sounds more like a space parasite," Zoey said.

"Nah!" Crusher honked.

Zoey held her hands in front of her. "A superior alien race that can navigate between the stars, but needs a human body to live?"

Crusher honked again and flopped around clumsily, staggering and nearly falling. Darren grabbed his shoulder to steady him.

"What's he doing?" Zoey asked, taking another step backwards.

Darren had a good guess. "He's demonstrating that if he were a career parasite, he'd have a lot better control of Crusher's body. He doesn't need a human body to live, just to get around in public without causing panic."

"Tah!" Crusher called.

Darren glanced at the tablet. "He says this became necessary when his incompetent companions destroyed their ship."

"He talks through that?" she said, pointing at the tablet.

"Well, he writes. He's something of a radio wizard." The message on the tablet changed. "Excuse me—'radio' is simplistic. He says that his natural mode of communication is a wide range of electromagnetic energy—another reason for using Crusher's body." He held his hand to his mouth, pretending to keep Crusher from hearing. "To tell you the truth, I think that was sort of a failed experiment. A two-year-old talks better."

Zoey seemed to be relaxing. She took a step forward, studying the hole in Crusher's forehead, as though waiting for a tentacle to reach out and wave. "Why are the fungal birds after you?" she asked.

"Fun-*gus* birds. They're about to invade and destroy humans, and we're trying to stop them. They've fooled the government into thinking we're the bad guys."

Zoey cocked an eyebrow. "Birds are going to destroy all humans?"

"They're really vicious birds. They can poison and electrocute you, maybe at the same time."

"Still."

"There's, like, a million about to come through hyperspace."

She turned her gaze on him. "That's why you were asking about the Anza Borrego Desert. That's where they're arriving?"

"Yeah. But our brainy leaders think that it's just a handful of bird ambassadors."

She nodded in understanding. "My boyfriend said that they're building like crazy out there. He thought it might be for some kind of military parade or something. There's temporary housing, and a big stage, like you might have for reviewing the troops."

"That would be to welcome the 'ambassadors.' Boy, are they going to be surprised."

"How are you going to stop them?"

Darren glanced at Adelaide, but she was avoiding him. "We haven't quite figured that out yet."

"When are they arriving?"

"Uh, tomorrow."

Her eyes sprang wide. "There's a million vicious birds arriving tomorrow, and you haven't figured out yet how to stop them?"

"Yeah, that about sums it up."

"We're fucked, aren't we?"

"We have him," Darren said, nodding his head towards Crusher.

"Him?" she said, nearly sputtering.

"He's really smart."

She was staring at him.

"The alien inside, I mean," he added.

She shook her head in amazement, and then shrugged. "I'll come with you."

"No."

"Why not? It's not like I have a job to go to."

"It's too dangerous. Two people have been killed already because they got in the way of Fungus Birds."

"Tah!" Crusher honked.

"What's it say?" Zoey asked, gesturing at the tablet.

"Nothing," Darren said after looking at it. "Just that you shouldn't come."

"Nah! Nah!"

"I don't think he agrees," she said.

He'd lied. Crusher did indeed want her to come. "He's not the boss," Darren said. "I'm the boss here." At this, Adelaide snorted. "And I say it's too dangerous for a kid."

"I'm eighteen."

"Like I said—a kid."

Zoey's eyebrows shot up again.

"Dammit, Crusher!" Darren yelled. "Cut it out!"

He'd extended two tentacles, and they flowed around each other in an intricate, sinuous dance. People had begun congregating from the growing fire, and they began to form a semi-circle around the alien zombie, pointing and jabbering. One woman screamed.

"Jesus, Crusher!" Darren cried. "Okay, I get it. Will you cut it out?"

"What's he doing?" Zoey asked.

"He's trying to show me that he's not under my thumb." To Crusher he said, "But you can't even drive a car. You *need* me, buddy."

Something whacked his elbow. It was Adelaide. She was pointing down the street.

"Oh, for the love of—let's go!" Darren said, grabbing Crusher by the arm and pulling him along towards their car.

It was McKinney, half a block away. He'd been aiming his pistol, but must have decided that there were too many people around. He let it fall to his side, and pounded down the street towards them.

The shop was completely consumed by now, and sirens wailed a few blocks away. Their car was fifty feet from the shop and the fierce wall of flame hissed as it whooshed cinders into the air, shooting heavenward. The heat was like a physical barrier, a searing hand pressing them back. Darren found some relief by squatting behind the car. The others followed suit, except for Crusher, who stood staring at the sidewalk as his collar began to char, and individual hairs on his forehead curled away in little wisps of smoke. Darren gave the back of his knees a karate chop, and the human taxis crumbled to the pavement.

Darren reached up and opened the driver's door. Trapped heat poured out like a living liquid. Adelaide opened the back door, and helped Crusher crawl inside. The fire was making popping sounds, like a row of champagne bottles uncorking. She then crawled through the open driver's door and on to the passenger seat. With a last glance back at McKinney who stood holding his hand up against the unrelenting heat, Darren crawled inside and turned the key, but there was no sound of the engine starting.

"Shit!" he called. "The heat must have melted something!"

"Go!" Adelaide yelled. "What are you waiting for?"

"The car! It won't start!"

"It's running! Go, you idiot!"

He stepped on the gas, and the car pulled ahead. He hadn't noticed above the roar of the fire that it had started. He turned out into the street and right into the path of an arriving fire truck. With its horn blaring loud enough to set his ears ringing, it swerved to miss him, and crashed into parked cars on the other side. Darren gunned the engine and climbed the sidewalk to get around the stranded truck, sending people scattering.

After four blocks, he slowed down and looked into the rearview mirror. There was nobody following.

There was something else amiss, though—two heads. He looked again. "What the hell are you doing?" he said into the mirror.

"I told you I was going along," Zoey said.

Adelaide turned to look and gasped. "Oh no!" she said.

Darren risked taking his eyes off the road long enough to glance back at what she saw.

A stream of blood was running down Crusher's shirt from a hole in his shoulder.

The popping sound wasn't the fire, it was McKinney shooting at them.

Chapter 14

"Shut up!" Adelaide said. "Just … shut up. You're heartless."

Darren sighed. "I tried," he said to Crusher who sat slouched in the back seat as Adelaide dabbed at his wound with alcohol, while Zoey held his shirt open. Darren looked at the tablet and held it up for them to see, but only Zoey looked. "See?" he said. "Crusher says to let it go. Just plug the bleeding."

Adelaide's mouth was tight with anger. It had been like that ever since he wanted to put Crusher out front when the Fungus Bird attacked. "'Crusher' said nothing of the sort," she said grimly. "He can't talk anymore. That hitchhiking alien is *not* Crusher, and neither you nor *it* have any right to presume what medical attention can be dispensed with."

Darren held up his hands in resignation and tossed the tablet on the front seat. "If McKinney finds us, nobody will be getting medical attention—we'll all be dead."

They had gone less than a mile before pulling off to take care of Crusher. Darren scanned the skies for the dozenth time. It wasn't government agents in black cars he was worried about. There! Cruising between two buildings along the adjacent block—a perfectly normal bird—the color of platinum. He squatted down behind the car and watched, but it didn't appear beyond the next house. It had either turned away, or was sneaking around to surprise them.

That was the last straw. "You're just going to have to deal with it," he said, climbing into the driver's seat. "We're getting out of here."

Adelaide didn't say anything beyond her signature snort as she braced herself with one hand.

"You guys understand that the world as we know it is about to end," Zoey said.

Darren glanced in the mirror. "Yeah. I was the one who told you."

"Well, you don't act like it. You two act like an old couple on vacation. An old couple who have nothing left but resentment."

"Hey!" Darren said. "*She's* the one who's wasting time. *I'm* trying to save the world."

"A world that cares nothing about basic human decency is not a world worth saving," Adelaide said as she placed Zoey's hand on the folded bandages to keep them in place while she wrapped tape.

"I'm going hoarse," Darren said, "repeating that there's nothing human left of Crusher."

"You are playing God—"

"Yo!" Zoey yelled. "You guys are giving me a headache. Can we call a truce? Addy, you've performed your Florence Nightingale duties, and Mr. Bewitched, you're making your Al Capone escape. Can we just get on with saving the Earth?"

"Yah!" Crusher honked.

"I hate the nickname 'Addy,'" Adelaide said.

"And I still hate my parents for my name," Darren said.

"There!" Zoey said. "See? We can all agree on some things. Now, how do we go about saving humans from a million Fungus Birds?"

The car went silent.

"You haven't even thought about it, have you?" she asked.

After a moment, Crusher blurted, "Yah!"

"Is that ironic, or what?" she said. "The only one thinking about saving the human race isn't even human."

The car was silent again.

"I'm the one who brought us here," Darren said quietly.

"That's a start," Zoey said. "Now if we could only get Addy to twitch her nose and make the bad Fungus Birds disappear."

"The name is Adelaide."

"Fine. Since we're being picky about names, mine is pronounced 'zow-ee,' not zoo-ee."

Darren bit his tongue about the reference to the sixties TV sitcom. He would show them how adults behaved. "We actually do have a plan. Sort of."

"Okay, what is it?"

"Uh, the last time we talked, we decided to, uh …"

"What?"

"Um, set off a nuclear bomb—but just a small one."

"Ha! You're joking, right?"

Darren wished he was. He really wished he was.

"Tah!" Crusher called.

Darren picked up the tablet.

"What's he saying?" Zoey asked.

Darren's brow furrowed and he looked up at them. "He wants us to capture a Fungus Bird."

"Now *he's* joking?" Zoey said.

"Um, he doesn't joke," Darren said, looking again at the words on the screen, trying to decipher some other meaning. "I don't get it, squidy. What good does that do?"

We can perhaps convince it to mobilize its companions to send a halt signal through the hyperspace portal.

"We already talked about that. It's too late to convince the government, and even if we did, the Fungus Birds know there's no time to amass a defense."

That is true in the case of the United States government.

"I hate to break your bubble, space-boy, but that's the only government we've got."

Indeed.

"Oh, come on. You have no sense of humor, but now you want to play games?"

My apologies. I assumed that we'd taken on a cynical mode with the addition of Zoey.

Darren glanced at her, but she couldn't see the tablet screen.

We could convince the captured Fungus Bird that we have contacted the Russians, and they are prepared to launch ICBMs at San Diego if the invasion begins.

"You're insane," Darren said. And then he thought about it. "But maybe a good kind of insane."

What did the Fungus Birds know about the realities of world

politics? The insanity of Russia targeting San Diego with a nuclear strike might seem a plausible scenario to them. After all, they invade and conquer other worlds—brutal tactics might seem the norm for them.

"Just for the sake of argument," Darren said, "how would one go about capturing an intelligent, agile bird that has the power to electrocute you or knock you dead with a prick of its beak?"

It would require Zoey's participation. In fact, it would place her in grave danger.

Darren held up the tablet for her to see.

"What's the alternative?" she asked.

The Fungus Birds would colonize the Earth. You could possibly live for a few months afterwards if you avoided developed areas, where they would sweep humans away first.

"That's an alternative? It sounds more like a threat."

A threat implies that I have control over the post-invasion carnage.

"'Carnage,' huh? You wouldn't be trying to manipulate me with exaggerated terms, would you?"

I believe carnage is an accurate prediction. However, I would manipulate you if I could. Dishonorable means are justified by the stakes.

"You're at least honest."

The tablet remained blank.

"Okay," Zoey said, "I'll do it on one condition."

"What's that?" Darren asked.

"The alien has to reach out its tentacle and pull my finger."

Adelaide rolled her eyes and turned away.

"Are you kidding?" Darren asked.

"Not at all," Zoey said. "I need to make sure this isn't some kind of elaborate prank."

Darren shrugged. "It's not up to me."

He looked in the mirror. A slim, silvery worm had already emerged, and curled into a hook, waiting for a human finger to engage. Zoey reached out, her forefinger curled and ready to mate.

Kids today are fearless, Darren thought. Maybe he had been at her age. If so, he was lucky to have survived.

Ж Ж Ж

Darren was sweating. It could have been the long-sleeve sweatshirt with the hood pulled over his head, and the scarf wrapped around his neck. It was, after all, a balmy seventy-six degrees, and the other patrons lounging around the outdoor Starbucks tables wore shorts and T-shirts. Also, they weren't wearing gloves. Customers peeked glances at his bizarre attire, but nobody engaged, probably fearing he was homeless and mentally unstable. Crusher had assured him that Fungus Birds couldn't distinguish odd human behavior from normal.

Half the sweat was obviously the outlandish getup, but the other half was raw fear. Crusher had mostly convinced Darren that all he had to do was protect his face with his metal mesh gloves, which could stop a razor sharp knife. The question was whether they were effective against a stabbing poison-tipped beak. If they weren't, he'd have about ten seconds to contemplate the fact.

Zoey sat at the next table, seemingly engrossed in a newspaper. With luck, the Fungus Birds wouldn't recognize her from the shop surveillance cameras. She was playing her part consummately. She hadn't even glanced at him since she sat down fifteen minutes ago. In fact, she was doing so well not noticing him, Darren began to wonder if she'd forgotten the plan. Sweat trickled down his temples.

What was taking so long? Crusher and Adelaide were inside, tucked away in a dark corner. The alien zombie would be hacking and probing the locked-down government secret stashes, killing two birds—or at least a single Fungus variety—with one cafe WiFi stone. Besides the obvious goal of baiting the nearest Fungus Bird, Crusher might be able to uncover more details about the "embassy" preparation.

Darren almost missed the Fungus Bird among the ubiquitous little chickadees flitting around, pecking at crumbs. Seemingly out of thin air, it suddenly appeared, hovering near the entrance door, maybe waiting for someone to come in or out. Somehow Darren had expected that it would recognize him immediately. All the damn winter clothing was camouflaging him. It would be a disaster if the alien went inside. He raised his gloved hand, as though attracting a nonexistent waiter. Zoey's eyes never left her paper. She clearly wasn't tuned in. Damn it! The whole thing was falling apart. Desperate, he raised the other glove and waved his hands. His heart climbed up into his throat. He was about to call out to catch the bird's attention when it finally saw him. It turned and stared at him.

Then, as though a button was pushed, it darted straight for him. The next instant, it was six inches from his nose. The breeze from the humming wings cooled the sweat on his face, creating again that weirdly welcome sensation as death poised to strike. He nearly peed his pants as he jerked his hands to cover his exposed face. At the same instant, a brilliant flash exploded. It was the Fungus Bird attempting to either kill or incapacitate him, and he felt absolutely nothing, other than a tickling vibration as the metal fibers drained off the electrical discharge.

Crusher's theory had worked perfectly. Beneath the concealing clothes, they had wrapped Darren in fine-mesh metal screen material they'd picked up at a hardware store. The metal mesh of the gloves was connected to this, and when he covered his face, he was completely shielded.

Darren's vision returned to find the bird gone. He swung his feet away from the rustling and banging below him. Zoey was on her knees, holding down the metal mesh that she'd thrown over the bird. Crusher had explained that the Fungus Birds had to temporarily shut down their own sensory inputs during a discharge. This had given Zoey a few seconds to make the capture.

"Here," he said, using his gloved hands to hold the screen so that she could move away. The Fungus Bird was struggling to turn and stab her unprotected skin. When he knelt, his chair toppled over with him, whacking his back. The cable grounding his mesh to a pipe had gotten tangled. The bird pecked at his gloves and wrist as he pulled the edges of the screen under it, drawing them together. Adelaide arrived and handed him a tie-wrap, which he used to secure the makeshift bag, struggling against the stiff, unyielding gloves. She then held a plastic garbage bag open, and he dropped their captured prey inside. "Uh, better hold it away from you," he said. The tip of a beak poked through here and there along the bottom.

Darren pulled off the sweatshirt, tore away and unwrapped the screen hugging him, and followed the others towards the car, leaving the whole mess behind. He walked past stupefied people who stared at him, mouths hanging open. "It stole one crumb too many," he said. "This should teach them all a lesson."

Adelaide dropped the bag in the trunk, slammed the lid closed, and they drove off. The people were still staring as they finally pulled out of view.

ж ж ж

"Your cousin needs medical care," Adelaide insisted.

"The bleeding has stopped," he said, glancing at her. He was watching Crusher—their alien—trying to goad the captured Fungus Bird into interacting. They had forced their prisoner into a bird cage. By grounding the metal enclosure with lamp cord, they'd created what Crusher called a Faraday cage, which shielded the bird—both from listening and talking to its colleagues.

Darren wished Adelaide would give it up, already. He hated being on the opposite side of her argument. "Look," he said, turning to her, "in less than twenty-four hours it's possible that the world will end. If we take Crusher to a hospital, it won't just be possible, it will be guaranteed. We really have no choice."

"That's assuming the alien birds actually are going to invade. You're just taking that … thing's word," she said, pointing at the long tentacle extending from Crusher's forehead, the tip probing the openings in the cage. The Fungus Bird ignored it.

Darren sighed. They were going in circles.

The sound of the toilet flushing was followed by Zoey emerging from the bathroom. This dumpy motel room had cost four times the one in Texas. And the tap water tasted terrible. "Poke it with a stick," she suggested. "A sharp one."

A tinny voice, like a cheap little radio, said, "This creature can't be trusted."

They all looked at the cage. The Fungus Bird turned its head to gaze at them. It was creepy. Where a real bird's eyes are featureless beads, its head turning in little jerks, constantly changing the view, this alien looked at them with the sedate eyes of a conscious intelligence. It had abandoned its pretense of imitating an Earth animal. The eyes took them in, one at a time, studying them, remembering them. When it spoke, its beak opened and the words emerged, formed by some mechanism within.

"What the hell would you know about me?" Zoey said.

The alien turned to look at her, and she backed up a step. "I wasn't referring to you," it said, "but to this Bloodsucker." As it said this, it gestured towards Crusher's tentacle with the tip of its wing, which had separated into three small fingers. They reminded Darren of a Pterodactyl's talons.

He was unnerved by the talking bird. They knew from Crusher that the Fungus Birds were sentient, but until now, their behavior might have been no more intelligent than a coyote. But talking—this was uncanny. Even Crusher didn't do that.

"He hasn't killed anyone," Darren said.

The bird turned its steely gaze on him, and he too backed up a step. "The Bloodsucker? He has commandeered a human body. Is this the action of a cooperative being?"

"He didn't kill him," Darren insisted, but he noticed that Adelaide had nodded in agreement. "Your friends murdered two people."

"In self defense," the bird replied. "Don't forget—they also gave their own lives in the pursuit of preventing a devastating invasion of Bloodsuckers."

The room was silent as the bird gazed at him.

"Tah!" Crusher honked, pulling the tentacle back.

Darren held up his hand to quiet him. "Did you say an invasion of *Bloodsuckers?*"

"Of course," the bird said. "This Bloodsucker has probably told you that it is we, the Tribbles, who are planning an invasion."

"Tah!" Crusher called. "Tah—"

Darren clamped his hand over his cousin's mouth. "Your ambassadors are arriving tomorrow?"

"That was the original plan."

"What do you mean? Why would the plan change?"

"Because of him," the bird said, flicking a wing-finger at Crusher.

"I thought that you can't communicate back to your planet, at least not until the portal opens tomorrow."

"That is correct. I don't mean that this Bloodsucker itself is changing the plans, but rather that his presence here on Earth means that the course of events tomorrow has already been derailed."

Darren shook his head. "Sorry, don't get it."

"Do you think it's a coincidence that we arrived on Earth at the same time as this Bloodsucker? They plan on using the open portal tomorrow to begin their invasion. They have obviously been tailing our advance corps. They are extremely sophisticated in their methods of scavenging on others' resources. After all, look at what your Bloodsucker has done to your friend. This is why they are invading the Earth. Your fellow humans have spent centuries building the infrastructure of your civilization—a ready-made home for Bloodsucking parasites—"

Crusher yanked his head away. "Tah! Tah!"

The bird flicked it's fingers dismissively. "You might as well let the Bloodsucker get on with its lies."

Darren nodded and picked up the tablet. The bird turned its head this way and that, as though trying to hear through the Faraday cage what Crusher was transmitting.

I'm sure you understand that Fungus Birds are intelligent, and will use any ploy to get the upper hand. We should proceed with the plan.

Darren looked at Crusher, the habit he couldn't break. He dropped the tablet on the bed. "Why are you allowing the portal to remain open tomorrow?" he asked the bird. "Why aren't you planning on immediately signaling for your home-side to close the portal if you know the Earth will be invaded by, uh, Bloodsuckers?"

"I only realized the true situation now after seeing your Bloodsucker."

"That seems to contradict the fact that you've been hunting us down ever since Houston."

"We knew there was another alien here on Earth, but we thought it was a more benign parasite variety—one that needed to be eradicated, but not one that posed a serious threat."

The other birds had seen Crusher up close, but they had been immediately destroyed, possibly before they had a chance to communicate their discovery. "It seems that space is crawling with parasites," Darren said.

The bird managed a viable imitation of a shrug. "Parasites are a natural consequence of evolution. On Earth, there are more species of parasites than there are hosts. Evolution works by the same rules throughout the universe."

Darren contemplated his next move. The Russian plan had seemed believable before the bird began talking so eloquently.

"We obviously must prepare to send a signal to close down the portal once it opens," the bird said. "We are wasting time here in this motel room."

Darren glanced at Crusher—the unbreakable habit. He sighed. "Here's the thing. You see, we've, uh, contacted the Russians— through their embassy. They understand—we told them—that there's an invasion coming tomorrow—that it's, uh, your people. Look, it doesn't matter whose invasion it is. If they detect this happening, well, they're going to nuke the site—with big bombs. Lots of them."

The motel room was silent. The bird said, "Russians?"

"Yes, they still have, you know, thousands of nukes from the cold war days."

"I understand. They will probably be using ICBMs to deliver them?"

"Exactly. Plus from submarines."

"I see."

The bird waited. Darren had the distinct impression it was letting silence underscore the ridiculous content of his message.

"Well, then," the bird finally said. "Even more reason to leave this motel room and get on with the signal preparations."

The ruse was both ridiculous and unnecessary. The bird had already offered to prepare a signal.

"Tah!" Crusher honked.

"Now that you know the truth," the bird said, "I suggest you throw that device away."

Darren picked up the tablet.

We need another plan. This Fungus Bird won't be fooled. It's just playing with you.

"What does the Bloodsucker say?" the bird asked.

Darren glanced at Adelaide and Zoey. "He says that we should get as far away from ground zero as possible."

"Darren," the bird said, "it's important that we trust each other. You know that. What did he really say?"

He tossed the tablet on the bed and turned away. He needed time to think. *What the hell was going on?* He went to the door and opened it, staring out across the parking lot at the gas station across the street.

Behind him, Zoey said, "So, your people are called Tribbles, eh?"

The bird didn't answer.

"What?" she said. "You only talk to men?"

"Yes," the bird said, "we call ourselves Tribbles."

"Golly! Well, talk about coincidences. First, the Tribbles and Bloodsuckers appear on Earth at the same time, and then it turns out that one of them has named themselves after alien characters in an old Star Trek episode!"

The bird was silent.

"Wait!" Zoey exclaimed. "Apparently that first coincident isn't a coincidence at all. Maybe neither of them are. What do you say, Tribble?" she said, emphasizing the bird's assumed moniker.

Nothing.

"Well," she said. "I understand that parrots can learn to repeat long passages, but they're not actually intelligent."

"Sarcasm may seem like a clever social weapon," the bird finally said, "but it actually demonstrates an unwillingness to participate in a true debate."

"So is silence."

"We're wasting time, when every minute of signal preparation is critical. We obviously don't refer to each other as 'Tribbles,' but we needed some label in your language."

"So you picked cute little furry balls. In fact, probably the only aliens on the show that weren't arrogantly superior."

Silence.

"Maybe you should have chosen 'Parrots' instead."

"Darren!" the bird called. "We must proceed with preparations."

A couple walked past and glanced curiously inside at the insistent tinny voice. "Our parrot," Darren said, and turned and closed the door. "We'll head inland, towards Anza Borrego. Whatever we do, it'll be there that we do it."

"Darren," the bird said patiently, "I can fly ahead and jump-start the signal preparations."

"You'd like that, I'm sure."

"Darren, I'm not sure you understand the importance of having sufficient time for preparation."

Repeating your mark's name is a tried-and-true tool of

persuasion. "Zoey," Darren said, "grab a bath towel."

"Darren!" the bird yelled. "You don't understand the magnitude of the mistake you're making. You are dooming the human race!"

When Zoey returned, he said, "Cover the cage. If he keeps talking, add a blanket as well."

"Darren!" the bird persisted. "You have to stop and contemplate—"

"I'm serious about the blanket," he said, pointing menacingly at the alien. "Now be quiet."

Adelaide had been sitting cross-legged on one of the beds listening. "Who appointed you our leader?" she asked.

Darren took a breath. How did she become so contentious? He looked at Crusher staring at the wall as though in a deep trance. One arm was just a stump, and the other hung useless from McKenzie's bullet. His pants were stained with urine. A small hole in his head allowed an alien tentacle to occasionally emerge.

He shouldn't complain. Anybody else would have run away and called the police.

Chapter 15

Darren watched through the plate glass of the convenience store as Zoey walked to the back and into the bathroom. "Okay!" he said, running back to the car. "Let's go!"

Adelaide had just gotten out after adjusting Crusher's bandages. "I have to use the bathroom!"

"We'll stop again soon," he said jumping into the driver's seat.

"I don't understand," Adelaide said, standing next to the car.

"I'll explain! Get in!"

She got in, reluctantly, and Darren pulled away. "You're leaving Zoey behind!" she cried, turning her head to look back.

"That's the whole point. She shouldn't have come in the first place. Crusher just wanted her along to catch the Fungus Bird."

"That's not fair! She *wants* to come along."

"I know that. That's not the point. It's too dangerous. She's just a kid."

"You can't just abandon her there!"

"I gave her fifty dollars—told her to pay for gas. I told the clerk to call her a cab."

Adelaide threw him an angry look, and sat fuming.

"You know how serious this is," he said gently, trying to sooth her. "People are getting killed."

She threw him another dark look. "In America, you have an expression—'What am I, chopped liver?'"

Darren blinked. "Right. I didn't leave you behind. Well, you see … I guess I need you. Sorry."

"I don't want to be left behind. I'm going to see this through.

The question is, what exactly are we doing?"

Darren sighed. "That *is* the question. Maybe it's time to consult with Crusher."

"Darren," the Tribble said from under its towel in the back seat, "we already have a plan. We need to begin preparations, and the best way to do that is to let me go."

"I brought a blanket to put over you," Darren warned. To Adelaide, he said, "What's Crusher saying on the tablet?"

"Um, he says …"

She held it up for him to see.

The Fungus Bird should not hear about our plan.

Of course. Despite their precautions, it might somehow get a message off.

Darren pulled the car over and popped the trunk. He lifted the cage out, and as he placed it inside, the bird said, "You're making the biggest mistake of your life, Darren. I think you know that."

"If you mean by not wringing your neck right now, you may be right."

He slammed the trunk lid, but worry nagged him. The Tribble was probably playing them as Crusher said, but what if it wasn't? Whatever the odds, it was a gamble he couldn't afford to lose, one the entire Earth couldn't afford to lose.

He would get Adelaide away from Crusher and talk it over. He knew her bias, but he owed it to the world to let her try to persuade him.

As he got in, Adelaide held up the tablet. "He says that the Tribble—he still calls it a Fungus Bird—won't voluntarily send a hyperspace signal," she said, "despite what it claims."

Darren checked the mirror and pulled out into the traffic. His cousin sat in the back staring at his knees. "No shit," he said into the mirror. "That's not a plan, that's a lack of one."

Adelaide read his response. "We'll need to revert to the original plan—create the signal ourselves."

Darren snorted. "Back to that pesky detail—we don't happen to have a nuclear bomb!"

Adelaide studied the tablet. "He says that there is a fallback method. It sounds like a long shot, but the science is sound. There's another source of energy that could be used as a signal. It's not as powerful as a nuclear warhead, but the energy emissions are tuned and would be much more efficient at being detected by the Tribble home planet."

Darren guessed that Crusher hadn't written *Tribble*. "Why are you only bringing this up now?" Darren said. "Why were we talking about atom bombs in the first place?"

Adelaide read. "We did not possess this energy source until recently." She looked at him quizzically.

"What the hell are you talking about?" he said, glancing back at Crusher.

Adelaide read the tablet, but her quizzical expression remained. "He says that this is the same energy source that the Tribbles—he's still using 'Fungus Birds'—themselves use for signaling a halt to the invasion." She stared at the screen, then looked up in alarm. "He says it's the birds themselves!"

Darren watched the traffic ahead of him and considered. It made some sense. The two birds they'd destroyed ended up burning down buildings within minutes. That's a lot of energy. What kind of animals *did* that?

"He says," Adelaide went on, "that one bird alone would not be enough. That's why he didn't suggest it at first. He says that we'd have to arrange it so that at least a half dozen birds emitted simultaneously—hold on!" she exclaimed, putting the tablet down "He's talking about murdering six Tribbles!"

"That true?" he said into the mirror. "Would the birds be destroyed?"

Adelaide looked at the tablet. "'Of course,' he says. Of *course?*" She turned to look at Crusher. "You are a monster, aren't you?"

Darren gestured towards the tablet in her lap. "What's he saying?"

She took an angry breath and read. "He says that they do this voluntarily when they need to halt an invasion." She scoffed. "He says that it's not murder, it's just part of a procedure." She gave Darren a hard look. "It's murder," she insisted.

She had stomped two of them to death. That had been in self-defense, but there was more to it. She was rebelling against the weirdness that was Crusher, and maybe the futility of the whole situation, Darren thought.

On the other hand, it would be hard killing something that has been talking to you, albeit in an ostensibly manipulative fashion. He'd never killed a being he knew was sentient. Could he, when it came down to it?

"I have to go to the bathroom," Adelaide declared.

Darren sighed and pulled up to a pump at the next gas station. She returned as he was putting the nozzle back. She stood looking at him. "What?" he asked.

"Maybe you should go too," she said. "You may not have an opportunity for awhile."

He shrugged. "Right," he said and walked off towards the glass doors. When he stepped inside, he paused. There would be gas stations and bathrooms all the way to the desert. He turned around. Adelaide was opening the trunk. "Dammit!" he said, and tore back outside.

She looked at him, and quickly tossed aside the towel covering the cage. He got to her as she was inserting the key into the padlock he'd put on the cage door. She held up one hand to ward him off, and he grabbed her wrist. He tried to grab her other hand, but she pushed him away, so he pushed back, and she fell, with him stumbling to avoid falling on her. "What the hell are you doing?" he yelled.

She lay on the pavement glaring up at him defiantly.

"Hey!" a man's gruff voice called, and Darren was spun around by his shoulder. A hulk of a man dressed in coveralls stood glowering down at him. "Whaddya think you're doin' bud?"

Darren shook his head. "You don't understand. It's okay."

"I don't think so. You don't go pushing women around." He swiped Darren aside with one arm and reached down to help Adelaide up. "You okay?" he asked her.

"Yes," she said, "I'm okay. But he's not," she added, giving Darren a whack with the back of her hand.

"What's it all about?" the man asked. "You need a ride, or something?"

"Oh shit!" Darren exclaimed, and made a lunge for the trunk, but the man caught him.

"Hold on, bud," the man said. "Just take it easy."

"Shit!" Darren said, straining against the iron grip.

The Tribble had reached through the narrow spaces of the cage with its fingers, and was manipulating to turn the key.

"What in God's name—" the man said, staring at the cage.

"It's going to get away!" Darren cried, struggling with the man, but he seemed mesmerized by the sight, seeming to have forgotten that he was holding Darren tight.

The back door of the car opened, and Crusher rolled out onto the pavement. The man turned his stunned gaze at him. With just one wounded arm, Crusher could only lie there. But a tentacle reached out from his forehead, spiraling up and up, like it was climbing an invisible tree.

The hulk man let Darren go, and turned a wide-eyed face to him. Silently, he shook his head slowly and backed away. After a few steps, he turned and sprinted.

Darren jumped for the car. The Tribble was pressing its beak through the cage, trying to see. It yanked at the padlock, and the shackle arm pulled out, still hooked through the door catch. Darren reached to grab the bird's fingers, but remembered the poison beak. *Damn!* He slipped off his shoe, and used it to bang at the lock. The bird pulled its fingers back, but not far. It was a stalemate.

"Adelaide," he said, "hand me the tire iron."

Wait, that was metal. "No!" he said. "In the glove compartment, I saw a plastic pen."

"Adelaide," the bird said. "You know the right thing to do. Trust your conscience."

"Shut up, bird!" Darren shouted, giving the cage another bang with his shoe. "Adelaide!"

She had gotten to her feet, and stood next to him.

"Adelaide," he said, "if you don't get the pen, then I'm going to use my fingers, and the bird is going to kill me. You'll know then what it's true nature is—and I'll be dead."

"I won't kill him," the bird said. "I promise, Adelaide."

"Oh, *verdammte*!" she exclaimed and stalked off.

Seconds later, she handed him the pen. It wasn't easy. He poked at the bird to keep it back, but it was quick, jerking around and slipping its fingers out here and then there. Finally, Darren just went for it, and reached in and pinched the shackle arm back into the lock. The next instant, he was sitting on the pavement, stunned.

His hand was numb.

The bird sat in its cage, staring at him glumly.

ж ж ж

"It says that the cage drew off most of the bird's charge," Adelaide said, and then let the tablet drop to her lap. When not relating what Crusher was displaying, she stared out the window, avoiding interaction with Darren. She refused to refer to Crusher's alien as anything except "it." She had been this way ever since they got back in the car and continued on.

"Look," he said, "I can't let the Fungus Bird—the Tribble—go. Not yet. It's not being hurt in the trunk."

She didn't say anything at first. "I know that. You blackmailed me back there."

Darren threw her a perplexed glance. "What? You mean because I threatened to risk being poisoned by the bird?"

"Yes. Of course. That is unethical behavior."

"Wait. No. I wasn't threatening, I was just stating fact. I *was* going to go in, with or without the pen ... wait a second! Talk about unethical behavior—you lied about stopping to use the bathroom!"

"I did not lie. I did go to the bathroom."

"Oh, come on. You know what I mean."

Silence. "I admit that I wasn't forthcoming about my intentions."

"You manipulated me into using the bathroom!"

"You went of your own volition. I did not manipulate you."

"That's what manipulation *is*! Do you even understand—"

"Tah!" Crusher honked from the backseat.

Darren sighed. "What does he say?"

"It says that this discord is exactly what the bird wants."

Adelaide made no comment about this. She just sat, looking at the screen.

"We have less than sixteen hours before the invasion begins," she read, still without looking at Darren. "The ... bird is intelligent in a way that I—that's our alien talking—am not. As parasites—" she finally looked at Darren. "I don't want to read this. It makes it seem as though I agree with its opinions."

"Tah!" Crusher honked.

Darren sighed again. "Please, just read what he's writing. I promise not to think it's your ideas."

Through a pinched mouth, she read, "As parasites, they have developed a keen ability to understand and manipulate target planet inhabitants. It's understandable that you—it means me—would develop empathy towards it, but you—I—must resist." She snorted. "The Tribble might say the same thing about Crusher," she said to Darren. She was beyond talking directly to Crusher.

"Tah!"

She muttered a curse and continued reading. "Remember, the … birds killed two people."

She looked at Darren. "As the Tribble said, it was self-defense."

He lifted his shoulders, caught between her and the zombie alien.

"Tah!" Crusher honked.

Adelaide growled. "Patience! Okay … it says … ha! It wants me to think about the details." She read on, then took a breath. "He says that the Fungus Bird had itself indicated that until recently they had thought that the alien commandeering Crusher was benign. Therefore, there was no reason for them to have come on so aggressively."

She let the tablet drop, and stared out the window.

Darren hadn't missed that she'd spoken the word "Fungus," and that Crusher was again a "he."

He was ready for another honk, but the car was silent. Adelaide finally picked up the tablet. In a quiet voice, she said, "He's asking if it makes a difference that the Tribble looks like a bird, whereas you've referred to him as a squid, a monster, a zombie, a parasite, a retard, a turnip, and a klutz."

She stared out the window.

"Does it?" he asked.

"Possibly," she said to the passing cars. She looked at the tablet. "He says that it's time to get back to the plan."

"As I recall, he was explaining that we'd need to pop at least six Tribbles at once, and that's when you suddenly had to pee."

Her look indicated that jokes weren't yet funny. "The Tribbles can be made to release all their stored energy instantaneously," she read, "but it's not easy. Typically when they are destroyed, the energy is released as large quantities of ultraviolet light over time. This is what happened when we destroyed them in the shops. Under certain conditions, however, the stored energy can be released catastrophically in a chain reaction."

"So they're little nuclear bombs?" Darren squeaked.

Adelaide frowned, and then nodded as she read. "No. The energy is not based on nuclear reactions, however the cascading chain reaction effect is similar. In a nuclear bomb, most of the energy is released as gamma rays, but when a Tribble implodes, almost all of the energy is ultraviolet, and this is non-ionizing."

"What a relief," Darren said.

"Do you know what that means?" Adelaide asked.

"No."

"It means that the energy isn't energetic enough to break molecular bonds, which in turn means that it won't damage your DNA."

"Did he write that?"

"No, it's common knowledge."

"Then I'm not even up to common."

"Well, don't forget that I have technical training."

"They teach you that stuff as an graphic designer?"

"In Germany, yes. But just because ultraviolet light isn't ionizing, doesn't mean it can't hurt you."

"I'm starting to peel from the last dose."

"Exactly. A stick of dynamite is non-ionizing as well. Wait, he's written some more. He says that for the same reason that the stored energy is released as ultraviolet light, the catastrophic cascade reaction is triggered by the same, except that it is only effective when the impinging ultraviolet energy is very dense."

"Meaning really bright," Darren guessed. "Like when a Tribble … oh my God! I get it! If you can get one of them to explode, others will go with it!"

Adelaide read the response. "He says that you are obviously more than up to common—"

"Gee, thanks."

"—but the tricky part is getting six or more birds close enough when one of them explodes. Remember that the light will radiate in all directions. Each bird will receive just a small portion of the total release."

"So," Darren said, "we have two parts to the problem—how to get at least six arriving hyperspace Tribbles to huddle around our bait-bird, and then how to get the bastard to explode." He shot a glance at Adelaide. "Oops. Sorry. That wasn't very sensitive."

She sighed and shrugged.

It was the most welcomed shrug he'd ever seen.

Chapter 16

"You going to finish those hash browns?" Darren asked.

Adelaide shoved the plate towards him. " 'Hash' must be English for grease."

She watched him shovel forkfuls into his mouth. "Do you eat this sort of food on a regular basis?"

He paused and looked at the slippery glob of shredded potatoes on his fork. "Occasionally. I normally have oatmeal, but sleeping in a car stokes a hunger for stick-to-your-ribs food."

"Stick to your veins, more likely."

"Or, maybe my waist. I could use a few more inches there."

She cocked an eyebrow.

"It was a joke," he said.

He felt okay. After a night in a car, he had expected to be dragging and grainy, but a splash of water on his face and a stomach full of greasy diner food had turned him around.

The fact that Adelaide didn't hate him anymore might have something to do with it. She'd slept with her head in his lap, and he'd thought that he would stay awake just to enjoy the experience. That was before he'd woken with the morning sun in his eyes.

They hadn't planned on sleeping in the car, but after buying the Tribble-busting equipment at the box hardware store, they had just thirty dollars left from the eleven hundred Aunt Melba had wired. The expensive piece was the arc welder—the most powerful one in stock—and Crusher wasn't even sure that this would be enough. The shotgun was the sticky point. Thanks to California's strict gun laws, that was purchased out the trunk of a car, with all eyes watching for the authorities.

When they came to the restaurant, they took a booth where they could keep an eye on the car. It wasn't that they were worried about the Tribble in the trunk, but rather that Crusher wouldn't stay put.

"Do you believe your alien?" Adelaide asked.

Darren looked at her, and then out at their stolen car. *His* alien. Was she baiting him? Was the truce over? "I'm not sure," he said, looking back at her. She seemed genuinely hungry for an answer. "I was probably running on mental momentum when we first captured our talking bird. For days, the Fungus Birds—the Tribbles—were the bad guys."

He moved the rest of the greasy hash browns around on his plate. "I still think it's the best bet, though. I have a gut feeling that the bird isn't being straight."

"But the alien sitting in Crusher's head is?"

Her eyes said she wasn't challenging him. "Yes." He hadn't thought about the question until now. "Yes, I think it is."

She looked sad. "How about you?" he asked gently.

She shrugged. "I wish it were over."

He looked at her, and then pushed the plate away.

"Physics wasn't my best subject," she said, "but I have to say that I find it hard to understand how an animal could store energy and then be made to explode like that."

He nodded. "I don't think they're animals."

Her brow furrowed. "You think they're … machines?"

"These Tribbles are obviously a very advanced race—or at least come from an advanced civilization. I suspect that the idea of a machine is sort of an anachronism for them. When I think of a machine, I think of gears and pulleys, or at least a bunch of metal and plastic parts that are assembled in a factory. The Tribbles aren't animals, but they're a lot more than machines. You've read about our own nanotechnologies—microscopic machines, sometimes made up of just individual molecules. It's only lab experiments now, but I can imagine—barely—billions of these things working together as a Tribble."

"But they're intelligent."

He lifted his shoulders. "Have you used Siri?"

"The personal assistant software that recognizes your voice?"

"Yeah. If you didn't know better, you'd think you were talking to a real woman."

She nodded slowly. "I've been thinking the same thing—that the Tribbles were some kind of artificial life." She looked at him, one eyebrow cocked high. "What about Crusher's alien?"

Darren took a deep breath. "We can ask him, but I can predict the answer."

Ж Ж Ж

It's complicated.

"Ha!" Darren exclaimed, throwing Adelaide a smirk as she held up the tablet from the passenger seat. "I told you."

"I never said otherwise," she replied as she watched the tablet. "He says that there will be plenty of time to talk about this after the invasion is stopped."

"That's an optimistic approach. On the other hand, if we can't stop it, then the whole subject will be sort of moot."

"He says that we're less than five miles from the probable turnoff—you should get into your disguise."

They were on Route 78, heading east, sixty miles from San Diego. They were leaving the pass through the Laguna Mountains, and the Anza Borrego desert spread out before them, a broad expanse of low rolling hillocks, like the surface of the ocean the day after a big blow. Scattered dry brush dotted the sand—life that might have been green a month or a century ago.

Darren pulled off at the next narrow road, which turned to dirt after a hundred yards. They came upon farm workers arguing in Spanish next to a beat-up old truck. Darren bumped along past them, and stopped once a second set of the mini hills hid them from the highway. "A disguise is suppose to include a wig and fake mustache," he said, smearing brown shoe polish across his cheeks. He looked at himself in the side mirror. "I look like I have shoe polish smeared on my face."

Adelaide looked at him. "You have to spread it evenly—work it into your temples, down your neck, and right up to your eyelids."

He grumbled. "I'll never get it off."

It had sounded so clever when they bought it. *Implementation brings home the devil-details.*

"I'll help you remove it," she said. "It's a problem that will be worth celebrating."

They'd be lucky if they were still around to take it off.

"The back of your hands, too," she said, and handed him a rag to wipe off the excess.

A pair of low-power thick-rimmed reading glasses and a baseball cap topped off the disguise.

Adelaide stood looking in at the backseat. "This is going to be fun," she said. She was being sarcastic.

"If you don't suffocate," he said, pulling out the heavy welder. She helped him set it on the dirt.

They'd been scratching their heads over how to disguise them all, when Crusher reminded them that they'd be looking for three, or at least two, people in the car. The question was how to hide two of them, with the car already stuffed with three of them, the Tribble in the trunk, and now all this equipment they'd picked up. The answer was to use the stuffing. "Crusher," Darren said, "you go on the bottom."

"No," Adelaide said. "His wounds might open if I'm lying on top of him."

Here we go again, Darren thought, bracing himself. "He'll crush you if you're on the bottom. Do you know why his nickname is Crusher? When we were kids, he sat on his dog to keep it from going after the mailman. He killed it."

"But his wounds. They'll never heal—"

"Dealing with opened wounds tomorrow will be what?"

She sighed and nodded. "A problem worth celebrating."

They helped Crusher lie down on the floor in the back, and then Adelaide gingerly lay down on top of him. "Honk if I'm hurting you," she said.

Darren chose not to remind her yet again that there was no sensation of pain to be felt.

Grunting, he lifted the welder back inside and set it on the back seat. The front of it rested on Adelaide's back, but she didn't complain, although she did groan a little. Darren then piled the rest of the tools inside, partially covering the stowaways, and finished off by positioning the shop rags they'd bought and sandwich wrappers to hide any visible areas. He climbed in the driver's seat, turned the car around, and re-entered the highway. He let the glasses rest on the tip of his nose so he could look over them.

Adelaide gave a little squeal.

"You okay?" Darren asked.

"Crusher!" she scolded. "Stop that! He's got his tentacle out. He's feeling my *hair*!"

"He's never had the chance before. Crusher! Cut it out! Now behave."

They had pulled off just in time. Topping the next rise, Darren saw two police cars along the side, and next to them, four cops stopping traffic in both directions. This explained the arguing illegal farm workers—they'd obviously gotten a heads-up.

Darren waited while one policeman queried the driver of a car ahead of him.

"Why are you stopping?" came the muffled voice of Adelaide.

"Shh! We're already being checked," he said, pushing the glasses into place. Everything more than two feet away became blurry.

It was his turn. He pulled ahead and stopped next to the cop, who leaned down to scan the interior.

"What's the problem?" Darren asked.

"Routine," the cop said. "The Army's doing some practice maneuvers up ahead—we're warning folks. Where you headed?" he asked.

Darren was ready. "Ocotilla Wells."

The cop's eyebrows went up. "Where abouts?"

"Some work with a garage there," Darren replied. The cop was supposed to ask what his business there was, not "Where abouts?"

The cop nodded. "Which garage?"

With a sinking feeling, Darren realized that the cop must be familiar with the little desert town, maybe even lived there. "It's, uh, on Main Street."

Every city had a Broadway, and every town had a Main Street. He held his breath.

"The Shell Station? Kransten's?"

"Kransten, that's it."

He waited, sweating. It could be a trap. There might be no Kransten.

The cop nodded again. He turned his gaze to the rear seat.

"Doing some welding?"

"That's right."

"Hmm. Donny said he'd just picked up a nice used unit."

Darren lifted his shoulders. "Maybe I didn't need to bring my own gear. Wish he'd told me."

"I guess you'll find out soon enough. Tell Donny I said hi, and watch for Army trucks. They're goofing around just a couple miles ahead."

He stepped back and waved him on, but just then from the trunk came the shrill voice of the Tribble. "Hold it!" the cop called. "What's that?" he asked pointing at the trunk. The Tribble doubled its cries.

"That sound?" Darren asked. The cop was walking to the back of the car. "That's just ... my CD changer—remember those? It's in the trunk. It has a problem. That's a, uh, rap album."

The cop bent down to listen better. "Doesn't sound like rap."

"Yeah, I know. The changer, well, it plays the CDs too fast— like, double time."

The cop listened and smiled. "Now, that's rap music I could almost listen to."

The driver behind them gave her horn a little toot.

"Yeah, yeah," the cop said, waving Darren on. "Hold your horses."

Sweat was running down the sides of Darren's face. He looked in the mirror. The brown polish was sweat proof. He was going to have a devil of a time getting that off.

"We're through," he called to the hidden bodies. "Stay put until we see what's next."

What was next was trouble. On the left were two Army troop trucks, one on each side of a dirt road heading off north into the desert. Soldiers lounged around the back, and Darren could see more inside, in the shade. A hundred yards along the one-lane road was a checkpoint, striped bars blocked the road, and MP sentries stood guard in the hot sun.

Darren drove on by, glancing at the bored soldiers smoking cigarettes. Their plan hadn't extended beyond getting to the desert and sizing up the situation. Now that they were here, Darren wondered why they ever thought they could get to the site at all.

Heck, they didn't even know where they'd get electricity for the welder.

A horn blared from behind, like a semi crawling up his tail. In the rear mirror, Darren saw green camouflage on the hood—an Army truck. He'd been tooling along below the speed limit, and he stepped on the gas, but the truck let loose with a second blast. He signaled and pulled off onto the shoulder, grumbling that the Army was too used to getting what it wanted. To his alarm, the truck pulled in front of him, blocking his escape. He sat, his heart pounding. Something large, covered in a tarp, sat on the truck bed.

"What's going on?" came Adelaide's muffled voice.

"We're under attack by the Army—wait, somebody's getting out."

A young soldier with a shaved head and sporting a big smile and an Army-issue camouflage cap opened the driver's door and got out. He sauntered towards them as though they were old friends getting together for a beer. Somebody else came around the back of the truck—a girl, dressed in the same T-shirt as Zoey. It *was* Zoey!

The soldier leaned in the driver's window next to Darren, and Zoey propped her crossed arms in the open passenger window. "You look like you've smeared shoe polish on your face," she said.

"Is that Zoey?" Adelaide called from the depths.

"Adelaide?" Zoey said, peering around the cluttered back seat. "Have the aliens freed your spirit from the confines of your Earthly corporal shell?"

"She's, uh, hiding down there," Darren explained, glancing nervously at the soldier, whose face hovered inches from his, a grin bridging one ear with the other. "It is shoe polish," he admitted, thinking that this was what the young man found so funny.

"That's Jordon," Adelaide said. "He thinks he's my boyfriend."

"Private Jordon Alexander," he said, sticking a hand through the open window and nearly crushed Darren's fingers. "Real happy to meet you, sir," he said. "Zoey tells me you're here to save the world."

Darren looked at Zoey. "He knows about the, um, invasion?"

"He knew before I got here," she said. "But, speaking of me, someone with thinner skin might feel a little rejected."

"Yeah, sorry. I was looking out for you. This is going to be dangerous. It's no place for a kid."

"You think I'm a kid?"

"Sir," Jordon said, "she's no kid. Believe me."

Darren didn't pursue that line. "How'd you get here?" he asked Zoey.

"I told the taxi driver to go until the fifty bucks ran out. I made it to Julian—a little tourist trap town about half way. I called Jordon, and he came in the Monster Mack."

"Monster Mack?"

"That's what he calls his truck."

"*Your* truck?" he said to Jordon. "You just drive it around wherever you want?"

"No, sir. At least not officially. You see, they had me bring in Big Mama—that's the satellite dish under the tarp—but it turns out that she's obsolete, at least for the com hookups they're using."

"But you're still here."

He chuckled. "That's the Army for you, sir. They're too busy to re-deploy me, so I'm in limbo for now. As long as I don't get in the way, they don't much care what I do."

"Hey!" Adelaide called from below. "It's really hot down here! And Crusher needs another bath. Badly."

"In a minute!" he said. To Jordon, he asked, "How did you know about the invasion?"

He stood up and gestured towards the truck. "We have a co-conspirator."

"Monster Mack?" Darren asked.

Jordon looked confused, then grinned. "No, sir. *In* the truck. Come on. We've been waiting for you."

"People!" Adelaide called. "Don't leave! I'm getting a little panicky down here! I think I have claustrophobia."

Jordon reached in his pocket, pulled out his phone, and looked at the screen. He looked up in surprise. "Uh, I think this is for you, sir," Jordon said, handing Darren his phone.

On the small screen, Darren saw: *Please show this to Darren—we have only 46 minutes until the invasion. We should talk to the co-conspirator.*

"That's *our* alien," Darren explained. To the back seat, he said, "You know who this co-conspirator is?"

No, but clearly this could be a windfall development.

Darren blinked. He handed the phone back to Jordon. This was really happening. Their mission had been so vague—so apparently impossible. Stop an invasion of a million space aliens. Use the captured Tribble as an ultraviolet bomb to in turn explode enough other arriving Tribbles to create a hyper-space signal. The whole thing was so ridiculously far-fetched, so one-in-a-thousand, that he hadn't had to take it seriously.

Now, though, they'd made it. They still had to get past the MP guards. They still had to set up the whole Rube Goldberg contraption without drawing attention. It was still ridiculously infeasible, but now they had a co-conspirator, and the odds had gone from one-in-a-thousand to one-in-a-hundred. He had bet on worse odds.

"I'm going to throw up," Adelaide's muffled voice said.

Darren took a deep breath and threw open the door. "Let's get her out of there—"

Just then, an Army jeep came over the rise. The two MPs slowed down to take a look, and Jordon waved them on, but they pulled off in front of Monster Mack. Jordon trotted off to talk to them, and Darren sat sweating.

"I taste bile," Adelaide said.

"Just a minute," Darren said, watching Jordon and the MPs. With a wave, they finally pulled out and drove away. "We're good for now," Jordon said running back, "but we shouldn't sit here too long."

"Pha!" Crusher honked from the depths.

"Pha?" Darren said.

"Ooo!"

"Ooo? Pha Ooo? Oh! Phone! Jordon, let me see it."

Take the phone with you, and leave it on. Watch for my communications.

"Right," Darren said. "Okay, time to meet the co-conspirator," he said, throwing open the door and sliding out.

"I'm going to be sick," came Adelaide's weak voice.

"I'll be back in a jiff," he said. "Hold tight."

Jordon walked them around the back of Monster Mack. The truck had an extended cab, and Jordon tilted the passenger seat forward so Darren could climb into the small rear row. A woman sat crouched, out of view. She nodded knowingly at him.

Darren froze. He turned to Jordon.

"That's her, sir," Jordon said. "She's been waiting for you."

Her face looked familiar, but he couldn't place it. He climbed all the way in, and Jordon closed the door. The seat was small, and their knees pressed together as they faced each other. She wore jeans and a loose, pale blue T-shirt. He remembered her face. Clearly. It came to him—the last time he'd seen her, she was dressed in crisp office clothes and wearing glasses. "Susanne," he said. "You're the NASA director's assistant."

She grinned. "Thanks—I already knew that."

"Right. Of course—it's just such a surprise. I wasn't expecting—"

"A woman?"

"No! Okay, yeah. But mostly ... well, you're his assistant."

Her grin expanded into a smile. "You mean I'm just his secretary? Good at keeping hot coffee at hand?"

"That's not what I meant." *It's what I thought.*

"Of course it's not. Let me explain. The director has critical talents. He's half politician, and half administrator. But his duties are mostly policy. His staff runs the day-to-day operation. Pick any one project, and a senior technical staff member sits at the top."

"And your project is ... ?"

"Aliens—the Tribbles. Also Bloodsuckers—your alien."

Darren stared at her. What was she trying to pull. A trap? Was a platoon of Special Ops soldiers about to come crashing out of the brush?

"Why are we hiding?"

"Because I'm the only one who believes that the Bloodsuckers are not scheming to invade the Earth."

"Why?"

"Why do I believe this? Because I don't trust the Tribbles. McKinney says that your Bloodsucker has killed two people—one in Houston, and one—"

"Here in San Diego. We guessed they'd blame it on us. It was Tribbles, of course, but why do you think so?"

"In the second case, there were witnesses. The accounts were confused, but the overlapping consensus matched what I'd already suspected. An FBI agent had died of unknown causes, and the coroner said that all the signs pointed to a paralyzing nerve agent, but the labs couldn't find a trace. A Tribble was the only witness. It claimed that it appeared as though the agent suffered a heart attack."

"If the witness accounts were so obvious, why don't others believe it?"

"Nobody else saw the report. McKinney immediately pulled it—national security."

Every mention of McKinney's name set the hair on the back of Darren's neck bristling. "Why? Why would McKinney cover for the Tribbles?"

"He believes that the knowledge the Tribbles can offer is worth some downside."

"Downside? It's worth lives?"

Susanne's grin found humor in his naiveté. "Men who take responsibility for millions of people sometimes get lost in the big picture. They lose perspective of all the little pictures—the point-oh-oh-oh-one percent of the group who are victims."

"Yeah, well in this case, the victims are going to represent one-hundred percent of the group."

She shrugged. "McKinney refuses to believe this. Because he doesn't want to. Some of the NASA scientists began finding holes in the Tribbles' story, and McKinney had the whole facility locked down—with the staff inside. Even the Director."

"But not you."

"He thinks my knowledge of the Tribbles is valuable."

She watched him, waiting for him to absorb it all.

"We called them Fungus Birds," Darren said.

She smiled. "And I suppose your alien doesn't call himself a Bloodsucker?"

"Actually, he doesn't call himself anything."

She watched him.

"I sometimes call him Squid-head."

One eyebrow went up.

"Because, you know, he looks like a squid. Sometimes."

Darren jumped when a loud thump landed next to his head. It was Jordon, rapping on the window for their attention. He opened the door. "Excuse me, sir. Your cousin is making noises," he said.

"Zoey says he does this to get your attention."

"Oh, right!" Darren said, pulling out Jordon's phone.

"He communicates to you over the phone?" Susanne asked.

"Uh, yeah. Wireless communication is sort of his specialty."

"What is he saying?"

"We have only thirty-three minutes until the Tribble invasion. We should get on with it."

Susanne's brow furrowed. "Zoey tells me that you've captured a Tribble and expect it to somehow convince the invasion to stop?"

"Sounds nuts?"

"Yes. Yes, it does."

"It was nuts. That's why we have a different plan. Much better."

Darren gave her a three-hundred word executive synopsis of the new plan as they got out of Monster Mack and walked back to where Zoey was standing with Adelaide and Crusher. "This plan is supposed to be much better?" Susanne said when he finished.

"At least we get to blow up a Tribble."

Chapter 17

The Monster Mack took a turn, causing Darren to fall against Adelaide, who pushed him roughly away. She was angry that he'd left her buried so long. His forehead still hurt where she'd smacked him with the heel of her palm. It was pitch black under the tarp, and he only assumed it was her sitting next to him. Zoey was somewhere off to the left softly whistling the theme to *The Great Escape*. Susanne was off to the left as well. She'd given up hushing Zoey, and sat tsk-tsking the teen's irascibleness. Crusher's presence was obvious by smell alone. To his general unkempt odor, Adelaide had added vomit. She hadn't been bluffing.

Darren sat back up and banged his head on the satellite dish, causing Adelaide to harshly shush him. The dish loomed ten feet above them, encased in a protective silver foil that made a crinkling sound when they brushed against it. The dish was normally positioned parallel with the road to reduce air resistance, and Jordon had unlocked the gimbal mounting and swung it ninety degrees to give them more room on the truck bed. Darren had asked him if he was worried that somebody might notice this, and he had only laughed, just as he'd laughed when Darren asked if he'd been worried about being caught hiding Susanne. As an Army private in limbo, he'd been used as a gofer, and he'd heard Susanne and McKinney arguing about the Tribbles as he delivered dispatches. When Zoey arrived, they had known exactly who to contact.

"You are dooming your species," came the barely audible voice of the Tribble.

The cage sat next to Darren. They had covered it with every blanket, tarp, jacket, and seat cushion they could find, and still Darren worried that the MP guards would hear it.

"How will you feel when you see thousands of Bloodsuckers pouring through the hyperspace portal?"

Darren wondered how that would work. Would thousands upon thousands of aliens come laboriously crawling across the portal threshold, dragging along with their tentacles? Would they come zipping through in little aircraft, like Snoopy on his dog house?

On the other hand, thousands upon thousands of lethal birds in massive attack formation, now that was a thought to raise goosebumps.

"It is sad and disquieting to think that Tribbles and Bloodsuckers sprang from the same source," the bird said.

Darren froze. He held his breath. Had he heard the Tribble correctly?

"Your Bloodsucker has told you this. Hasn't it?" the bird said.

Darren wondered if Crusher was listening.

"It has not, has it? Don't you find that interesting?"

He was about to give the cage a shake when he had to hold on as Monster Mack braked to a halt. From deep inside the pile of muffling, the Tribble began shouting in its high, toy-like voice. On schedule, Jordon turned up the hip-hop tune in the cab. The bird's cries were out of rhythm with the music, but that was hardly noticeable.

The truck jerked to a halt, and the voice of the MP could be heard. "Turn that damn noise down! Where've you been?"

"Old Monster Mack needed some fresh air. All the brass around here makes her run rough."

"You know, you're never going to make P-F-C."

"Okay with me. That would just be something to be demoted from."

"Yeah, well Captain Segorski's been looking for you. He's not happy." The MP's voice became softer, but closer. "Hey, have you heard anything about the North Korean president flying in?"

"Nah. That's crazy."

"Then, what's going on in there?"

"Secret."

"I know that. What's up with all the generals? It's like half the Pentagon's here."

"I think they've got a high-stakes poker game going."

"Okay, I get it. Thanks for nothing. You know, you're going to be driving trucks the rest of your life. Now, get out of here."

The truck jerked, and they rolled on.

Darren couldn't resist. He crawled to the edge of the tarp and peeked under. There was nothing but sand and scattered desert scrub. He slid back to his seat against the base of the dish. The Tribble started in again, and he thumped his fist against the soft pile, and it shut up. Adelaide still wasn't talking to him, and they rolled and bounced along the dirt road in silence.

She spent a lot of time being mad at him. She always got over it. That was a good sign, wasn't it? Besides, it wasn't like they were dealing with normal life problems. It wasn't like they were on vacation or anything. The last few days had been stressful. Heck, under the circumstances, the fact that she hadn't left or killed him probably boded well—

His thoughts were interrupted by a whump on the rear window of the cab—Jordon's signal that they were just about there. The truck stopped, started, turned, made a few more maneuvers, and then the engine went silent. Voices came from different directions—calls and shouts, directions and arguments. The general tension was obvious. Even without knowing, it was easy to guess that something was about to break.

The urge to peek again under the tarp was almost irresistible, but it was obvious from the voices that there were people nearby, seemingly just a few feet away. Darren didn't even know in which direction to face the hyperspace portal.

Suddenly Darren was blinded by an intense light. It was Jordon, lifting one end of the tarp. "Hey," he whispered, "I think we can take it off."

Darren made his way to the opening on his hands and knees. Outside, in the achingly bright light of the desert sun, were a variety of people milling about, carrying boxes, waving their hands to get somebody's attention, setting up tripods. Some were wearing Army uniforms, but there were many in civilian clothes, both men and women.

"It's filming crews," Jordon explained. "The brass wants to make sure their part in history is preserved. 'The day the alien allies arrived.'"

Darren scanned the scene. It was chaos. The film crews were scrambling to get set up. They would have been brought in at the very last minute to avoid rumors. Jordon had parked Monster Mack right next to them.

Darren turned to the dark interior. "Hey! Great news! We're taking off the tarp."

Susanne started to protest, but Jordon was already tugging at the pulley lines that raised the tarp like a theatre curtain. Darren went to the other side and together they uncovered the giant dish with the motley crew crouched underneath.

This was good news indeed. They had planned on preparing everything underneath the tarp, raising it only at the very last moment. Zoey sat cross-legged, hand over brow blocking the sun, gazing at the melee. "I feel like I've just been born—in the middle of Times Square."

Monster Mack was a couple of hundred feet from a temporary ten-foot-high platform facing an empty space in the desert, as though a miniature Woodstock concert was waiting for the audience to arrive, except that in this case the show was reversed. This was the observation deck. A dozen chairs lined the rear of the platform, but they were empty. The military elite stood talking, shaking hands, slapping each other on the back. You don't sit when your competition is standing. "Word about the aliens leaked out," Jordon said. "Every branch of the military demanded representation. It's literally the Joint Chiefs of Staff up there. Even the Coast Guard wiggled in. You'd have to use a wheelbarrow to haul away all the stars on that pack of generals and admirals."

An older, harried looking woman in civvies called up to them. "What crew are you with?" She stared at Crusher, soaked in blood from the stub of one arm and a hole in the other shoulder as he stared through her at some unfathomable point in the far distance.

Darren looked at Jordon, who said, "Zoey Productions."

The woman blinked, looked at them, and shook her head. "Never heard of it. Who's in charge?"

Jordon pointed to Zoey, still sitting cross-legged.

"Her?" the woman said.

Jordon put his hand to his mouth, as though preventing Zoey from hearing. "She's Bill Gate's niece."

The woman frowned. "Well, you're encroaching on our area." She eyed the giant dish. "You doing a live feed?"

Jordon looked at Darren. "Yeah," Darren said. "Live."

The woman nodded, calculating. "Tell you what. You can stay where you are if you let us in on your feed."

"No," Darren said. "Sorry. We're, uh, going high-definition. It's all the link can handle."

The woman's face hardened. "In that case, you're going to have to move away."

"Sorry, ma'am," Jordon said, "General Bringam told us to park here. You'll have to talk to him."

Her eyes went wide with anger, and she sputtered a bit. "We followed the same instructions as everybody else! This is unacceptable. Army! No wonder we lost the Iraq War. I've got them right here …" she said and strode off.

"What if she asks General Bringam?" Darren asked quietly.

"He's not here. He's a character from a movie."

"Private Alexander!"

It was an Army officer striding towards them. "Uh, oh," Jordon whispered. "That's Captain Segorski."

"What in God's name are you doing with that truck there?" Segorski demanded, standing on the ground before them, fists on hips.

"Sir!" Jordon piped, snapping a salute. "General Garrard told me to!"

Darren guessed that this must be a real person.

The woman had returned, flapping a piece of paper in victory. "Wait a second," she said. "He told me that General Bringam told him to park there!"

Segorski's eyes narrowed. "That was the last straw, mister. MPs!" he shouted, waving two of them over. "Hold this man until I can deal with it. Don't let him out of your sight," he said, and hurried away.

Jordon jumped down and let the MPs lead him away. He

turned, though, and grinned. He had lifted just enough of the truck keys from his pocket for Darren to see. Monster Mack was going nowhere anytime soon.

"Well?" the woman demanded.

Darren shrugged, and she stalked away.

"Is he going to be okay?" he asked Zoey.

"Don't worry about him," she said, standing up. "He spends more time in the brig than on duty."

Adelaide came past and gave him a nudge. "You going to help?"

"Right." He looked at his watch. "Oh, man—only eight minutes left."

A wave of panic rose, starting at his calves, and shivering its way up his spine. Time was up. The mad scheme seemed all the more ludicrous, now that the moment had arrived. It was like trying to convince a dozen cats to sit quietly in a row while you squirted each one in turn with a water pistol, but not directly—you had to bounce the stream of water off the wall. Through a keyhole.

A horn blared, and everybody around them began scurrying in double-time to their positions. The sense of excitement buzzed in the air. If they knew the truth, the buzz would be a scream of terror.

"Electricity!" Adelaide yelled.

"What about it?" Darren asked, as he squatted for the third time to check that the shotgun was loaded. He was keeping it out of sight under a scrap of tarp until the last minute.

"I *need* it for the *welder!*" she cried, nearly in tears. "Jordon has the *keys!*"

"It's okay," he said gently. "The generator has its own." He showed her by firing it up at the base of the dish. The sound of the motor drew some looks from the filming crews beside them, but everybody was busy with last minute preparations.

"Thank you," Adelaide said, barely audible. She fiddled with the welder controls, and sniffed. She was crying. He knelt down next to her and gave her shoulder a little squeeze. She reached up and placed her hand on his. "I'm scared," she whispered.

"It'll be fine," he said. He smiled. "What can go wrong?"

He watched her adjust the current setting. "I'm scared too," he whispered into her ear.

"Come out, come out, wherever you are," Zoey said, peeling away the pile of cushions covering the Tribble.

It was going to be all about timing. And luck. First, they'd have to get the attention of the first Tribbles through the portal. That was going to be Crusher's job. He spoke their electromagnetic language. Crusher would have to draw them close—they'd need at least six of them within thirty feet. Then came the tricky part, where Zoey, Adelaide, and Darren would need to perform their roles in precise succession.

In preparation, Zoey needed to strip away the sound proofing from the bird cage down to the very last blanket. Predictably, the Tribble began squawking. They were ready, however. They'd borrowed Jordon's wireless music box, and they now turned up the radio. The bird's yelling was only partially masked, and the film crews were giving them occasional quizzical looks. Zoey did a little dance across the truck bed and sang along. She didn't know the words, and made up nonsensical phrases, hip-hop style, in and out of key.

She was doing a better job hiding the Tribbles calls than the radio. Darren joined in the song, humming and slipping in and out of falsetto, mimicking the bird's high tones. Adelaide looked at them both as though they'd lost their marbles, but caught on, and joined in the acoustic fray.

The film crews shook their heads in disgust, which was the goal.

"Pha!" Crusher called from where he stood stone-still in the background.

Darren took Jordon's phone from his pocket.

Just a few minutes left. They'll come through precisely on time.

He looked at his zombie cousin. The Tribble's jabs about Crusher were meant as subversive wedges. Darren knew this, but they still nagged at him. "How do you know this?"

Our peoples have had long contact.

This wasn't the best time to delve into a potentially difficult subject, but Darren realized that he had to know. Within minutes, the truth was going to open up in the cleared area in front of the viewing platform, and he needed this to trust Crusher with what would be either a desperately heroic attempt to vanquish a mass invasion of lethal Tribbles, or a cleverly orchestrated diversion so that Crusher's own people could conquer the Earth.

"The Tribble said that your and their kinds sprang from the same source. What did it mean?"

It's complicated.

Darren sighed.

But I will try to explain. You had asked earlier whether I am artificial. This is a simplistic question, like asking whether a Ming Dynasty porcelain bowl is made from dirt. The technical answer is yes, but you'd have to agree that an adequate description requires a more sophisticated question.

"Fine. Help me ask the right question."

What if we asked whether the mechanisms of life could be improved for specialized circumstances?

"Sounds like we're back to artificial."

And porcelain is made of dirt.

"Okay, okay. Improved in what way? Better blood? Bigger brain?"

I have neither blood nor an organ you would call a brain.

"And yet you are somehow alive—I know, and porcelain is made of dirt."

Science's classic definition of life is an organism that can grow, adapt to its environment, respond to stimuli, and reproduce.

"And by that pretty general definition, you can obviously do all of that. Uh, what about the reproduce part?"

Yes.

That gave Darren pause. What kind of sex would they have? Or would they simply exchange genetic information digitally?

"Fine," Darren said, "but I think our engineers could probably build a kind of robot that could do all that if they set their minds to it. And that would clearly be artificial."

Perhaps it comes down to degree. I doubt your engineers could build something like me. Not with all the money in the world.

"That's true." But the sex part … "What about DNA? Do you have that?"

Now, that is asking the right type of question. I do. Obviously not identical to your double helix molecular structure, but information that serves the same purpose.

"Hmm, you use the word 'information' rather than 'molecules.'"

Information is always stored using molecules. I'm afraid our time is up. By the way, McKinney is here.

Darren's heart skipped two beats. He spun around and scanned the crowd.

He's not in our immediate vicinity. Jordon provided some misdirection. He lied and told him that we had disguised ourselves as Mexican farm workers— the ones we passed when we stopped to don our actual disguises. McKinney has gone off to check it out.

"That's good. Not for the Mexicans. I hope he doesn't give them a hard time."

He clearly cares nothing about illegal immigrants. Darren, are you sure you are ready? This is not going to be easy.

"I don't know what else to do, now, but wait."

That won't be long. Remember that the arriving Tribbles know absolutely nothing about Earth. They will be concentrating on understanding the situation. They don't have much time—it takes tremendous energy to keep the portal open. Once they get their bearings and determine that there's no immediate threat, they'll start taking out leaders. That will be the military officers on the platform.

Darren nodded. He remembered that Crusher always looked straight ahead, and was about to confirm verbally when he saw that his cousin's eyes had swiveled and were looking at him.

"Darren."

He jumped at the sound of his name. It came from the radio. Very loud. It was the voice of calm authority. It reminded him of the Methodist minister of his youth.

"I want you to know that I am gratified that I picked the right person to trust after landing on Earth."

Darren looked from the radio to Crusher. "Is that ... you?"

"Of course, Darren."

"You can ... talk?"

"I am not dirt, remember."

"No," Darren said quietly. "You are porcelain."

Adelaide and Zoey were staring at the radio. In unison, they turned their gaze on Crusher, blood-soaked, disheveled, smelling. The people standing around the truck had gone silent, and were watching.

"They are here," the radio announced calmly.

At that instant, a sound like a giant champagne bottle uncorking rocked the crowd, and Darren felt his ears pop. A blinding light forced him to squint, a light composed of colors all intermingled together and yet maintaining their individual identities. A collective gasp had sprung from the crowd surrounding the portal area, and this was followed by a chorus of awed rapture as the unearthly light faded to reveal the arriving stellar travelers. Against a background of nothing, where once there was a view of the desert receding into the distance, each Tribble arrived as first a deformation in the surface of the nothingness, which grew and extended outward until it dissolved, leaving behind a Tribble ... which fell, until it gained its bearings and found its wings.

These Tribbles were no common silver birds. In fact, they looked nothing like a bird. The wings seemed thin as gossamer, and waved in the air like the fins of an angel fish. Where a bird's beak would normally be, sprouted a thin, sharp needle, half a foot long. Waving like the snakes of Medusa's hair, were tentacles, long, thin, curling and twisting in a mesmerizing dance.

Darren noticed that each Tribble, as it emerged from the dissolved hyperspace bubble, was no larger than a cat, the wings and tentacles folded back compactly. Once the creature unfurled, a butterfly merging from its cocoon, it rivaled a giant condor for size and majesty. Whereas an Earth bird was flesh and bone, however, a Tribble ambassador was mostly air, the dancing tentacles creating the illusion of substance.

No Fungus Bird had ever shown even a hint of a tentacle. Crusher, on the other hand, seemed to be nothing but tentacle.

Darren threw his cousin zombie a glance, but the eyes had turned back forward, staring once again at his own nothingness.

Six aliens had now arrived, and they hovered a moment above the crowd, either for dramatic effect, or studying these new creatures, aliens to them.

Adelaide nudged him and pointed. People in the entranced crowd were being jerked to one side or the other. In the middle was McKinney, pushing forward. He seemed to finally see what all the rest were staring at, and he stopped dead, gazing upward.

The six alien ambassadors rose, higher and higher, swiveling their heads to scan the human gathering. Then, on some shared, silent signal, they started forward, purposefully, straight for the platform where the country's top military leaders stood in awe. The dancing tentacles had folded back down, and the wings beat in drum-like rhythm. The needle beaks glinted in the sunlight. What a moment before had been delicate, esthetic creatures had suddenly become menacing bullets.

At the same time, Darren's ears popped again, and the span of nothingness began expanding. The edges shot outwards, seemingly too fast to see. Within seconds, hundreds—thousands—of bubbles of deformed hyperspace began forming, stretching as far as could be seen from one horizon to the other.

Darren jumped when the radio blasted a shattering screech—that banshee again. Crusher had stepped forward, and stood, his one arm and stub flung wide. A tentacle emerged from his forehead, and rose into the air, higher and higher, longer than Darren imagined possible. He was challenging the Tribbles, daring them to attack.

People were being flung to the side now as McKinney forced himself towards them screaming, "Here! Here they are!" He called to the attacking Tribbles. He didn't understand that English was gibberish to them. The crowd, panicking at the turn of events, surged away, leaving the special agent standing alone before Monster Mack. He pulled a pistol from a holster under his coat.

"Adelaide, Zoey, you ready?" Darren asked.

"Yeah," they both replied, their voices shaking.

"*McKinney! No!*" It was Susanne, running towards him. "It's happening!" she cried breathlessly, planting herself in front of him and gesturing at the infinite wall of nothingness. "Just like I warned."

"Out of the way!" he yelled, pushing her aside. "We're not going to lose this."

"Lose what?" she said, pacing him as he moved forward. "Our planet?" She ran ahead, and stopped in front of him.

"You know what," he replied, pushing her again to the side.

"Military technology? You still think they want to be partners with America? Together, become the benevolent leaders of the world?"

She ran and gave him a push, hardly more than a nudge,

considering the size difference. He turned and pointed the pistol at her chest. "Yes," he said and pulled the trigger.

Chapter 18

McKinney's gunshot was like a punch in the face. Time seemed to stop. The geyser of blood bursting from Susanne's back, and her fall to the ground appeared to happen in slow motion. Utter silence followed, broken by another banshee screech from the radio.

Zoey squatted next to the captured Tribble, and she tugged at Darren's pant cuff and pointed. Two of the Tribble ambassadors had turned and approached them, but stopped where Susanne lay lifeless on the ground. Crusher filled the desert with a mighty honk.

"Get him!" McKinney implored to the two Tribbles, pointing at Crusher. "It's one of 'them'!"

The agent lifted his pistol and fired up at Crusher. From behind, Darren saw Crusher jerk, and his shirt tugged backwards as droplets of blood splattered across Darren's face. Crusher staggered, and caught himself. He brayed again.

McKinney cursed, held the pistol carefully with both hands, and fired again, this time hitting Crusher square in the chest. Again, the zombie staggered, leaned forward, and then stood straight again. The rest of the Tribble ambassadors turned and started for them.

Screaming with rage, McKinney tore off his jacket, reached up, over his shoulder, and pulled out a short-barrel shotgun. With one continuous motion, he pumped it, aimed, and shot. The blast of pellets caught Crusher in the shoulder, and his arm flew off. McKinney pumped, aimed, and fired again, and Crusher's torso exploded, this time covering Darren in his cousin's blood. Crusher fell to the bed of the truck and lay there.

People were screaming now, rushing madly to gain distance

from the carnage. Adelaide was sobbing. The six Tribbles beat the air with their wicked, droning wings fifty feet away.

Adelaide's sobbing froze, and she gasped. A tentacle lifted into the air from the remains of Crusher, and was followed by another, and another. Within seconds, Darren was looking at the poised Tribbles through a web of weaving, swaying silver filaments. The screeching noise from the radio swelled, and, as though answering the challenge, the Tribbles started forward. One, though, dipped towards McKinney. He turned just in time to meet a sharp snap and flash of light. The agent fell to the ground. The Tribbles had given up the pretense of human allies.

Darren watched entranced as the deadly alien Tribbles advanced. They spread to each side, approaching in a semicircle. The tentacles of Crusher's alien whipped in place to meet them, and crackling snaps and flashes of white light filled the air as the lone defender battled the multitude of foes.

Over top of the radio's screech came the calm voice of their alien. "Now."

"Go!" Darren called to Adelaide, but she sat, staring in terror at the battle unfolding just a few feet away. "Now!" he yelled, and she jerked her head to look at him, then nodded, and flicked the switch on the welder. A moment later, a point of light, painful to look at, sprang to life, accompanied by the hiss of the electric arc, the most powerful source of ultraviolet light they could bring to bear.

Zoey, tough as nails, had already yanked off the blanket, revealing the Tribble bird, which stood staring straight at Darren. The glare from the welder glinted off a dozen points of the bird's silver surface, imbuing a regal effect.

Darren grabbed the shotgun. It was up to him now.

But the radio's banshee screech rose even higher. At the sight of their caged comrade, three of the Tribble ambassadors had moved back, far beyond the thirty-foot limit. Whether they guessed what was coming or not, there were now too few Tribbles in range to create the signal.

Darren cursed. They'd almost pulled it off. If only he'd been sooner with the gun.

An image appeared in his imagination—an expanding balloon, growing thinner as it stretched outward, the ball of UV light from their Tribble captive. Did it have to grow thinner? A flashlight focused the beam … he looked behind him. The foil covering of Big Mama caught the white-hot arc of the welder in a hundred sharp points of light, a slice of the Milky Way galaxy glinting in the noonday desert.

He dropped the gun and ran to the base of the dish. He'd watched Jordon unlock the gimbal support. The latches were right … *there*! The dish was big, and it was heavy. He grunted as he swung it around. The battle, as Crusher's alien struggled to keep the Tribbles at bay with whipping, snapping tentacles, appeared in miniature on dozens of foil surfaces before him.

He ran back, grabbed the shotgun, and knelt on the truck bed. He aimed point-blank at the bird inside the cage. "Adelaide!" it called. "Look out!"

Even as Darren turned to look, he knew it was a ruse. He caught himself and turned back. Out of the corner of his eye, he saw movement. He pulled the trigger just as a loud snap sent pain exploding in his shoulder. One of the Tribble ambassadors had slipped through the defense.

His shot had missed. Instead of crushing the bird, it blew the corner off the cage, sending it spinning sideways, coming to rest against Crusher's corpse. As Darren struggled with a numb arm to pump the gun for another shot, the bird found its footing and left the cage.

And then something happened that made Darren wonder if the Tribble's shock had somehow rattled his brain. A hand grabbed the bird. There was nobody within reach. But there it was, a hand clutching the bird. With a realization that made his world spin, he saw that the hand was part of Crusher's detached arm.

He tore himself from the mental vortex, and aimed the shotgun. In the gun's sight was the bird, struggling to get free, and the hand of his cousin. He pulled the trigger, and the shotgun slammed back against his shoulder.

What followed, as the innards of the Tribble were exposed to the bath of UV, was a full body slam, and an immersion in a sea of impossibly bright blue light, an intensity so complete that he would later swear that the radiance had substance. Their Tribble captive had obviously undergone chain reaction obliteration.

Darren was on his knees, his fists jammed against his shocked eyes. He was *hot*! He smelled burnt hair. *His* hair! He slapped his head, and realized that his shirt was smoldering. *Roll over when on fire!* He obeyed the lessons from his youth, and rolled and rolled, until he hit up against something hard—the base of the dish.

Adelaide! Zoey! How had they fared? He pushed himself up, and staggered back. He couldn't see! The world was dizzying swirls of light—multi-colored comets orbiting within his field of vision. "Adelaide!" he called, but there was no answer. In fact, the world had gone eerily silent, except for the distinctive crackle of fire. "Zoey! Crusher!" Still nothing.

His shocked retinas slowly recovered. Among the swirling comets he could discern objects—the abandoned arc welder, Crusher's mangled and blood-soaked body with the black and twisted bird cage next to it, and nearby … another body, tendrils of smoke rising from it. "Adelaide?" he cried, and fell next to it on his knees. He grabbed a blanket and threw it over, patting it down where he could see the glow of smoldering cloth. Was it Adelaide? Yes! These were her clothes. But the person inside them … was a man. With sickening realization, he saw that it must indeed be Adelaide. The dark complexion was her seared face, and the short hair was just what was left after the rest had burned off.

He gently rolled her over. Her eyebrows and eyelashes had been whisked away. He wouldn't have known it was her if not for her clothes. Her eyes opened. Her hairless brow furrowed. "Darren?" she said.

He smiled, even though it hurt. "Yes! Of course!"

Her furrowed brow deepened. "Are you … okay?"

He shrugged, and that hurt his neck. "A little burnt, I guess. Listen, we need to get you to a hospital—"

"A *little* burnt?" she said. "Darren, you look like a deep-fried mummy." She reached up and turned his head. "At least one half still looks like you."

He touched one side of his face, and then the other—"Ow!"

"That's the burnt side," she said. She pulled the blanket off, rolled over, and got to her feet. "Where's Zoey?" she asked, gazing out over the receiving area. The crowd had fled. Suzanne and McKinney's bodies lay all alone in the dirt.

"Zoey!" Darren called.

"Here!" the teenager called. She was running towards them, her clothes still smoking. Jordon was in hot pursuit. "I had to make sure this clod was okay."

Adelaide tugged at Darren's sleeve and pointed out across the desert. "It's gone," she said wonderingly.

Where there had been nothing, there was now the blessed sight of the Anza Borrego desert all the way to the far horizon. The hyperspace portal had closed. The Tribble ambassadors were gone, obliterated along with their captive comrade.

"We did it!" he said.

"You sound surprised."

"Aren't *you?*"

"Yes, I am." She laughed. "Ouch! I shouldn't do that. You know, I didn't trust Crusher—the alien—right to the end. When those … things came through covered in tentacles, my heart sank."

"I know. I had the same thought."

She tugged his arm again, and pointed.

"What?" he asked.

"Look!" she said, alarmed. She was pointing off into the distance.

He saw it. Something was hovering in the air, something silver. It was too far to see details, but it looked vaguely like a bird. "Some of them would have made it through before the portal closed," he said. "Hell, maybe hundreds of them. The Army can finally make itself useful."

"Hunt them down?"

"Yeah."

She shook her head, frowning. "They're intelligent. They'll know there's no point in fighting."

He shrugged, which hurt. "Maybe. We can let that be somebody else's problem."

He sighed, which didn't hurt. He walked across the truck bed to where the torn and mangled body of his cousin lay.

"Poor Crusher," Adelaide said softly next to him.

"Crusher my cousin? Or the alien?" he asked.

"Both, I guess. Where is your alien?"

"Gone."

"Gone ... burned up?"

"Exploded. He was made of the same stuff as the Tribbles."

"How do you know?"

"They're the same color, they both change shape, they both communicate using radio. Our captured Tribble said as much. I think it's true."

"Maybe human bodies wouldn't survive passing through a hyperspace portal. Maybe that's the way space-faring beings always develop."

"Convergent evolution. Perhaps. They know so much about each other, though."

"But ... he would have known that he too would be destroyed."

"Of course."

"He ... he sacrificed himself for us, you think?"

"Yes, I think so."

She was silent. "I feel so bad. I was mean to him."

"I'm sure he understood why. You were upset that he'd commandeered another human being. That speaks a lot about our species. I bet he found that commendable."

"You think so?"

He smiled, and it hurt. "He gave his life for us."

She nodded, but stopped. It probably hurt. "Do you think he really was alive?"

"He thought so."

She smiled, but winced and stopped. "Maybe that's all that counts. Maybe that's the final test of life."

Zoey and Jordon had crawled onto the bed of Monster Mack, and Jordon was staring in astonishment at them, all three of them. Zoey's face was fine, but most of the hair was gone from the back of her head. She'd been turned away when the UV blast had hit. "Shouldn't you guys be, like, lying down or something?" Jordon said.

Adelaide lifted her shoulders and winced. "They're flash burns. Not deep. I've seen this before—"

"She's had technical training," Darren explained.

"We'll blister and peel, but we'll be fine in a few weeks."

Zoey was rubbing her hand along the back of her head. "Maybe you. My hair is going to grow back half an inch in a few weeks.

That's not exactly fine."

"You didn't think I was in love with your looks," Jordon said, "did you, babe?"

She stared at him. "You just said you loved me."

"Not exactly."

"Close enough. I have witnesses."

Crusher's bloody carcass caught Jordon's eye, and he stared in horror. The alien had made a mess exiting the head. "His arm!" he uttered, looking at Darren, perplexed. "It came *off?*"

The arm! Darren had forgotten. Shivers ran up his spine as he remembered the severed limb clutching the Tribble.

He approached slowly, curious, yet fearful. The arm lay there next to the twisted cage. The hand was gone. That wasn't a surprise. He watched a moment, and then toed it gently. There was no reaction. But then he jumped back with a shout.

"What happened?" Adelaide asked.

"It moved!"

"It couldn't have."

"It did," he insisted. He stared at it, waiting for another sign of unholy life.

The radio whistled, and then said, "Dar-ren."

They all spun to look at it. Another whistle swung up and down in pitch, and then the voice—uncertain, artificial in texture—spoke again. "My mother told me to find you. Are you there?"

"Your ... mother?" Darren said, looking around, desperate to find the source.

"You called her Crush-her."

Silence.

"*What?*" Darren finally said.

"I said that you called her—"

"I know what you said, I just don't understand it. Where *are* you?"

"I haven't moved."

"Okay, but *where?*"

"You just touched me. I'm under—"

"The arm!" Darren cried, stepping back.

"Yes, the arm."

They all watched transfixed as Crusher's severed arm jiggled, and a tiny red crab crawled out from under it. Two black-tipped stalks extended up, and one leg lifted and waved at them.

No one spoke.

"Do you see me?" the radio said.

Darren shook the trance from his head. "Yes, we can see you just fine. We're just having a hard time understanding."

"It's complicated, I know."

"That's Crusher, all right," Adelaide muttered.

"I have been … gestating for fifteen days, and I reached … I'm sorry—I have many words to choose from. I reached solo status just yesterday. Mother decided that I should stay … attached until ten minutes ago."

"Let me get this straight," Darren said. "You're Crusher's *baby*?"

"That's a close word."

"He was a *she*!" Zoey exclaimed, and Darren held his hand up for her to be quiet.

"Where is your mother?" Darren asked.

"She does not exist anymore," the radio said.

Darren sighed.

"That is why she made me … go solo."

"So you wouldn't, um, be gone along with her."

"Correct."

"What should we call you?"

"What would you like to call me?"

Darren turned his head to look at Adelaide and smiled, and it hurt. "How about 'Junior'?"

"Maybe if Crusher had been a 'he.'" Adelaide said. "How about 'Crushlet'?"

"How about it?" he said to the little alien. "Is Crushlet okay?"

"My name is your choice," the radio said. "I have a request."

"Shoot."

"I don't understand."

"I mean, go ahead. What's your request?"

"Could you move me to a safe place? I can hear Tribbles, and they will destroy me if they have a chance."

"Of course." Darren looked around, and it hurt. "How about this?" he said, opening the lid of a utility box built into the base of the dish.

"That would work well, as long as you remain nearby."

"Sure. Somebody will always be here—but why?"

"Mother explained that if we were successful in closing the portal, the remnant Tribbles would be careful not to harm humans."

Adelaide harrumphed.

Darren knelt next to the hand-mangled arm. From here, it was obvious that Crushlet's red color was blood. The little guy was practically swimming in it. It came to Darren. "It was *you*!" he said peering closely at the tiny crab, which stared back through expressionless black beads.

"Yes. You are looking now at me."

"No. I mean, you were controlling the arm—hanging on to the Tribble."

"Yes. I thought you knew that."

"How would I know that?"

"That's a good question. I made an assumption."

The child alien's voice was gaining confidence, losing the artificial quality.

"How?" Darren asked. "How was it possible?"

"Mother instructed me."

"She told you how to do it while she was fighting off a squadron of Tribbles?"

"Apparently our relational thinking processes work faster than yours. You are most efficient at reflex operation—the parts of your brain that operate without your conscious knowledge."

"That doesn't explain how you got a severed arm to work."

"Nerve stimulation. The arm had been detached for less than two minutes. The cells had not yet expired. The local muscle storage of glycogen would have lasted another minute or two, at which point I would have lost the hold on the Tribble."

"Frankenstein," Zoey said ominously.

Darren again held his hand up for her to be quiet. "Your mother figured out a lot about us."

"Perhaps. I'm not in a position to gauge that."

"Well, I guess it's good she did."

"Darren," Crushlet said, "would you please take me to a safe place. I am scared."

You can be scared? he thought. *You have emotions?* "Sure, little fella," he said, and placed his hand palm-up next to it, and it hurt.

The little crab walked up to his hand, and the legs stretched and lengthened to reach up and over the edge of his palm before pulling the body up as well. Apparently the trick of shape-changing started early.

Darren stood up, carefully holding his hand out. "Are you a 'he' or a 'she'?" he asked as he walked slowly across the truck bed.

"Since I will be capable of reproducing, I presume you would consider me female. However every one of my kind would then be considered female."

"But, um, you know, you exchange, uh, genetic material?"

"In a manner of speaking. Of course, mother explained that there will be no others of my kind for that procedure."

Darren felt a lump in his throat. How would he feel? Stuck on an alien world with no chance of ever having a mate?

Of course, if he were less than an hour old, he wouldn't be thinking about much except getting some milk.

"Hey," Zoey said, "do you need a human to live in?"

"I don't understand the question."

"She means," Darren said, "do you need a human host—like your mother did?"

It was a question he'd eventually have to ask, but he wasn't sure he'd ever be ready for the answer.

"My mother thought she had arrived at a world that knew nothing of aliens. Her means of transportation, along with her mission, had been destroyed. She saw an opportunity with your cousin. She was surprised at the degree of your sentimental attachment to the otherwise useless body. It was too late, at that point, to find other means."

Darren stood, holding the tiny creature in his cupped hands. It seemed so pathetic, homeless, covered in blood. The featureless black-bead eyes looked up at him with trust, and devotion. He knew he was probably imagining it. "Do you need anything?" he asked. "Maybe some water? Wash off the blood?"

"Rhodium."

Darren glanced at Adelaide, and it hurt.

She laughed. "Ouch! That's why she was always after rhodium.

She had a growing baby in her tummy."

"She had no stomach," Crushlet said, "but, yes, that was why she needed it."

"Look," Zoey said, pointing out towards the empty desert.

"What?" Darren said. "I don't see anything."

"That's my point. Where's the Tribbles?"

She was right. "They're gone." He felt the hairs on the back of his neck, and he turned, half expecting a dozen of them in attack formation. And it hurt.

"They have gone into hiding," Crushlet said, "until they can work out how to survive here. They don't have friends like I do."

Darren smiled. "Ouch!"

"Here come the brass," Zoey said.

Officers with their assistants were gathering again on the platform, shouting orders, calling for status, generally being generals.

"They don't have a clue about what happened," Adelaide said.

"They probably don't even know how close the world came to ending," Darren said. He looked at Crushlet, nestled in his palm—so small, so vulnerable—who considered Darren his friend. "Maybe it would be best to just slip away," he said.

Adelaide nodded enthusiastically, then winced. The film crews were returning, picking up equipment they'd abandoned in a panic. They still seemed in a daze. Many had red faces and arms, but none were burnt as badly as the defenders of Earth.

A young man tossed a tripod into the back of a van and slammed the door shut, then walked around to the driver's side. "Hey!" Darren called. "Can we catch a ride?"

The man looked at Darren with concern. He shrugged. "I'm only going as far as Julian. Looks like you need to get to a hospital."

"No, that'll do," he said.

Darren turned to Zoey. "Coming?"

She shook her head. "The Army geniuses are going to put two and two together and realize that Monster Mack had something to do with destroying their plan to own the most bad-ass weapons in the world." She gestured at Jordon. "Left to himself, this lunkhead will be court-marshaled, and maybe executed. He'll need somebody to explain that he actually saved their asses."

"Okay, then," Darren said smiling, and wincing. "Thanks for not letting us abandon you back there."

"No problem," she said. "It just cost me half a bald head, but jarhead here says he loves me anyway."

"I didn't say—" Jordon started.

"What didn't you say?" Zoey asked.

He shook his head, grinning. "Nothing."

To Crushlet, Darren said, "Will you be okay in my pocket?"

The little alien curled into a compact package the size of a ping-pong ball. "I'm not fragile," he said over the radio.

The van driver glanced at the talking radio and then at Darren. He didn't say anything. This was just another bizarre part of his most bizarre day.

Adelaide had already gotten down and she said, "Hold on!" and ran to Monster Mack's cab. She returned with the trusty tablet.

"Good catch," Darren said. "Can you use this?" he said, holding Crushlet out on his palm.

One eye stalk rose as Adelaide watched the tablet. "Something's happening." She shook her head. "No, it's just a smear of lines—wait!" She frowned and winced. "It looks like—" She turned the tablet one way, and then the other.

"Hold it up," Crushlet said over the radio.

She held it so the baby alien could see, and almost instantly, the jumble coalesced into words—*My name is Crushlet.*

"Like mother, like child," Zoey said.

"You guys coming?" the van driver called.

"Ready?" Darren said to Crushlet, who retracted the eye stalk. Darren placed the little ball of alien carefully into his pocket and slid off the truck bed, ouching the whole way. Adelaide was waiting for him, and they stood together and waved to Zoey and Jordon. Darren thought about Crushlet's isolation, how she would never have a mate to reproduce with, laugh with, argue with, or just be together, silently sharing existence by knowing what the other was thinking.

On impulse, he turned to Adelaide, and she seemed to have the same thought. He wrapped his arms around her, and she returned the hug.

"This hurts," he whispered into her ear.

"Yes, it does," she replied. "A lot."
Neither let go.

Ж   Ж   Ж   Ж   Ж   Ж

About the Author

Blaine C. Readler is an electronics engineer, inventor of the FakeTV, and surprisingly, a writer. He lives in San Diego, where the weather allows him to walk around outside year-round thinking about stories.

He encourages you to visit him:
http://www.readler.com/